MR. PRATT'S
PATIENTS

MR. PRATT'S PATIENTS

BY

JOSEPH C. LINCOLN

AUTHOR OF

"THE RISE OF ROSCOE PAINE," "CAP'N WARREN'S WARDS,"
"MR. PRATT," ETC.

GROSSET & DUNLAP

PUBLISHERS   NEW YORK

By arrangement with D. Appleton-Century Co.

MR. PRATT'S PATIENTS

CHAPTER I

I WAS having my fortune told. Sophrony Gott
was telling it, with tea leaves. She had drawn
off the tea and was shaking the leaves in the
bottom of the cup around in circles. After she'd
shook for a minute or so she drained off what little
tea there was left and then stared solemn at the
leaves. I stood by the kitchen window looking out
at the yellow sand strip that they call a road in
East Trumet. 'Twas early June, the new grass was
flourishing everywheres, the posies in the yard—
peonies and such—in full bloom, the sun was shining, and the water of the bay was blue, with light
green streaks where the shoals showed. It was a
mighty fine afternoon and, by all that was fitting,
I ought to have felt like a yacht just off the ways.
But I didn't. I felt like an old hulk just ready to
be towed in and broke up for junk. For the first

time in my born days I was out of a job. Me, Solomon Pratt—only fifty-odd year old and used to scratching for a living since I was knee high to a horse-foot crab! Out of a job!

Sophrony give the tea leaves and her head another shake. Fur's that was concerned, she shook all over, being terrible big and fleshy. Adoniram, her husband, drifted in through the doorway and stood looking at her, interested as could be. It always interested Adoniram to see somebody else doing something.

"Well!" says Sophrony, solemn, "I'd have scarcely believed it. There's a whole lot here, Mr. Pratt. I can see a lot of things in this cup."

Adoniram thought 'twas time for him to say something, I cal'late. He most likely judged that I was finding fault with his wife's table board.

"That's nothing," says he, cheerful. "Them accidents are li'ble to happen anywheres. Sol won't blame you for that, Sophrony. Why, one time, over to Peleg Ellis's, I was eating a piece of pie and I see——"

I never found out what 'twas he saw. Maybe it's just as well. I was born with a pie appetite; it's one of my few natural gifts, as you might say, and I'd hate to lose any of it. Anyhow, Adoniram hadn't got any further than " see " when Sophrony

2

swung round in her chair and looked at him. You wouldn't have believed a body could shut up the way he did and leave his mouth standing open.

His wife kept on looking until he shut even that. Then she turned to me.

"I can see a great many things, important things, in this cup, Mr. Pratt," says she, dignified.

"That's good," says I. "You don't see a fifteen dollar a week job down in the no'theast corner, do you?"

"No," she says. "No——o, not exactly. And yet there's money here, a lot of money."

"That would do on a pinch," says I, sarcastic. "If I had the money maybe I could manage to worry along a spell without working for it. I never tried the experiment, I'm free to confess, but I'd chance it just now. Never mind the job, Mrs. Gott; just keep your eye on the money. Say, there ain't a crack in that tea cup, is there?"

She didn't pay any attention. Fur's jokes was concerned she was an ironclad old frigate. A comic almanac man might have practiced on her all day and never dented her broadside.

"Yes," she went on, "there's money here. And a letter. I seem to see a letter with good luck in it. You ain't expecting any letter, are you, Mr. Pratt?"

"No," says I. "My girl's gone back on me, I'm

afraid. Took up with a handsomer man, I suppose—if there is such a person living. Don't seem
hardly possible, does it, Adoniram."

But Adoniram was as solemn as his wife, just
then. Solemn, and a little mite excited.

"Why, Sophrony," says he, "don't you suppose
that means——"

"Don't interrupt the reading."

"But, Sophrony, I was only going to say——"

"Be still. Yes, Mr. Pratt, the lucky letter's there;
I can see it plain. And there's a journey; you're
going to take a journey."

"Humph! I hope 'tain't a long one. Walking's
all right, fur's it goes, but I'd just as soon it wouldn't
go too fur. There ain't any railroad ticket under
them tea grounds, is there?"

"No. . . . Let me see." She took a spoon and
poked around in the cup with the handle of it. "Let
me see," she says again. "Why, what's this? I can
see two spirits hovering over your life; one's dark
and the other's light. They're going to have consider'ble influence. And here's two men. One of
'em's a sort of thin man with—with kind of thick
hair, and the other's a—a——"

"A thick man with kind of thin hair, hey?" I finished for her. "Well, all right; I wouldn't bother
any longer if I was you, Mrs. Gott. You've found

more in that cup already than the average person could dredge out of a wash-boiler. If you'll excuse me I cal'late I'll trot along and see if I can locate any of that money."

"But you haven't heard it all. There's lots more. I can see a bottle—that means sickness."

"Maybe it has something to do with the spirits; hey, Adoniram?"

"No, it ain't. Adoniram, you be still. It means sickness. You're going to be mixed up with sickness, Mr. Pratt."

"Going to be! *Have* been, you mean!"

"And here's a dark blot—that means trouble. I'll stir it a little, and——"

"No, you won't. I don't need anybody to stir up any more trouble for me. I'm ever so much obliged to you, Mrs. Gott, but I must be going. Morning, Adoniram."

I was on my way to the door when Adoniram got in my way. He was so excited that he actually forgot to be scared of his wife, which is saying something.

"The letter!" he says. "The letter, Sol!"

"Yes," says I. "Well, when I get it I'll let you know. Don't hinder me now."

I brushed past him and went out on the front piazza. There I stopped. After all, I hadn't much of anywheres to go. I'd been about everywheres in that neighborhood.

That winter and spring was the worst I'd ever put in. A chap named Eleazir Kendrick and I had chummed in together the summer afore and built a fish-weir and shanty at Setuckit Point, down Orham way. For a spell we done pretty well. Then there came a reg'lar terror of a sou'wester, same as you don't get one summer in a thousand, and blowed the shanty flat and ripped about half of the weir poles out of the sand. We spent consider'ble money getting 'em reset, and then a swordfish got into the pound and tore the nets all to slathers, right in the middle of the squiteague season. We'd no sooner got that fixed than Eleazir was took sick with something that the doctors couldn't label for much as a fortni't. Time they decided 'twas walking typhoid, brought on by eating sp'iled clams, I'd got it, and mine wa'n't the walking kind by as much as two trots and a gallop. 'Twas January afore I cared whether school kept or not, and mid-winter afore I could do anything the way a healthy man ought to, except cuss. Then the doctors, and the nurses they'd hired when I was too crazy to stop 'em, had run up a bill that was higher than our weir poles, enough sight—for the ice had come into the bay and scraped every last one of *them* out to sea.

MR. PRATT'S PATIENTS

In March Eleazir and me got together—we was so thin that we had to hug each other to make a lump big enough to cast a shadow—and decided we'd give Setuckit another try. We had just enough cash, after paying the doctors' bills, to buy stuff for a new weir; but Coxton and Bragg, the fish dealers up to Boston, owed us a good deal, so we didn't call ourselves poorhouse candidates, exactly. We built the weir, caught seven hundred barrel of mackerel inside of a month, and shipped 'em to the Coxton and Bragg folks. Then the mackerel stopped running and Coxton started. He run to South America or somewheres, taking the heft of the firm's money with him. Bragg had enough reserve on hand to fail with, and he done it. Eleazir and I set down in the sand and looked at the empty weir and counted our fingers. They was all we had to count.

Well, we counted till May. Then we drawed lots to see who'd stay by the weir and who'd go hunting some other job. I lost—or won, whichever way you look at it—and 'twas me that went. I'll never forget Kendrick's parting remarks.

"So long, Sol," he says. "Think of me down here on the flats with a typhoid appetite and nothing to satisfy it but the clams that made me sick in the first place. It's what you might call the—the flat-irony of fate, ain't it?"

7

He was a real droll feller, with some consider'ble education, and was always making jokes like that. I liked Eleazir; we got along first rate together.

The first place I headed for after leaving Setuckit was the Old Home House at Wellmouth Port. My catboat, the *Dora Bassett,* was still in commission— Coxton and Bragg hadn't got *her* away from me—and I thought maybe I could get the chance of running party boat for the hotel—taking out boarders on fishing and sailing cruises, you understand. 'Twould be only a summer's job, if I got it, but a summer job is a heap better than no job.

I didn't get that party boat job for the same reason that Abel Simmons stayed an old bach. Abe used to say that he'd have got married two or three times if no had meant yes. If another skipper hadn't signed up with the Old Home folks in April, I might have signed in June. As 'twas, I got a lot of sympathy and a five cent cigar to pay me for my trip. I didn't really appreciate the sympathy till I started to smoke the cigar.

I put in another week cruising from Provincetown to Ostable, but 'twa'n't no use. An able-bodied typhoid relic by the name of Solomon Pratt seemed to be about as much in demand just then as a fiddler at a funeral. Finally I drifted around to East Trumet and hired a room on the hurricane deck of

Sophrony Gott's boarding house. Sophrony kept hens and a pig and two or three boarders and a husband. I mention 'em in that order because that's the way they was rated on the ship's books, the hens first and the husband last. Adoniram, the husband, was little and thin. The hens didn't have any special names, but they was big and fat like Sophrony. Me and the other boarders averaged in between the pig and Adoniram. And at Sophrony's I stayed, feeling the tide going out in my pocketbook every day and my pluck going along with it. I was bluer than a sp'iled mackerel and all hands noticed it. That's why, I cal'late, that Sophrony took the notion of telling my fortune. She thought 'twould brace me up, I shouldn't wonder. It didn't; 'twould have taken something a plaguey sight stronger than boarding-house tea to do that.

I came out of that setting-room, as I said, and stood there on the piazza, looking at nothing in particular—which is all there is to look at in East Trumet, and thinking hard. What should I do? I'd got to do something, but what?

And, as I stood there, I heard the biggest sort of pow-wow bust out in the house behind me. I hadn't more'n swung round on my anchor, as you might say, when the door flew open and Sophrony and Adoniram hove in sight under full steam. The doorway was like them in most Cape houses, not any too wide, and they both tried to get through it at the same time. 'Twas a mistake in judgment, on Adoniram's part, anyhow. One of these summer boy's canoes trying to shove an iceberg out of the channel wouldn't have been wrecked any quicker than he was. He went up against the port door jamb with a smash that a body'd think would have stove in his poor little timbers, and his wife swept out into the fairway without even rocking. There is some advantage in being built broad in the beam.

"Oh, Mr. Pratt!" says Sophrony.

"Ugh!" says Adoniram.

Then they both said something about a letter.

"It's here," says Sophrony. "It's here, Mr. Pratt. I didn't think of it till——"

" 'Twas me that thought of it first," puts in her husband, gasping but game. "When she see that in the tea cup about——"

"And all at once it come to me. I don't know what made me think of it, but——"

"I do. *I* made you. I says to you, says I——"

"Here! here! hold on!" I interrupted. "You sound like one of them choir anthems in church. Make it a solo, can't you? What's the matter?"

"Why, you see——" begins Adoniram.

"Be still," orders Sophrony. "Mr. Pratt'll think

you're crazy. Mr. Pratt, it's the most amazing thing. When I saw that letter for you in the tea leaves I never thought of the mantel-piece. It had been there for three or four days, too. You hush up, Adoniram! Can't you let me tell him?"

"Well, you be telling him, ain't you. All I can see you've told so far is that the mantel-piece has been there three or four days."

"Not the mantel-piece! The idea! The mantel-piece has been there ever since the house was built. It's the letter, Mr. Pratt. It came three or four days ago. You was away, over to Wellmouth or somewheres, and so we put it behind the clock. 'Twa'n't till just this minute that I remembered it."

"You wouldn't have remembered it then if I hadn't gone and got it," says Adoniram.

He may have been the one that got it first, but 'twas his wife that had it now. She gave it to me and the two of 'em stood close alongside when I started to rip open the envelope. I don't patronize Uncle Sam's mails to any great extent, but, generally speaking, a letter for me wasn't such a miracle as all this fuss amounted to. 'Twas account of the fool fortune-telling business that they'd got so excited. If you believe that the past, present and hereafter can be strained out of a teapot you can get excited over anything. I could hear Adoniram breathing hard close at my weather ear and Sophrony was saying: "It's a lucky letter. It'll bring you luck, now you see!"

There was only one sheet of paper in the envelope. This was a bill for eighteen dollars and forty cents for some canvas and a new anchor and some running rigging for the *Dora Bassett* that I'd bought of old man Scudder over at Wapatomac the fall afore I was took sick. I'd paid for it, too; but, like an everlasting idiot, I hadn't took any receipt. And now here was a bill with "Please Remmit" on it in red ink, and underlined at that. A bill for eighteen dollars; and I had less than twelve in my pocket! This was the "luck!"

About an hour later I was setting in the stern of the *Dora Bassett* bound for Wapatomac. Why was I going? I didn't know scarcely; and yet I did, too. I was going to talk Dutch to Nate Scudder. Not that 'twould do any good. He'd swear blue that I'd never paid him, and I didn't have a scrap of writing to prove that I had. He'd threaten to sue me, probably. All right; the way I felt just then he might have something real to sue for after we got through with our talk. The low-down swindler! What did he think I was; a fool summer chap from the city?

You think it's queer, may be, that I didn't write,

instead of cruising that distance. If it had been any-body else I would have wrote, but not to Nate. I knew him of old. No, the more I thought of the trick he was trying to play me the madder I got, and the quicker I wanted to tell him what I thought of him. So I asked Sophrony to put up a snack for me to take along for supper, and marched straight down to the shore.

Adoniram went with me, fur as the dock. I hadn't told him nor his wife what was in that "lucky letter," and he was just bubbling over with the won-der of it all. He talked a steady streak every foot of the way and all the time while I was casting off and making my skiff fast astern, and the like of that. I tried not to pay attention to his clack, but he made me nervous, just the same. The "letter" part of the fool fortune-telling coming true, as he saw it, had gone to his head and made him drunk, as you might say. He kept preaching over and over what a wonderful woman Sophrony was.

"You know she's a Spiritu'list," he says. "She's way up in Spiritu'lism. Sort of a—of a clair-voyum, that's what she is. She can see spirits just the same as you and me can see humans. That's how she saw them two hovering over you in the tea cup, Sol. And the spirits can see her."

"Don't have to put on their specs to do that, I

cal'late," says I. "There's enough of *her* for a blind spook to see in the dark."

"You don't understand," he says. "She's a clair-voyum, I told you. Suppose you wanted to talk to your grandmarm, say——"

"I don't," I cut in. "Nor anybody else just now."

That ought to have shut him up, but it didn't. He never could see a point until after he'd set on it.

"But if you did," he says, "you'd go to her and pay her a little something—fifty cents or so, maybe—and then she'd go into what they call a trance. Wouldn't speak a word for much as five minutes."

"Godfreys!" says I, "you don't mean it! It's wuth the money, ain't it. *You* don't ever take a trance, do you, Adoniram?"

"No, I ain't got the gift. I wish I had. But Sophrony's got it. When she's in one of them trances, and there's somebody there that the spirits want to talk to, they come and talk to 'em through her."

"Want to know! All the way through? Have to holler some, don't they?"

'Twas no use. He went gassing along, and the only relief I got was when the engine—the two-and-a-half horse power motor I'd put into the *Dora Bassett* when cash was something more to me than a typhoid memory or a tea-leaf hope—got gassing, too. And even then he wa'n't quite through. As I swung out of the dock and got the boat's nose headed for the bay, he commenced to holler again.

"Oh, Sol!" he sung out. "Oh, Sol! Hold on a minute! I just thought of something! I bet you ain't thought of it neither! You know what you're doing?"

I might have told him I was trying to get away from a graduate of the feeble-minded school, but I didn't. I just looked at him over my shoulder.

"You're taking a journey!" he hollered, actually hopping up and down, he was so excited. "You're taking the journey Sophrony see you taking in the tea. It's coming true! It's all coming true, every bit of it! Goodbye! Keep your eye out for the luck."

I didn't answer. The kind of luck that was coming to me nowadays I wanted to keep my eyes out of the way of. If I didn't, I figgered it was liable to black both of 'em.

That cruise to Wapatomac was a long one. 'Twas pretty fur into the afternoon when I started and I had a little mite of engine trouble to hinder me, besides. It was almost sunset when I made out the Denboro shore, and I had some miles to go then. As I sat there in the stern sheets, hanging on to the tiller and crunching the dry ham sandwiches Sophrony had put up for my supper, I couldn't help thinking of the last trip I took to Wapatomac, the one with Martin Hartley, when he and I sailed across that very bay in a howling gale to get the doctor for little "Redny," the Fresh Air youngster.

That's all been told about afore, of course, so I sha'n't tell it again. But I got to thinking what a lot of changes had took place since. Van Brunt and Hartley, the New York fellers that had come to Wellmouth to live what they called "The Natural Life," was back on Fifth Avenue and Wall Street, living, from all accounts, about as complicated a life as a body could live. Nate Scudder, who rented 'em his island, "Horsefoot Bar," had moved from Wellmouth to Wapatomac. He and his wife, Huldy Ann, was keeping a little store there, and Nate had managed to get himself made postmaster. His character hadn't changed any, though; my "bill" proved that. As for me, I was a little older and considerable poorer, otherwise about the same. But Eureka Sparrow and "Washy" Sparrow, her dad, and Lycurgus and Editha and Dewey and all the rest of the Sparrow young ones—I wondered where they was and what had become of 'em. They'd moved from the shanty on the Neck Road years ago, and 'twas common report that they'd gone to

Brockton, where Lycurgus had a good job in a shoe factory. I hadn't heard a word from 'em since.

Seemed as if I could see Eureka right then, as I set thinking of her. I couldn't help grinning as I remembered how she looked when she first came to "Ozone Island" to cook for us. Thin, she was, and straight up and down—not a curve in her any-wheres. She must be a reg'lar rail by this time, I thought, 'cause her kind generally stretch out as they shoot up, like an asparagus sprout. Never mind, I liked her, in spite of her looks. Her dad might be the laziest critter on earth, same as Nate Scudder was the meanest, but his daughter was all right. I was for Eureka, first, last and all the time.

The sun had set and 'twas dark when I came abreast of Wapatomac Neck. Wapatomac harbor, where Hartley and me had come so nigh getting wrecked, was further on, and the more I thought of navigating that channel in the dark the less I liked it. I could do it, of course, when I had to, but just now I didn't have to. I see a little cove in the shore and decided to anchor the *Dora Bassett* there and go ashore in the skiff and walk the rest of the way. I could have my séance with Scudder and then come back and sleep aboard the boat. I put what was left of the ham sandwiches in my pocket and swung in for the mainland.

The place where I beached the skiff was a deserted hole, not even a fish shanty on the beach. However, some ways back amongst the pines was the roof of a big building sticking up and I judged that the road must be somewheres there or thereabouts. After I'd carried the skiff's anchor up above tide mark, and hid the oars in the bushes, I was ready to start. By that time 'twas getting pretty dark.

I stumbled along through the young pines and huckleberry bushes. Pretty soon I struck into a sort of path that, I cal'lated, might lead to the road I was hunting for. It twisted and turned, and, the first thing I knew, made a sudden bend around a bunch of bayberry scrub and opened out into a big clear space like a lawn. And, back of the lawn, was a big, old-fashioned house, with piazzas stretching in front of it, and all blazing with lights. 'Twas the house I'd seen the roof of from the beach.

Thinks I to myself, "Sol, you're run off your course again. This is some rich city man's summer 'cottage' and if you don't look out there's likely to be some nice, lively dog taking an interest in your underpinning." So I started to back away again into the bushes. But I hadn't backed more'n a couple of yards when I see something so amazing that I couldn't help scooching down behind the bayberries and looking at it.

From around the corner of the house come a procession of men, four of 'em together, running at a dog trot. At first I couldn't make out much about 'em except that they was running, but as they swung round the edge of the lawn in my direction, I made out that every last one of 'em was fat as a porpoise and puffing like the engine on the *Dora Bassett*. And, trotting easy on t'other side of 'em and not puffing the least mite, was a big square-shouldered chap, bare-headed and bare-armed. Against the lights from the house they stood out like black shadows cut out of cardboard, though 'twould have taken a sight of cardboard to cut the fattest out of, and that's a fact.

Just as they got abreast of me the square-shouldered feller stopped and slapped his hands together. Then the four fat ones stopped, too—all but their puffing, they kept that up—and one or two of 'em groaned dismal as a funeral. Didn't speak, but just stood there and puffed and groaned.

"Now then," says Square-Shoulders, "that's enough for to-night. Into the house with yez—lively."

There was more puffing and more groans; then the procession tacks ship and begins to move slow toward the piazzas. Only one hung back, the fleshiest one of the lot.

"Oh—oh, I say!" he pants, "just let us have one drink, won't you? The well's right here."

"Nothing doing," says Square-Shoulders. "It's the house and the hay for yours. Come! Get a move on now."

"But—I'll give you a dollar for a drink of water."

"Nothing doing, I tell you! Beat it."

They beat it, though they was too much out of breath to have beat a mud turtle in an even race. One after the other I saw 'em go in at the door. Then the lights in the house begun to go out, the downstairs ones. Inside of five minutes there was only one or two feeble gleams on the main deck.

I woke up and stepped out of the bushes. I'd been too much interested in the circus to move afore. I couldn't make out what sort of a place 'twas I'd struck. It might have been a fat men's home, but, if it was, they wa'n't over tender with the inmates. I'd gone about ten foot and had just discovered that a black, square thing in front of me was a wooden well-top, with an old-fashioned windlass, when I heard a door creak in the house. I had just time to dodge back to my bayberries when somebody come tiptoein' across the grass. I could hear him wheeze afore he got much more'n half way, so I didn't need the little light the stars give me to prove

'twas one of the inmates, probably one of the four
that had just gone in.

Down he comes as fur as the well, and I could
see him leaning over the top and fiddling with something inside. Then I heard the old windlass begin
to squeal. Every time it squealed the fleshy feller
would turn his head and look at the house and say,
"Oh, Lord!" or something more emphatic, under
what breath he had left. 'Twas the most mysterious,
ridiculous performance ever I come across.

At last I couldn't stand it no longer. I just *had*
to find out what was going on. So *I* done some
tiptoeing—'twas catching, I cal'late—and I reached
that well just as my hefty friend dragged the bucket,
brimming, slopping full, over the curb.

"Good evening," says I.

He jumped as if I'd stuck something into him.
I expected he'd drop the bucket back into the well
again, but he didn't; he clung on to it as if 'twas the
"Ark of Safety" that old Amos Peters used to be
always talking about in Come-Outer meeting. He
raised his head, glared at me, says "Oh, Lord!"
again, and then ducked down to the edge of that
bucket and begun to drink as if he'd never stop.
I never see a human being suck up water the way
he did; a sponge wa'n't a circumstance to him.

He drunk and drunk till I expected to see the

bottom of the bucket come out at the top. Then he fetched a long sigh and set the bucket down.

"There!" says he. "I've had it, anyhow. You can't take *that* away from me, blast you!"

I shook my head. This was a good many fathoms too deep for me.

"Yes," says I, "you've had it. I should say you'd had about all there was."

"I needed it," says he, stuffy and sulky as a young one; "I needed it, by thunder!"

"I should think what you needed now was a pump. What was you trying to do; drink the well dry?"

He leaned over the curb and stared at me through the dark.

"You ain't McCarty," he says. "I never saw you before. Who the blazes are you?"

"My name's Pratt," says I. "I hope you'll excuse me for——"

He didn't wait to hear any excuse.

"I never saw you before," he says again. "You're a new victim, I suppose. What ails *you?*"

"Nothing ails me, 'special," says I, grinning.

"Humph! you're in luck. What are you doing here?"

This was the most sensible thing he'd said yet,

'cording to my notion. I tried to give him a sensible answer.

"I'm here by mistake," I told him. "Just landed down abreast here on the shore and I'm trying to find my way to the road to the Neck. How do you get to it?"

He didn't seem to believe me; acted awful funny.

"Here by mistake!" he says, slow. "Then it's the biggest mistake of your life, I'll tell you that. Isn't there anything the matter with you?"

"Nothing, except that I could use a meal's vittles with consider'ble comfort. Ain't had nothing to eat but dry sandwiches since noon."

He jumped again and come around to my side of the well.

"Sandwiches!" he whispers, excited. "Sandwiches! What kind of sandwiches?"

"Well, they was labeled 'ham,' but there wa'n't scarcely enough substance to 'em to make the christening worth while. My landlady, she——"

"Say! you haven't any of 'em left, have you?"

As a matter of fact, I did have a couple of 'em in my pocket.

"Why, yes," says I, "there's one or two——"

"I'll give you a dollar apiece for the lot."

I stepped back. I'd begun to suspicion that I'd run afoul of a private crazy asylum; and this was

23

the proof I needed. Anybody that would give five honest cents for a barrel of Sophrony Gott's sandwiches was too much of a loon for me to keep company with.

"Come!" he snaps, impatient. "Are you deaf? I say I'll give a dollar apiece for whatever sandwiches you have left."

I'd read somewheres that the way to get on with lunatics was to pacify 'em. I dove into my starboard pocket and resurrected the sandwiches.

"Here you be," says I. "I don't want your dollars either."

He grabbed the sandwiches the way a shark would grab a herring. Inside of a half second his teeth was rattling amongst the dry bread.

"By George!" says he, through the crumbs, "that's good. I never tasted anything so good in my life!"

I couldn't help laughing. I was a little worried, too—I didn't know where he might break out next—but I laughed just the same. He struck me funny.

"You ain't lived very long, have you?" I says.

He didn't answer; or, when he did, it wa'n't rightly an answer. 'Twas another question.

"What's that other thing in your hand?" he sung out.

"Well," says I, "it's a . . . humph! it's a sort

of heirloom. In the beginning 'twas a doughnut, I presume likely; but now it's what a summer woman would call a genuine antique."

He held out one of his hands; the other was full of sandwiches.

"Give it to me," says he.

"You don't want it."

"Give it to me."

I passed it over. When a strange Bedlamite talks to me in that tone of voice he generally gets what he asks for; but I did think I'd ought to warn him.

"You listen to me now, whoever you are," says I. "That doughnut ain't fit to eat. It's as old as——"

"Shut up!" he snaps. "You don't know what you're talking about. Anything's fit to eat when you're starving—anything but nuts and raw oatmeal and——"

He didn't get any further. There was a click and out of the dark about twenty foot to one side of us—the side we hadn't either of us been watching—blazed a stream of light that hit that fat loon right plumb in the face and eyes. Then a voice, a female voice, said:

"Um! I thought 'twas you. What do you s'pose the Doctor'll say to this kind of doings?"

I was too surprised and set back to move or say a word. The fat man didn't say a word neither.

but he moved. I heard him give one gasp, and the next second I was left alone on the well platform. My sandwiches and doughnut and the critter I'd give 'em to was going through the bushes the way the swordfish went through Eleazir's and my fish net; and making full as much fuss about it.

Then the lantern light—that's what 'twas, the light from a dark lantern—swung over in my direction and the voice says:

"Now who are you? And what are you doing, sneaking around, interfering with the patients? Well, why don't you answer?"

I tried to answer. I done my best. There was something about that voice that sounded familiar, too. If I could have seen who was talking to me I'd have felt better, but the blaze in my eyes dazzled me.

"Ma'am," I stammers, "I cal'late I've made a mistake. I got into your—your asylum by accident. I was——"

That's as far as I got. The person that was holding the lantern almost dropped it. She took a step toward me and sung out:

"Why! Why! *Mr. Pratt!* What in the wide world fetched you here? I'm awful glad to see you! Don't you know me? I'm Eureka Sparrow."

No wonder I thought the voice was familiar.

CHAPTER II

"WELL! well! well! Eureka," says I; "this does seem like old times for sartin."

We was inside the kitchen of the big house by this time. I was setting in a chair by the table and Eureka was flying around, busy as a wasp in an empty molasses hogshead, getting supper for me. She'd insisted on doing it; nothing I could say would stop her. She was terrible glad to see me, she said, and I own up that she acted as if she meant it. Well, fur's that goes, I was mighty glad to see her.

"Don't it?" says she. "I declare if it don't! You haven't changed a mite, Mr. Pratt. I should know you anywheres."

I shouldn't have known her. She'd changed, all right enough. When she did the cooking for me and the "Heavenlies" at "Ozone-Horsefoot-Bar Island" she was thin as an August herring, and as for her looks—well, her face mightn't have stopped a clock, but 'twould have fixed it so's you'd had to wind it every few days to keep it from losing time. Now she was round and plump; her hair, that always used to be pulled back so tight she couldn't scowl without running the risk of cracking her forehead, was fixed real wavy and pretty; and her gown was white, and fitted her first-rate. And she'd growed rosy-cheeked and good-looking, in a wholesome, healthy kind of way. I could scarcely believe 'twas her, unless I shut my eyes; then the way she talked, and the brisk, snappy way she had of moving, and the way she sung when she worked— all these was the Eureka I used to know and like. When my eyes was shut she was natural as life, and when I opened 'em she was twice as handsome, as the saying is.

She asked me more'n a shipload of questions and I answered 'em best I could, trying hard to get a chance to ask one or two on my own hook. When I told her about Kendrick's and my luck with our weir, and our typhoid and all, she was fairly bubbling over with sympathy. And when I got to Nate Scudder's bill her eyes snapped and she stamped her foot just as I'd seen her do so often in the old days.

"There!" says she, "ain't that just like that Scudder thing! The contriving old scalawag! I knew he was here at Wapatomac. Miss Emeline and me hadn't been in this house more'n two days when round he comes to see if he can't sell us groceries.

I guess likely he'd have talked Miss Emeline over, for he saw her first, but I got into the room just in time. You ought to have seen his face when he laid eyes on me. Ho! ho! Miss Emeline was surprised. 'Why!' says she, 'Eureka, have you met Mr. Scudder afore?' 'Yes'm,' says I, 'I have; and that's the only safe way to meet him, unless you want to spend the rest of your days trying to catch up.' Oh, I give her *his* character, all right! Old cheat! He's just the same as ever, ain't he? Pa always used to say that you couldn't teach an old dog new tricks."

"Humph!" I says, "you don't need to teach Nate any new ones; he's got enough of the old ones to keep the average person busy. But who's this Miss Emeline you're talking about? And what are you doing in this asylum?"

"It ain't an asylum," says she.

"It ain't! Then what's all the lunatics doing loose around the premises?"

"They ain't any looneys here; we don't take 'em."

"Don't take—say, look here, Eureka; don't that fat man—the one I run afoul of out in the yard just now, the one that was trying to drink up the well a bucketful at a time—don't he belong here?"

"Yes, course he belongs here. That's Colonel Applegate, from Providence. He's a stock broker man with barrels and barrels of money and he's been in the milishy and on the Governor's staff and all that. He's a Rhode Island first family, the Colonel is."

"He's big enough to be a family. But do you mean to tell me he ain't crazy?"

"Course he ain't."

"Then—why, what are you talking about? If he ain't out of his head, then I am. Why, he et one of Sophrony Gott's sandwiches and vowed and declared 'twas the finest thing ever he tasted in his born days."

"He did! O—oh, won't he catch it when the Doctor finds it out! I wouldn't be in his shoes for something."

"*He* wa'n't in 'em when I met him; he was in his stocking feet."

"I bet you! that's how he sneaked out without making any noise. But I suspected he was up to some kind of capers. My! my! but we have to watch 'em all the time. Just like young ones at school, they are. You wouldn't believe grown up people could——"

"Eureka Sparrow, stop it! Stop where you be! What sort of a place is this, anyway?"

"Don't you know? I thought everybody knew. The papers have been full of it."

"Maybe so, but I've had something else to do with my money besides buy papers. And, if I had bought 'em, nobody but a web-footed person could deliver 'em at Setuckit Point. What sort of a place is this, I ask you?"

"It's a sanitarium, that's what it is."

She give this out as if 'twas a sort of Gov'ment proclamation that ought to settle everything. But I was about as settled as a cup of fo'castle coffee.

"Sanitarium," says I. "I want to know! *In*sanitarium, you mean, don't you?"

"No, I don't. There ain't any crazy folks here, I tell you. It's a sanitarium, a place where sick folks come to be made well."

I let this sink in a spell.

"Do you mean to tell me," says I, "that that fat man—that Cap'n Appetite, or whatever his name is—is sick?"

"He's fat, and fat's a kind of sickness."

"'Tis, hey! Humph! Then Sophrony Gott's a desperate invalid, and I'd never have guessed it to look at her. Well! well!"

"It's a sanitarium," says Eureka again. "The name of it is 'Sea Breeze Bluff.' There! you've heard of 'Sea Breeze Bluff Sanitarium for Right Living and Rest,' ain't you?"

I shook my head.

"No," says I. "I hate to lower myself in your opinion, Eureka, but I ain't."

"Ain't heard of Sea Breeze Bluff? Or the salt air cure? Or the sand baths? Or Doctor Wool?"

"Nary one!"

"Not of Doctor Lysander P. Wool? Why, I thought everybody had heard of *him!* His advertisements have been in the papers for ever so long. And his picture, too."

Then I begun to get a glimmer of light. The word "advertisement" give it to me.

"Hold on," I sung out. "You don't mean 'Wool's Willow Wine for the Weak'? Not that feller?"

"Um-hm," says she, nodding emphatic. "That's the one, but he ain't a feller. 'Wool's Willow Wine for the Weak' and 'Wool's Licorice Lozenges for the Liver,' and 'Wool's Perfect Plasters for Pleurisy.' That's him. Well, he is running this place. You see, Miss Emeline, she——"

"Belay, Eureka!" I cut in. "If you and me are going to get anywheres on this cruise, I cal'late we'd better go back and start over again at the mark buoy. Suppose you commence by telling me about yourself and how you come here."

"Why, I come here along of Miss Emeline."

"You don't say? And Miss Emeline come along

of you, I presume likely. But you ain't told me
who Miss Emeline is yet."

She stopped rattling dishes in the sink—she'd
been washing 'em as fast as I cleared 'em—and
says she:

"I see," she says, "you want me to tell you everything, right from the beginning."

"That's the idea. You commence at the first
chapter of Genesis and work down slow. Time you
get to Revelations I may be where I can understand
why a sane man—even a fat sick one like this Cap'n
Applecart—trots around in his stocking feet after
dark offering to pay a dollar for three square inches
of stale bread and canned ham. Don't say any
more; just heave ahead and tell."

So she towed a chair up to the table abreast of
me and commenced. And she commenced at Genesis, just as I'd ordered her to.

Seems that after the Sparrows had flocked to
Brockton, about everybody in the nest worked for
a spell—everybody but the babies, that is, and the
oldest ones of *them* took care of the younger. Lycurgus and Editha and Napoleon was in the shoe
factory and doing first-rate. Even Washy—Pa
Sparrow—got a job, night watchman in a drug
store. He slept under the counter and answered
the night bell and the telephone, provided they rung

loud enough and long enough to interfere with his naps. As for Eureka herself, she went out at housework. She got a place with a single old maid, name of Miss Emeline Adams, and had been with her ever since. 'Twas her that Eureka called "Miss Emeline."

Well, this Miss Emeline had been poor and every-day and healthy once on a time, but now she was rich and high-toned and ailing. She was born in New Bedford, but when she was twenty she went to Brockton and lived with a couple of old ladies who thought the world of her and kind of brought her up, as you might say. 'Twas from them she got her aristocratic notions and, after they died, her money. They left her all they had, which was consider'ble, and part of the inheritance was this big old house and grounds at Wapatomac. For three years Eureka and Miss Emeline had lived together, winters in Brockton and summers at Wapatomac. They got along fine together. 'Twas plain enough to see why, too. Eureka was a smart, capable girl and a good housekeeper, and, besides and more-over, I judged there was a kind of romantic nobil-ity, so's to speak, about this Adams woman that hit Eureka where she lived. As I remember her—Eureka, I mean—she was always reading story-paper yarns about counts and lords and earls and earlesses. Miss Emeline, with her high-toned ideas and her worship of "family"—'cording to Eureka's tell, she had a pedigree like a trotting-horse and was possessed with the conviction that the name of Eve's husband in Scriptur' was a printer's mistake and there should have been an *s* on the end of it—all this was just the sort of thing Eureka would love. Keeping house for Miss Emeline Adams was the nighest thing to being hired help for an earless that you're liable to find this side of the big salt water.

'Twas after Miss Emeline got her money that she begun to collect symptoms. Afore that she was well enough, but she hadn't been cutting coupons long afore she begun to feel feeble and to read all sorts of doctors' books and take all kinds of medicine. At last she run afoul of "Wool's Willow Wine," and, later on, of Doctor Wool himself. From that time she and the Doctor had been mighty friendly.

"And last winter," goes on Eureka, her good-looking face all lit up like a binnacle lamp, with excitement and enthusiasm; "only last February 'twas, just think of it!—last February Doctor Wool came to see us and told us of his great discovery. And what do you suppose that discovery was?"

"Land knows!" says I. "What was it?"

" 'Twas that all his life his theory of curing folks had been wrong. Yes, sir, all wrong! He's discovered that medicines wa'n't what really cured at all. The real cures was those provided by Mother Nature."

"Whose mother's that?" says I. "His wife's?"

"No, no! He ain't married. Don't you understand. Mother Nature; everybody's mother, yours and mine and everybody's. Mother Nature means the earth we live on and the sun and the sand and the fresh air and salt water—and—and all. Those are what cures, not medicines at all. And he'd just found it out."

"Humph!" says I, remembering some of the advertisements; "how about the million or so souls that the 'Willow Wine' and the 'Licorice Lozenges' and the 'Pleurisy Plasters' yanked out of the grave? Land sakes! I've read more letters testifying to——"

"I know. That's what I said to Miss Emeline. But she explained all that. Doctor Wool had explained it to her, you see. 'Twa'n't the 'Wine' and the 'Plasters' they took that really cured 'em. They wa'n't cured by them at all."

"They're a set of awful liars, then," says I. "They ought to take something for *that*. Never mind; heave ahead."

She went on, explaining that the medicines helped some, in a way, because the folks that took 'em thought they was helped, but that really they was only what she called "stimulated," and stimulants wa'n't lasting cures. I told her that I'd seen plenty of folks in temperance towns "stimulated" by Jamaica ginger, but she didn't even smile. This was a serious business for her; I could see that.

"No," says she. "Doctor Wool had discovered 'twas Nature that done the curing, and he'd decided to give up his medicine making and start in curing in the right way. He was figgering to open a sanitarium. Well, he'd no sooner said that than Miss Emeline had an inspiration. Says she, 'I'll help you open one.' And she did. This is it. This is 'Sea Breeze Bluff Sanitarium for Right Living and Rest.' Miss Emeline owns it, and Doctor Wool runs it. There! *now* you understand."

I didn't understand any too well. There was nine hundred and ninety-nine odd points that wa'n't clear in my mind even yet. I mentioned one of 'em.

"This Cap'n Apple—Apple——" I begun.

"Colonel, not Cap'n," interrupted Eureka. "Colonel Applegate, his name is."

"All right, Colonel it is. Do I understand he's one of the Right Livers?"

"Um-hm, I told you so."

"I know you did, but it don't seem hardly possible. And the other three heavyweights I see sachaying around the yard—I suppose likely they was Livers, too?"

"Sure."

I thought this over.

"Well," says I, "maybe so. If you say so, Eureka, 'tis so, of course. But if ever a gang acted as if they was living about as wrong as could be, they did. And for the land sakes, answer me this: Why did that—that Colonel man drink a gallon of cold water? And why did he grab that sandwich and doughnut like a shipwrecked fo'mast hand on a raft? And what made him———"

She moved her hands for me to stop. Her eyes was snapping with the glory of it all.

"I'll tell you," says she; "I'll tell you. 'Twas account of his treatment. He's being cured of his flesh. Every morning he gets up at five and goes for a walk, a mile or so. Then he runs a half a mile. Then he has his breakfast, some weak tea, and some toast with no butter on it, and some uncooked cereal without sugar or milk. And four prunes. He has four now; at first he only had three, but he's been advanced to four. And———"

"Hold on!" I sung out. "Do you mean to say that's *all* the breakfast he has, after turning out at five and running a mile and a half?"

"Yes. And——"

"And are the rest of his meals like that?"

"Not exactly. He has some rare steak—awful rare, hardly cooked at all—at noon. Four ounces of rare steak; we have to be awful careful and weigh it just right. He has that, and a quarter of a pint more weak tea, or b'iling hot water, just as he likes, and five more prunes. And at night, after his sand bath, and his different kinds of exercises, he has——"

"Belay again! My soul and body! Four ounces of raw steak and five prunes! No wonder the poor thing was starving! But why was he so crazy to get at that well?"

"Because he was thirsty for something cold, I suppose. They all get that way first along. You see, cold water is terrible bad for fleshy folks, and we don't allow 'em but one glass of it a day. It's all in the treatment."

"Well, I wouldn't stand such treatment. I shouldn't think he would neither. Great grown-up man like him! and a Colonel, too. Why don't he——"

"Oh, my sakes! Don't you see? It's a part of

39

the treatment, same as I say. He's paying for it, and——"

"*Paying* for it! Eureka Sparrow, are those poor, wheezing, puffing, suffering things I saw limping across that yard paying *money* to be treated so?"

"Of course they are. They pay five hundred dollars apiece for it. And they have to pay it ahead of time, too, else they might get discouraged and quit afore they was cured. They *can't* quit after they've paid, or they lose the five hundred. That's pretty smart, I think, don't you?"

I rubbed my forehead. "Well," says I, "I can see one thing plain enough. Nate Scudder is in the primer class alongside of this Wool doctor of yours. I suppose that was him I see bullying the lunatics— the patients, I mean. He talked like the second mate on a cattle boat, and he looked like one, too— what I could see of him in the dark. So that was your Doctor Wool, hey?"

If I'd said a swear word on the meeting-house steps I couldn't have shocked her more. She gave a little scream and jumped half out of her chair.

"My sakes, no!" she squealed. "That was Mike McCarty, the physical director. He is pretty rough, and Miss Emeline don't like him very well, but Doctor Wool keeps him 'cause he ain't been able to get anybody else. I don't believe he'll keep him very long, though; they. had a big row the other day. I suspicion that this McCarty man used to drink liquor and that he's beginning to do it again. I've thought two or three times I've smelt it on him lately. Him and Thoph Pease, the hired man, are awful thick, and——"

"Hold on," says I. When she got started talking she was as hard to stop as a young one's sled going down hill. "If that wa'n't the Doctor that I see, where is he?"

"He's gone to Boston to fetch down a new patient. Oh, he's a wonderful man, Doctor Lysander P. Wool is! You'll say so, too, when you see him, Mr. Pratt. *He* don't bully. He's as gentle and grand and—and noble as a duke or—or a Seneschal in a story book. Talk! You never heard anybody talk the way he can. It sort of flows out of his face, the talk does, and all you have to do is set and listen. Such talk! Full of high thoughts and uplift and such, like a 'Poet's Corner' in a paper. After he's talked to you for a spell you don't know where you are, scarcely. And you don't care, neither. You're willing to be anywheres so's you can rest back and hear him. He's——"

The praise service broke off there, 'count of some folks coming to the back door. I cal'late 'twas a mercy, fur's I was concerned. I'd never heard the Wool man talk, so I couldn't judge the effect, but I did know that Eureka's talk had got me whirling. I'd always figgered that my brains was as hard as the average alongshore, but now they was softening up fast. I couldn't understand more'n half I'd heard, and that half was pretty foggy. So the noise of somebody else talking, and steps on the kitchen piazza, was the blessed relief I needed, as the feller with the p'ison-ivy rash said when the cat scratched him.

I got up to go, but afore I could get started the folks was in the kitchen. There was a pair of 'em: one the square-shouldered feller I'd seen in the yard, the McCarty one, and the other a long-legged, red chin-whiskered critter that Eureka called "Thoph" and introduced to me as "Mr. Theophilus Pease, who does the gardening and such; you've heard me speak of him, Mr. Pratt."

I didn't remember that I had, but I said I was glad to hear of him now, and him and me and the McCarty man shook hands.

"I do hope you've chained up that dog of yours, Mr. McCarty," says Eureka. "He's got the most terrible bulldog ever was," she adds, turning to me. "He'll mind Mr. McCarty fine, but the rest of us don't feel safe unless he's chained up. He's a good watchdog, though; that's why the Doctor lets him stay here. His name's Pet."

"That's a pretty name," I says, for the sake of saying something. McCarty laughed.

"He's a pretty dog, all right; ain't he, Thoph?" he chuckled, turning to the Pease man. "Do you like dogs, Bratt?"

"Some kinds," says I.

"He'll like you. He can eat a guy about your size for supper."

"He'll have to have good teeth. I'm fairly tough for my age," says I, getting up to go. I didn't take much shine to McCarty, nor the other feller, neither. And, speaking of liquor, it did seem to me that there was a floating smell of it on the premises just then.

"Don't hurry, Mr. Pratt," Eureka says.

"Got to hurry, or I'll be too late to catch Nate Scudder afore he turns in for the night."

"You're too late now," says she. "He's turned in long afore this, ain't he, Thoph."

Thoph said he cal'lated so. He didn't seem to be in what you'd call a good humor with himself or anybody else. McCarty, though, was talky enough for two. He was looking me over, with a kind of condescending grin on his face.

"Sure he's turned in," he says. "It's after eight

o'clock and all you hayseeds down here hit the mat-
tress soon as it gets dark, so's to save kerosene and
spite the oil trust. Scudder's place was pitch dark
when we came by it, so you might just as well camp
where you are, Spratt. Say, are you a relation of
the guy in the book the kids read—the one that
licked the platter clean?"

"No," says I, pretty crisp.

"His name ain't Spratt, Mr. McCarty," says Eureka, coming to the rescue. "It's Pratt."

He laughed louder than ever. "Oh, all right,"
he says; "my mistake, Pratt. No hard feelings,
hey?"

"Not a bit," says I. "I can make allowances, Mc-
Ginty."

"McCarty," he says, sharp.

"Oh, I beg your pardon. I had an idee you
might be a brother of the critter that went to the
bottom of the sea, in the song."

Afore he could think of an answer to this, Thoph
took a notion to say something.

"Has the old man got back yet?" he wanted to
know.

Eureka looked at him. "If you mean Doctor
Wool," she says, dignified, "he ain't. But we expect him 'most any time."

"That's who I mean. When he comes, I've got a

word to say to him. By time, I'm getting sick—
that's what I'm getting, sick!"

He seemed to be talking to me as much as anybody, so I answered him.

"That so?" says I. "Well, I should judge you'd
come to the right place to be cured."

"Humph! No sir-ee! I'm sick. And McCarty's
sick, too. Ain't you, Mac?"

"You bet your life!" says McCarty ugly.

"Maybe you ain't took your prunes reg'lar," I
put in, by way of suggestion.

Neither of 'em smiled. Pease looked sourer
than ever, and the square-shouldered chap leaned
for'ard in his chair and scowled at me.

"Say, Rube," he says, "you may not know it, but
you're pretty blamed fresh, if you ask *me*."

"I don't recollect asking you," says I, "but I'm
much obliged for the information. Now that you
mention it, I had noticed there was something around
here that needed to be pickled pretty soon, or 'twas
liable to spile."

I don't know what might have happened then.
The weather was thickening up and it looked to me
like squalls. But Eureka took charge of the deck.

"There, there!" says she. "That's enough of
this kind of talk. Mr. Pratt's a friend of mine,
Mike McCarty, and if you and Thoph Pease can't

be civil to him, you needn't stay here. You can take yourselves and your sulks right out of here this minute."

Pease didn't say anything; he looked kind of scared. But McCarty had a shot left in the locker.

"Are you running this joint?" he wanted to know.

"I'm running this kitchen, and it ain't a joint, whatever that is. You get right out of here, Mike McCarty. If you don't, I'll report you both to the Doctor when he comes."

I didn't want her to get into any trouble on my account, and afore anything else happened I grabbed my cap and headed for the door. She followed me to the back piazza.

"It's a shame," says she, snappy as a bunch of firecrackers. "The sassy, impudent things! You stay here, Mr. Pratt. Don't you go till you get good and ready."

"I ought to have been ready half an hour ago," I told her. "Don't worry, Eureka; I'm going because I want to, not because of them two. What ails 'em, any way?"

"Oh, I don't know. Thoph Pease has a notion that he don't get pay enough for what he does."

"What does he do?"

"Nothing mainly. He's supposed to be male hired help around the place, take care of the hens and the cow and cut the grass and so on. Make himself generally useful, that's what Doctor Wool said when he hired him. But what he does is to be generally useless. I never saw anybody do that better'n he does. It comes natural to him. But he don't count. It's McCarty that's responsible for most of the fuss. He's a trouble-maker, that's what he is."

I laughed. "Yes," says I, "that's plain enough. Well, I've dodged the trouble that Sophrony Gott saw in the teacup when she was telling my fortune this afternoon, and I'm going to keep on dodging long's I can. Good-bye, Eureka. I'm awful glad I run across you again and I'm much obliged for the supper."

I was stepping off the porch, but she wouldn't let me go. The mention of that fortune-telling was like a chunk of sp'iled fish to a crab, 'twas the kind of bait she liked and she wouldn't let go till she had the whole of it. Nothing would do but I must tell her all about it.

"Well!" says she, when I'd finished. "Well, I declare! Ain't that wonderful! Just like a story! And some of it's come true already, ain't it? You did get a letter, even if 'twas only a bill; and you have taken a journey. Maybe it'll all come true. There was two female spirits hovering over you, she said, didn't she? I wonder who they are. Why, perhaps I'm one of 'em."

I shook my head. "When *you* get to hovering over me, Eureka," I says, "I'm going to stand out from under. You weigh too much nowadays to hover comfortable."

But joking wa'n't in her log just then. She held tight to my arm and, though 'twas too dark to see, I could feel that she was awful excited.

"And the money!" she says. "There was a lot of money coming to you from the journey. How do you s'pose that. . . . Oh, my goodness gracious! I do believe. . . . You don't s'pose——"

She stopped. There was a rattle of wheels and the "thump-thump" of horse's hoofs coming along the drive. A covered wagon, a depot wagon it looked like, hauled by an old white horse, came rolling past us and up to the front piazza.

"Whoa!" says the feller on the driver's seat. The door of the wagon opened and a big, heavy-built man got out.

"It's the Doctor!" whispered Eureka in my ear. "It's Doctor Wool himself. I'm so glad! Now you've *seen* him, anyway."

I couldn't see much of him. There was a lamp burning now, in a glass frame by the front door,

but it wa'n't a Highland Light lighthouse by consider'ble.

"Who's the other critter with him?" I asked,

"I guess likely it must be Professor Quill, the new
patient," says Eureka. "He was coming with the
Doctor."

The Professor was long and lanky. Against the
light his clothes hung on him as if he was framed
with laths. He had on a tall hat, and he knocked
it off getting out of the carriage. When he stooped
to pick it up his hair fell down all around his face.

"Too bad, too bad!" says the thick-set man, in
a voice like a church organ, 'twas so deep and kind
of musical and purry. "No harm done, I trust?
No? No? Good! Good! Walk in. Enter, if
you please. After you, Professor. Our arrange-
ments here are a bit primitive, a bit primitive and
rural—yes, but homelike, we—er—hope. Walk in,
walk in."

They walked in, the big voice purring along till
the door shut it off. Eureka hadn't said a word
since the accident to the hat. Now I heard her give
a kind of gasp.

"Did you see?" she sung out. "Oh, did you see?
It *is* coming true! It is! It is!"

I pulled my arm loose. "Stop!" she called after
me. "Wait! Please wait! Mr. Pratt, you must

promise me that you won't go back to Wellmouth till you've come here again. Come to-morrow morning. Promise!"

I'd have promised 'most anything to get away. I was sort of anxious to make sure the *Dora Bassett* was safe and sound; and, besides, I was sleepy.

"All right, I'll promise," says I. "I'll have my little folksy chat with Scudder and then I'll run up and say good-bye to you. So long, Eureka."

"Good-night," says she. "It's wonderful, ain't it? I never knew anything so wonderful. You did see, didn't you?"

"I saw your Wool doctor, if that's what you mean."

"No, no! the other one—Professor Quill. You saw him. You know who he is?"

"Who he is? What do you mean?"

"I mean you realized who he is. I did; it came to me just the minute his hat fell off. He's the thin man with the thick hair, the one Mrs. Gott saw in the teacup. Of course he is! Isn't it wonderful!"

CHAPTER III

I CHUCKLED to myself all the way down to the skiff at the ridiculousness of the whole thing. But I made up my mind to keep my promise. I wanted to see more of that "Rest" place and the "Right Livers." They was the most curious combination I'd run across for a good while. On the way down the path I heard a dog growling somewheres off to the left; I judged 'twas "Pet," chained up. I was perfectly satisfied to have him chained; bulldogs ain't as much in my line as dog-fish, although I have about as much use for one as t'other.

The skiff was all right, and so was the *Dora Bassett,* when I'd rowed off to her. I turned in and slept sound all night, cal'lating to start for Nate's first thing in the morning.

But in the morning, when I turned out, that pesky appetite of mine got to reminding me that I hadn't had any breakfast. As a general thing, I don't chuck overboard much advice about making over creation, but it does seem to me there's been a mistake in this appetite business. A poor man's appetite and digestion is usually first class and able to tackle anything—but there's precious little for him to tackle; and a rich man, with all the world on ice, so to speak, has dyspepsy and must worry along on hot milk and such. Now, the way I look at it, there's a misdeal here somewheres. You think it over and see if I ain't right.

Well, as I said, my appetite was on deck that morning, and 'twas a troublesome cargo. I'd given Colonel Applecart all the sandwiches and dough-nuts I had left from Sophrony's luncheon, and, hungry as I was, I didn't shed any tears over the memory of them. But it did look like a long wait till I got to Wapatomac, and, as the tide was going out, I took my clam hoe and a dreener, and got into the skiff and rowed ashore, hoping to locate a few clams to stay myself with till I got where I could buy something else.

My hopes wa'n't disappointed. I never saw clams thicker than they was along them inshore flats. I filled my dreener in no time, and then it come to me that 'twouldn't be a bad idee to get a lot more, take 'em with me to Wellmouth, and peddle 'em out. Clams was fairly scarce over that side of the bay and ought to fetch a fair price.

So I went back to the *Dora Bassett*, taking my full dreener with me, lit up my little ile-stove that I always carry aboard, and put on a kettle of clams to steam while I was digging some more. Then I rowed ashore again. As I was on my way out I'd noticed a heap of old barrels and such piled up at the edge of the pines; the rubbish pile from the sanitarium, I judged 'twas. I ransacked the pile and resurrected a big box that, according to the markings on it, must have had crockery in it at one time or 'nother. I lugged the box down to tide mark and left it there, cal'lating to fill it with clams soon's I'd filled the dreener again.

But I'd hadn't got the dreener more'n half full, when another notion struck me. The further out from shore I got the bigger the clams I found. Thinks I, "Why not go to see Scudder first, and then come back and do the rest of my digging?" The tide would be further out then, and I'd stand a better chance for the big fellers. So I left my clam dreener right where 'twas, in a hole where the water covered it a foot or more, and rowed back to the *Dora Bassett,* anchored my skiff, started up the engine, and headed for Wapatomac and Nate. I ate my steamed clam breakfast as I went along.

'Twas only half-past seven, and a fine morning with an off-shore wind. The long stretch of narrows leading up to Wapatomac harbor didn't look much the way it did when Martin Hartley and me came through it that time in the gale. The *Dora*

Bassett chugged along, slick as a greased eel, and I run her up to the wharf and made fast.

There was a feller setting on a mackerel keg on the wharf, same as there always is on any wharf or around 'most any railroad depot. And he was a fine specimen of the average run of such fellers. I don't know why his kind are always there, but they always are. Maybe they're anywheres where there's a chance to set.

I climbed up over the string-piece and hailed him.

"Morning," says I, cheerful.

"Ugh," says he. A hog would have said about as much and in pretty much the same way.

"Is there a man name of Scudder running a store in this latitude?" I wanted to know.

"Um-hm," says he. "Ain't got no smoking terbacker on you nowheres, 'tain't likely?"

"Oh, yes, 'tis," I says. "It's the likeliest thing ever you saw. Want some, do you?"

"Yup, I shouldn't wonder if I did."

"Then I shouldn't wonder if you could have it."

I rummaged out my plug and handed it to him. He dug an ancient and honorable old clay pipe out of his overalls and set looking at it, mournful.

"Got a knife?" says he.

I passed over my knife. He whittled up a quar-

54

ter of the plug and filled his pipe with part of the whittlings; what was left he put in his pocket.

"Speaking of Scudder's store," I says, by way of suggestion.

'Twas like a poor vaccination, it didn't take. He seemed to have suggestions enough of his own.

"Ain't got a match you can lend me, have you?" says he.

I grinned. I was in kind of a hurry, too, but I couldn't help grinning.

"I might," I says, "if you give it back when you get through with it."

He didn't answer, but held out his hand.

"Don't you want me to light it for you?" says I.

"No-o, I don't know's I do."

He lit it himself and got the old pipe to going. Then he crossed his legs and looked me over.

"Where'd you come from?" says he.

"Wellmouth Neck. I——"

"What in time do you want to find Nate Scudder's store for? Want to buy something there?"

"No, I don't."

"Looking for mail at the office?"

"No."

I said it pretty sharp, I cal'late, and he looked at me again. He actually leaned for'ard a little on the keg, too, which was the first symptom of interest he'd shown.

"Say," he says, "you ain't going to try to *sell* Scudder something, be you?"

"No."

"What do you want of him, anyhow?"

I'd been heating up slow and by now I was pretty well het.

"I want to break his everlasting neck," I snapped. "And I may do it afore I get through. Now will you dry up on the catechism and tell me how to locate him; or won't you?"

He jumped up off the keg and slapped me on the shoulder. I was so surprised I pretty nigh fell down.

"I'll do more'n that," he says. "I'll go along with you and see that you take the short cuts. Come on! Break old Scudder's neck! Gosh!"

I never see a body look happier at a prospect. I judged Nate was about as popular in Wapatomac as he had been in Wellmouth.

The store wa'n't but a little ways off, standing by itself, and wa'n't much to look at when we got to it. The sign over the door was "Wapatomac General Store. Groceries, Dry Goods, Yacht and Boat Supplies, Confectionery, Boots and Shoes and Cigars. Hulda A. Scudder, Proprietor." There

was a little one by itself that said, "Post-Office." I
grinned again, in spite of my temper, when I see
those signs. I hadn't noticed it on the billhead,
but you could always trust Nate to keep his weather
eye out for squalls and put everything in his wife's
name; he run the post-office in his own, but that was
all he'd risk.

My pilot stopped when we got as fur as the platform.

"Ain't you comin' in?" says I.

"No-o," says he, "I cal'late I won't, not just now.
There's a little mite of a bill that. . . . No, I'll
stay out here till the neck-breaking begins. Say,"
he whispers, with the first sign of a smile I'd seen
on his face, "don't do it too quick, will you? Kind
of stretch out his sufferings long as you can, for my
sake. So long."

The store was as dingy inside as 'twas out. Nate
wa'n't nowheres in sight, but Huldy Ann was astern
of the counter; she hadn't changed a mite, fur's looks
went. Setting in a rickety old wooden armchair
close by was a middle-aged, prim-looking woman,
dressed in black, with a prim-looking hat on her
head and gray silk gloves on her hands. Her hair
was fixed smooth and plain, not a wisp of it loose
anywheres, and if ever "Old Maid" was wrote large
on a person, 'twas on her. Yet what she was wear-

ing was good quality, and she looked as if she was used to her clothes.

"I cannot wait, Mrs. Scudder," she was saying, as I came in. "I cannot. I must get back. Is there no one with a horse and vehicle whom I can hire to drive me home? When do you expect your husband?"

Huldy Ann looked sort of troubled.

"He won't be back afore noon," she says, regretful. "He's gone over to Brantboro to collect a . . . on a matter of business. I'd drive you back myself, only I can't leave the store very well, and Nate's took the horse, besides. Can't you get a team down to the livery stable?"

"I suppose I can," says the other woman. "If I may use your 'phone, I'll try."

Huldy shook her head. "Well, now, ain't that too bad!" she says. "It does beat all how contrary things act sometimes. Our telephone ain't working. My husband had some little argument with the company about—about a charge they put on our bill, and the unlikely critters cut off the service. That's the trouble with them big corporations, they ain't got any souls. I——"

The other woman interrupted her. "Very well," says she, sort of impatient, but resigned; "then I will walk home. Good-morning, Mrs. Scudder."

She was turning to go, but when she turned she saw me standing by the door. Huldy Ann looked up and saw me, too.

"Well," says Huldy, brisk, "what can I do for you, Mister?" Then she looked a little closer and sung out: "Why! why! I do believe it's Solomon Pratt!"

"Your belief's orthodox so fur, Huldy," says I. "How are you?"

"Solomon Pratt!" says she again. "Solomon Pratt from Wellmouth! What in the wide world are you doing way over here?"

"Oh, I couldn't stay away from you and Nate any longer, 'specially since you took the trouble to write and invite me."

"I invite you? Oh!" She looked a little queer, seemed to me, and sort of flustered. "Oh!" she says again, "you mean that little statement Nathan sent you. You needn't have come way over here to pay that."

"I didn't," says I, prompt. "So don't let that weigh on your conscience, Huldy. Nate's out, I understand."

"Yes. No—— Oh, are you going, Miss Adams? You're really not going to walk way back home!"

"It looks as if I should have to," says the other

woman. "It is a long way for one in my state of health, but I must get back."

"Well, I must say it's a shame. If there was anybody I could get to drive."

"I wish there was, but it appears there isn't. It is almost as far to the livery stable as it is to the sanitarium, so I may as well walk home, if walk I must. Oh, dear!"

She looked at me, sideways, when she said it. I had been looking at her. The name Adams had given me the idea who she must be. The description Eureka give me fitted her to a T. She was the Miss Emeline I'd heard so much about: Doctor Lysander Wool's star patient; the one that owned the "Right Livers' Rest Place."

"I would gladly pay two dollars for a horse and carriage—and driver," she said, still looking at me sideways.

Maybe 'twas the two dollars. I could use money about as well as the next feller, just then. Anyhow I says:

"I'll take you back home, ma'am, if you want me to."

She started and looked me over again.

"Thank you," says she, kind of hopeful but doubtful, so to speak. "I am much obliged to you, I am sure. But I——"

"Oh, I'm fairly respectable, in spite of my looks," I put in. "Huldy Ann here'll give me a recommend, I shouldn't wonder; though she ain't much in the giving habit. How about it, Huldy?"

Huldy looked more fussed-up than ever, and a little mite put out besides.

"Mr. Pratt is an old fri—neighbor—of ours at Wellmouth," she says, short. "He's all right; you can trust him same as you would my husband, Miss Adams."

"There!" says I. "Now I *am* proud. You couldn't ask more'n that, ma'am, could you?"

She never smiled. I judged all my good sarcasm was going to waste. However, she acted a little more satisfied.

"I am sure I can trust him," she says to Huldy. "You must excuse my hesitation, Mr.—er—Pratt," turning to me, "but I have had a very disagreeable experience this morning with one whom I had trusted heretofore, and perhaps I am over-cautious. I thank you. But do you know where I wish to go?"

I told her I cal'lated I did, if she was Miss Emeline Adams of Doctor Wool's sanitarium. She seemed surprised that I knew her name, and Huldy Ann acted similar. I explained that I had a friend who knew her.

"Eureka Sparrow, her name is, ma'am," says I.

"Oh," says she, as if this settled it. "Are you *that* Mr. Pratt? Eureka has spoken of you often. I accept your offer, of course, Mr. Pratt. Is your horse and carriage outside here?"

I shook my head.

"No, ma'am," says I; "but my power boat, the *Dora Bassett,* is right down to the wharf. She'll get you home quick as any horse, now I tell you."

This opened up a whole lot more trouble. She wa'n't used to boats and was scared of going in one. However, after consider'ble pow-wow she agreed to run the risk, and we started. Huldy Ann got me to one side afore I reached the door.

"If you want to pay that bill, Solomon," says she, "you can leave the money with me."

"If I wanted to, Huldy, I would," I says. "It's awful kind of you to think of it."

She flared up in a jiffy. "Look here, Mr. Pratt," says she, "if you expect my husband to go clear to Wellmouth Neck to collect that bill you owe him you're——"

"There, there!" says I. "I don't. *I'll* tell him where he can go, when I see him. So long, Huldy."

The long-legged critter that had piloted me up from the wharf was waiting around the corner.

"Have you broke it?" he whispers, eager.

"Broke what?"

"Old Scudder's neck. Have you? I didn't hear no row."

"No, I ain't broke it yet."

"Humph! Why not?"

"Well, for one reason, he's gone to Brantboro and taken his neck with him."

He was awful disappointed. "Humph!" he says again, "then you ain't done nothing to him, after all."

"Oh, yes, I have. I've been trying a little Christian Science, giving him absent treatment. Right this way, Miss Adams."

The tide had gone out consider'ble while I was up to Scudder's store, and I had a good deal of a job getting the Emeline woman to climb down the ladder into the boat. However, I got her there finally and I cranked up and got under way. On the run down to the Narrows she asked me a lot of questions about myself, what I'd been doing, and the like of that.

"Can you cut grass, Mr. Pratt?" says she.

I shrugged my shoulders. What on earth she asked that for I couldn't make out.

"Cal'late I can, ma'am," I said. "If I don't get a job pretty soon I'll have to l'arn to *eat* it, like Nebuchadnezzar in Scriptur'!"

She smiled then. 'Twas a kind of uncertain smile,

same as if she guessed there was a joke round the premises somewheres, but wa'n't sure, not being used to the breed.

"I do hope you won't think me unduly curious, Mr. Pratt," she says. "I am not asking these questions merely from idle curiosity, I assure you."

"That's all right, ma'am. Heave ahead and ask."

"I have an idea that perhaps—— Well, I'll say no more now. We will discuss it later, after I have spoken with Doctor Wool. I presume you wonder why I happened to be at Mr. Scudder's store so early with no way of getting back. I will explain. I have had such an experience!"

I had been wondering what such a precise female as she was doing, hunting for somebody to take her home at half-past eight in the morning. Now she went ahead and told me. Seems she always turned out about six, that being a part of the particular "treatment" she was taking. Eureka, who was sort of over-seeing housekeeper at the Rest shop, had just been told by the cook that they needed some more oatmeal or prunes or something right off. Thoph Pease, the feller I'd met the night afore, had been given his orders to hitch up the horse and drive over after it. Miss Emeline took a notion to go along.

"'Twas such a beautiful morning, Mr. Pratt,"

says she. "I thought the drive would do me good. I should have asked permission of the Doctor, but I did not."

"Asked permission," says I. "What for? You own the place, don't you? Eureka said you did. What do *you* have to ask anybody's permission for?"

She looked at me as if I'd said something unreligious.

"It is true," she says, dignified, "that I own the property itself, but Doctor Wool is in full charge of the sanitarium. I am merely one of his patients and we abide entirely by his directions and advice. The Doctor is a wonderful man."

Eureka had said the same thing, and in the same reverent, meeting-house kind of voice, too. I was more anxious to meet Lysander the Great than ever; anxious and a little mite nervous. I'd never run afoul of any saints and heroes alongshore, and I wa'n't sure that I'd know how to behave.

"But that is immaterial," she went on. "I did not ask his permission and I did start for Mr. Scudder's with that dreadful Theophilus. I thought he behaved queerly when I got into the buggy, and it seemed to me that I noticed a peculiar odor about him."

"Yes, ma'am," says I, "I noticed it last night. Rum and molasses, wa'n't it? I wouldn't take my oath on the molasses, but the rest of the prescription was there."

"It was some sort of spirits," she says, kind of shuddering. "He frightened me, Mr. Pratt, and when I remonstrated with him for driving so recklessly he used the most dreadful language. Before we reached the village I insisted on getting out of the carriage. I thought for a moment he was going to detain me by force—yes, physical force. But he did not quite dare and I got out and walked the rest of the way. I told him to go home at once; that I would see he was discharged. He was—— Why, Mr. Pratt, the man was—was actually—— I'm ashamed to speak the word!"

"I'll speak it for you, ma'am. You was going to say he was drunk, tighter'n a b'iled owl, wa'n't you. He was on the way to it last night, and his McCarty friend wa'n't much better. I cal'late the pair of 'em have been keeping it up ever since. What did he say when you bounced him?"

"He was dreadfully ugly. He said I had better not mention it to the Doctor or it would be the worse for me. I was frightened and hurried away and left him. I think he drove back then, but I'm not sure. What is it? What are you looking at?"

I was bending for'ard to stare over the port bow ahead. It had seemed to me that I'd noticed a couple of fellers in the bushes on a point of land we was passing. However, I didn't see 'em any more and I didn't mention 'em to her. She went on talking about this and that, principally Thoph and his dreadful actions. I was busy keeping clear of the flats and shoals. The tide had gone out a lot and I wa'n't used to the coast.

However, everything went first rate till I turned the last point and swung in where I'd left my skiff. Then I had a shock. The skiff wa'n't there any more—'twas gone.

I was surprised and pretty mad, at myself, of course. I thought I'd anchored that skiff hard and fast, but it seemed as if I hadn't. I looked out over the bay, but she wa'n't nowheres in sight. A good, four-year-old skiff, too, worth fifteen dollars of any man's money; and fifteen dollars was a Standard Ile salary to me just then.

"What is the matter?" says Miss Emeline. "Oh, what is it, Mr. Pratt? We are not in any danger, are we?"

"No, no," says I. "You couldn't find any danger here if you dredged for it. My skiff's drifted out to sea, that's all. I'd like to go and hunt for her, but I cal'late you're in a hurry to get back to the house, ain't you?"

Indeed she was! She must get back at once. No

67

one knew where she had gone and they would be worried.

"All right," says I, "then I'll get you back somehow. It's all right; don't you fret, Miss Adams."

I run the *Dora Bassett* as close inshore as I dast to, but that wa'n't so awful close. There was a good fifty yards of shoal water between me and the beach when I got the anchor overside, but not more'n a couple of foot under the keel.

"Now, Miss Adams," says I, beginning to take off my boots and socks, "if you'll just not be scared and set still in my arms I'll hop overboard and lug you ashore."

Well, sir, you wouldn't have believed a sane person could have made such a fuss over a simple thing like that. If I'd proposed hitching that Emeline woman to the anchor she couldn't have made more objections.

"But there's no danger," says I. "I'll see that you don't get wet, and I'm a kind of half fish, anyhow. Salt water's good for me. I'm like old Tony Peters, the Portygee. He fell off the wharf and got wet all over for the first time in ten years, I cal'late. When they fished him out he acted sort of surprised. 'No, no!' says he. 'Tony no hurt. Tony feel better. I go in again sometime, maybe.'"

I laughed. I always laugh when I think of Tony.

But that Emeline woman didn't laugh. No, sir-ee! I give you my word I thought she was going to cry. She would not let me lug her ashore, that's all there was to it.

"All right, ma'am," says I, losing patience. "Then there's nothing to do but set here and wait till somebody comes, fur's I see."

"But no one ever comes down here," says she. "Not oftener than once a week."

"All right, then we'll wait a week; unless you're willing fur me to leave you here and go ashore by myself and hunt up a dory or something."

No, no! she wouldn't be left alone in that dreadful boat for anything. That would be worse than being toted in my arms. So there being nothing to do, I set still and did it.

Pretty soon she begun to whoop for help. You'd think she was drowning. I was so ashamed I didn't know what to do.

"Look here, ma'am," says I, after the nineteenth whoop, "I'd just as soon you wouldn't do that, if you please. There's an offshore breeze anyhow, so it don't do us no good; and, besides, I ain't so proud of this pickle we're in that I want to advertise it. . . . I . . . . Say, keep still, will you!"

I guess my tone wa'n't any too peaceful; anyhow she kept still. Then, for five minutes or so, there wa'n't hardly a sound. From ashore somewheres a dog barked, but his bark shut off sudden in the middle.

Then, all at once, Miss Emeline spoke up.

"You are sure it would be safe?" says she.

"I've told you so, ma'am, ain't I?"

"And you won't drop me?"

"Nary drop."

"Then—then I'll trust you. I—I'm ready." She said it as if she was going to be led out and hung.

However, she didn't have to say it but once. Next second I was overboard in water above my knees and holding out my arms for her. She flopped into 'em with her eyes shut and groaning as if she was dying. I started for shore.

The first fifteen yards was all right, except that I was pretty nigh strangled from the death grip she had on my neck. And every second step she screamed, not loud screams, but, being as they was straight into my port ear, they was loud enough. Then we come to a channel and the water deepened up some. It deepened till 'twas up to my waist. Miss Emeline stopped screaming and begun to give orders.

"I'm going back," says she. "I'm going back."

"No, no, you ain't," says I; "you're going ahead. Just keep still and we'll be out of this in a shake."

"I'm going back! I command you to take me back at once! I command you!"

"Ma'am," says I, "you keep still. Keep still! If you don't I'll—I swan to man I'll put you down!"

I was mad enough to do it. I guess she realized I meant it, for she stopped kicking. On I went.

"Ouch!" says I.

"Oh!" she gasps. "What is it? What *is* it? Is this the end?"

"Which end? I stepped on a crab, if you want to know. There! now she begins to shoal up again. Your troubles are 'most over, Miss Adams."

But they wasn't; they was just beginning. I hadn't no more'n said this when from astern of us come a hail. I stopped and looked over my shoulder. What I see made me forget all about crabs and women and such trifles.

Back of us, between where we stood and the *Dora Bassett,* was a skiff—my skiff, the one I thought had floated adrift. And in that skiff, grinning the ugliest grin ever you saw, was Mike McCarty, Physical Director of the Right Livers' Rest. He had—so I found out afterwards—waded off and got the skiff and had been hiding in it behind the next point, waiting for us to come. He had one oar in the water, steadying the skiff where it was, and the other balanced across the rail. I stared at him and he grinned at me. *I* didn't grin much.

"Hello, Spratt!" says he. "How's the water; wet?"

I could have punched his head; the only reason I didn't was that I couldn't get at it.

"What in thunder are you doing in that skiff?" I hollered.

"Taking a little fresh air," says he, cheerful. "You two make a classy picture, Spratt. Pity I ain't got a kodak."

"You'll make a whole panorama when I get hold of you," I sung out. "Come here with that boat."

"Oh, no, I guess not. We'll have a little talk first. How's the old girl; heavy?"

I don't know how Miss Emeline liked being called "old girl." I didn't wait to find out.

"I'll see you in just two minutes, chummie," says I. "Wait till I put this lady on dry ground and I'll talk to you—more'n you want, I shouldn't wonder."

He just grinned again. "We won't wait, Spratt," he says. "Stop where you are! Hi, Thoph! Thoph!. . . . Humph! Now you'll stop, maybe."

And stop I did. I had took a couple of long steps toward the shore when out of the bushes walks that Thoph Pease critter, the hired man, the rum and molasses one. He was holding tight to one end of a rope. At the other end of that rope was the savagest, ugliest, hungriest-looking bulldog I'd ever run acrost in my born days.

I saw that bulldog and Thoph, and, as I say, I stopped. Miss Emeline saw 'em and screamed. From astern of us I heard McCarty laugh.

"Pretty, ain't he," says he. "Let him go, Thoph! Hi, Pet! Look out for 'em! Sic 'em, boy!"

Thoph let go of his end of the rope. "Pet" turned loose a growl like the first rumblings of an earthquake and come tearing to the shore. There he pranced up and down, with his forepaws in the water, and stood, ready for his breakfast. There wa'n't much doubt in my mind that we was the breakfast.

"And now," says McCarty, "we'll have our little talk. Miss Adams, you listen to what me and Pease have got to say."

I was too much set back and surprised to get a word loose, but I felt Miss Emeline kind of stiffen in my arms.

"Theophilus Pease," says she, stern and sharp, "how dare you! Call off that dog! Take the creature away immediately."

Thoph acted a little mite scared, in spite of his rum and molasses.

"I—I can't, ma'am," he says.

"You bet he can't!" This was from McCarty. "I own that dog and he minds nobody but me. Miss Adams, you stay right where you are until you promise on your word of honor not to tell Wool or anybody else about Thoph's row with you this morning. You've said you was going to have him fired. Well, you ain't. Him and me are standing together in this thing and we'll see it through. Hey, Thoph?"

"Bet your life!" drawls Thoph, uneasy but ugly.

I'd found my tongue by this time and I was b'iling over.

"Don't you promise nothing, ma'am," I bellowed. "I'll settle this business myself. Don't be scared."

I swung round and commenced to make toward the skiff. Miss Emeline gave another gasp.

"What are you going to do?" she sung out.

"I'm going to take you back to the *Dora Bassett*. Then I'll do a little physical directing on my own hook."

But I hadn't got into the deep water again afore McCarty made his next move. In that skiff he had a big advantage over me. Two strokes of the oars and he was alongside the *Dora Bassett* and his jackknife was out.

"Nothing doing," says he, with a snap of his jaws

74

"You come this way another inch and I'll cut the anchor rope and let her go adrift."

Well, I never wanted to keep moving more, but I didn't—I stopped. The wind had been breezing up and 'twas dead offshore. If he cut that anchor rope the boat might drift to Jericho. Ten to one I'd never see her again. And she was about all I had left in the world.

"Ha! ha!" laughs McCarty.

"He! he!" chuckles Thoph.

"Gr-r-r! Bow-wow!" remarks Pet.

And the water was getting colder and Miss Emeline getting heavier every second.

'Twas McCarty that spoke next. He was boss of the situation for the time being. More'n that, he'd had plenty of time to think in, which I hadn't.

"We ain't unreasonable, Miss Adams," he says, more polite and coaxing. "We don't want to lose our jobs, that's all. I'll own that Thoph has been tanking up a bit, but that's nothing; maybe he won't do it again. All we want of you is to keep still about it and give us another show. If you promise I know you'll keep your word. And you don't get out of that water till you do."

She opened her mouth to scream, but McCarty shut it up in a hurry.

"There's no use to yell," he says. "Nobody'll

hear you. The Doc and his new guy, old Quill, have gone for a walk. The patients are all over on the exercise ground, quarter of a mile off. The Sparrow girl has gone to the store to find you. There's nobody in the house but the cook and maid, and they're busy. There's nothing doing in the rescue line, so you can promise us to keep still, or you can stay there—and drown."

Miss Emeline's clutch on my neck got tighter than ever, if that was possible.

"What shall I do?" she groaned in my ear. "What shall I do?"

I managed to gurgle out a word or two over her wrist.

"Do!" I choked. "Do nothing, of course. You couldn't drown on these flats unless you dug a hole and put your head in it. Don't you promise a single thing."

"But—but——"

"Hold on! Ease up on my throat a jiffy, will you. Whew! Much obliged. I'll tell you what you do. Promise, same as they say. *You* needn't tell a word. I'll do all the talking's necessary. Promise."

She hesitated.

"I hate to," she gasped. "It is against my principles. I——"

"Well?" says McCarty. "Going to be sensible, are you?"

"I—I don't know."

"I guess you know all right. Now, Spratt, or Pratt, or whatever your name is, you've got to promise, too."

"Promise be—keelhauled!" says I. It's a good thing Miss Emeline choked me off when she did, or I'd have made it more lively. "I'll promise to break your figurehead for you; that's what I'll promise."

"No, you won't. I'll risk my figurehead. But you'll promise to keep your mouth shut or I'll cut this anchor rope. And see here, Miss Adams, if he does promise and then blabs, you've got to swear he's a liar. You'll have to promise that, too."

She almost jumped out of my arms.

"What!" she says. "You expect me to tell a falsehood! You—you—I never did such a thing in my life!"

"You've missed something," says McCarty. "It ain't too late to begin."

"Never!" says she, "never! I'll stay here till I drown first."

"Right you are, ma'am," says I. "And we won't drown nuther. Come on, we'll go ashore."

And for shore I headed. But I didn't get very far.

"Watch 'em, Pet," yelled McCarty. Pet watched us, all right. It's a bad thing to have too much imagination. I could feel them teeth in my underpinning already.

"Is—is that critter very ferocious?" I asked, easing up in my stride.

"Dreadful! Oh, dreadful! He has bitten several people. He would kill us, I do believe."

Well, I didn't hanker to be fresh meat for a bulldog. And it sartin did look as if 'twould take a lot to fill that mouth. I kept on edging in, but mighty slow. McCarty and Thoph noticed the slowness and they both laughed.

"He don't like the scenery, Pease," giggles the physical director.

I was thinking awful hard. As for Miss Emeline, she was trembling, but quiet. It was plain she'd ruther die than lie. I begun to have more respect for that old maid.

I edged in a little further, and then I spied something that give me an idea. Just in front of me, in the hole where I'd left it, was my dreener half full of clams. I remembered something Obed Nickerson, of Orham, told me about an experience he had with a dog.

"Ma'am," I whispered. "Miss Adams, I want you to do just what I tell you. I'm going to put you down."

"Oh, no, no!" says she. "No, no!"

"Yes, yes! 'Tain't more'n up to your—up to the tops of your shoes. I'm going to set you down."

"No, no! you mustn't! I——"

She hung on to me as if I was a life preserver. I grabbed her wrists and pulled 'em loose.

"I've got to," says I. "There's a limit to being choked and froze, and, besides, you weigh all of fifty pounds more'n you did when I picked you up. Down you go! There!"

I stood her on her feet in the shallow water. I heard McCarty yell, but I didn't pay no attention.

"Now," I whispers, not asking, but ordering, this time, "you start for the beach up there," pointing off to starboard. "Go, as fast as you can."

"I can't—I can't—the dog——"

"I'll look after the dog. Or he'll look after me. When I start you start, too."

I didn't wait to see whether she did or not. I made one jump for'ard, grabbed up the dreener of clams, and ran pell-mell for the beach. Only I took a course in the opposite direction from what I'd sent her.

Through the sand and water I went, yelling like

a loon. Thoph and Pet danced around on shore, not knowing which of us to take after. The Mc-Carty swab, though, kept his head and he yelled his orders.

"Look out for the woman, Thoph!" he roared. "Sic him, Pet! Sic him!"

So after Miss Emeline went Pease, and after me came Pet, mouth open and teeth snapping.

'Twas what I'd cal'lated on and I was ready for him. I grabbed a handful of clams out of the dreener and let him have 'em, hard as I could throw. Four out of the half-dozen missed, but 'tother two bust right in his face and eyes. He yelled and jumped, and I gained a lap in the race.

When he come on again he got another handful. A clam shell is pretty sharp when it lands edgeways on your nose, and, for the average pup, two broad-sides would have been enough. But not for Pet— no, sir! On he came, coughing and snarling.

By this time I was on the beach and heading straight for that big empty box I'd found early in the morning, and had figgered to put my extry clams into. He was at my heels when I reached it, and I fired all my ammunition, dreener and all, at him. It hit and over he went as if he'd been blowed up. He wa'n't discouraged, not him, but neither was I. I had the big box, open side down, in my arms in front of me by now, and, when he made his next jump, I jumped, too.

It was more luck than anything else, but if anybody ever had luck due 'em, I was that feller. I jumped up in the air, box and all. When I come down the sharp edge of the box caught that dog about six inches from his tail and right acrost his back. Naturally, he jumped for'ard to get out from under. When he jumped he went inside the box. Down it came "plunk" in the sand with me sprawled on top of it. As for "Pet," he was inside the box, for all the world like a rabbit in a trap.

Well, 'twas some situation. There I was, sprawled on top of the box; underneath was the dog, humping up and snarling and growling and yelping and sneezing all at once; up the beach was the Adams woman, running best she could, with Pease after her; and McCarty in the skiff was rowing for shore and yelling orders to his messmate and brimstone remarks to me.

And then a voice right alongside of me says:

"You go and help Miss Emeline, Mr. Pratt. I'll set on the dog."

I twisted my neck and looked up. Eureka Sparrow was standing there, calm and cool as an iced codfish.

"My soul! Eureka!" says I.

"Yes," says she. "Don't get up all to once; just shove over a little and give me room. I weigh a hundred and fifty-two, and I'll stay put, I guess likely. It's all right, Miss Emeline. Mr. Pratt's a-coming."

CHAPTER IV

WELL, I shoved over; I don't know why, nuther. I'm mighty sure 'twa'n't because I sensed what Joash Howes, when he talked politics at the post-office, used to call the "true inwardness of the crisis that's onto us." I didn't seem to sense much of anything, except that *my* inwardness was awful scant of breath. However, I shoved over on the box and down set Eureka. The solid, everyday way she did it kind of brought me to myself. I scrambled to my feet and took after Pease. He had caught up with the Adams woman by this time and was dancing around in front of her, waving both fists and telling her to stop. He didn't hardly dast to actually lay hands on her. McCarty would have grabbed her and thrown her into the bay, for what I know; but not Thoph. He was the weak end of that rum and molasses concern, and his partner wasn't there to help him.

And I got there afore the partner did. McCarty wasn't over halfway to the beach when my boot hit that Pease critter and pitchpoled him same

83

as I've seen a boat pitchpoled in the surf when a summer boarder tried to make a landing. Thoph's nose—and there was consider'ble of it—made a furrow in the sand. I grabbed Miss Emeline by the waist. I thought maybe she was going to faint— women do that sometimes, they tell me—but I was mistaken. She was on dry land now and the first word she said proved there wa'n't much faint about her.

"Is—is that dog out of the way?" she panted.

"Yes'm," says I, "he is."

"Where is he?"

"He's—he's under Eureka."

"Eureka! Where is Eureka?"

"Over the dog. Over there, I mean."

She looked where I pointed. Eureka smiled and nodded.

"He's all right, Miss Emeline," she called. "He can't get out. Mr. Pratt, McCarty's 'most here."

I turned around. The skiff was almost to the beach. Thoph was getting on his knees again. He seemed sort of undecided in his mind whether to run away or stay there and hold onto his nose. I was undecided, too. I hated to leave Miss Emeline, but I didn't want McCarty to get ashore. Two to one's a big majority, and I'd ruther have the two separate.

Miss Emeline settled it for me. She twisted out of my arm.

"Look out for that creature," she says, pointing toward the skiff. "I am all right now."

"But—but him," says I, pointing toward Thoph. He was on his knees still. It looked almost as if he was praying—but it didn't sound that way.

"He!" snapped Miss Emeline. "I'm not afraid of *him!* I'm ashamed to think I ever was. Let me be, Mr. Pratt."

I let her be. I was glad of the chance. I run down to the shore and stood there, waiting. For the first time in twenty minutes I was happy, actually happy.

"Come on, Mr. Physical Director," says I. "Come on, and get your morning exercise."

He kept coming; I'll give him that much credit. But all at once he stopped and jumped to his feet. There was a rustle in the bushes astern of us, and a voice, the big, purry, organ voice I'd heard the night afore, said:

"What is all this? Tut! tut! tut! I am surprised! What does this mean?"

All hands looked, I cal'late. I know I did. For a jiffy 'twas still as could be; then everything happened at once.

Thoph Pease give one gulp, or groan, or swear,

or combination of all three, and put for tall timber as if the Old Scratch was after him. McCarty sat down again in the skiff and looked sick. Miss Emeline collapsed in the sand and looked thankful. And Eureka, perched on the dog coop, spoke up, resigned and contented.

"It's the Doctor," says she. "There! *Now* we're all right."

He come marching down the beach, big and calm and serene, like the admiral of all creation on parade. He was dressed in white, generally speaking— white flannel pants and white vest and a white broad-brimmed hat in his hand. His coat, though, was long-tailed and black like a parson's, and his neck-tie was blue with white spots, and clewed up in a big, floppy bow. All these things I noticed afterwards; what I was watching just then was his face.

'Twas a big face and smooth, no whiskers, no mustache, no nothing, and his forehead run up over the top of his head. His nose was big, and his mouth was big, and his hair, what there was of it, was brushed back astern of his ears. When he walked he stepped deliberate; when he moved his big white hands he moved 'em deliberate; everything he did he did deliberate and grand. Somehow he made you feel little and—and—well—young.

He looked us all over, one after the other. Then he took command of the deck.

"McCarty," he boomed, in his big voice, "bring that boat ashore immediately."

And, by time! McCarty done it. I was expecting a row, but there wa'n't any. That physical director hesitated for half a shake, but that was all.

"McCarty," says Doctor Wool, "did you hear me? Bring that boat ashore."

I took one step into the water.

"Yes, McCarty," says I, "bring it ashore. And don't forget to come yourself, 'cause I'm waiting for you."

McCarty was just stepping out of the skiff. He glared at me and doubled up his fist.

"McCarty!" booms the big voice again. "And you, sir, kindly let him pass, if you please."

I let him pass; I don't know why; one thing's sartin, I hadn't been intending to.

"Go up to my office and wait for me," orders the Doctor.

"Aw, now, Boss!" pleads McCarty. "I—'twas all just a mistake. I——"

"To my office. I will hear your—er—explanation later. Go!"

And he went. Yes, sir, he went! And I, who had been jumping up and down with the hankering to get at him, let him go and never said a word. As for Thoph, he'd been gone quite a spell.

The Doctor paraded majestic over to Miss Emeline.

"Miss Adams," says he, and when he spoke to her the purr in his voice got stronger and sweeter and more wonderful than ever, "I trust you have suffered no actual—er—harm. I trust not."

"Oh, no—no—I think not, Doctor. I—I am— my nerves——"

"Nerves, my dear madam, are what we permit them to be, as you know. I am certain that a strong, womanly nature, such as yours. . . . Ah, you are better already, are you not? Yes. Quite yourself again. May I assist you to rise?"

He put one hand under her elbow and hiked her up out of that sand as easy as if she'd been a feather-weight, which she wa'n't, according to my experience. I don't mean he really lifted her by main strength—not by no means. He kind of purred her up, if such a thing's possible.

"You are yourself again?" says he.

"Yes. I—I—think so."

"As we think, we are. Er—Eureka," he swung around and looked at the Sparrow girl; "Eureka," he says, "may I ask why you continue to decorate

88

that—er—box; and why you do not come to Miss Adams's aid?"

Poor Eureka looked scared and troubled.

"I'm setting on the dog," says she.

Even he was surprised, I cal'late.

"The dog?" he says.

"Yes, sir. Mr. McCarty's dog—Pet, you know. He set him onto Mr. Pratt."

"Ah! I see—I see. And now you are—er—returning the compliment. Very good, very good."

He smiled, and that smile on his big face was like sunshine breaking through and lighting up half a mile of white beach.

"And this—er—gentleman?" waving a big white hand at me.

"That is Mr. Pratt," says Eureka, prompt. "He's a friend of mine. I used to know him over to Wellmouth."

"He saved my life, Doctor Wool," puts in Miss Emeline, getting fussed up again and beginning to tremble. "I verily believe he saved my life. If it were not for him—— Oh, Doctor, if you knew——"

"There, there! My dear madam, calm yourself. Force your thoughts in the right direction. I shall know all very soon. I shall make it my business to know. Meanwhile, suppose we return to the—er—sanitarium, if you please."

He offered her his arm and they paraded toward the bushes. At the edge of 'em he stopped.

"Eureka," he said, "perhaps your friend here will assist you in securing the—er—dog. Afterwards I shall be obliged if you will bring Mr.—er—Pratt to me. I shall wish to thank him for the service which it—er—appears he has rendered our dear Miss Adams."

"I'll fetch him right up," says Eureka, quick as a flash.

"Why! I don't know," says I. "I ought to be getting back home. I was cal'lating to dig a few clams and then I ought to see Nate Scudder. That's what I come over fur."

"Doubtless, doubtless. But I am certain you will not go without giving me a moment. I shall count upon your doing so, sir. Say no more; I shall count upon it."

And, by the everlasting, I *didn't* say any more. Somehow or 'nother I couldn't. Contradicting him seemed sort of ridiculous and useless, like a hen's trying to stop a funeral by getting in the way of the hearse.

"And now, Miss Adams," says he.

They went away together. I looked at Eureka and she looked at me.

"Ain't he the *grandest* thing!" says she, in a sort of whispering hooray. "Ain't he?"

I shook my head. "I don't know," says I. "He's something, sartin. Anyhow, I never see anybody like him."

"That's 'cause there ain't anybody like him. And now what'll we do with this Pet nuisance. I do believe he's et a hole half through this box already."

He hadn't, but he'd dug himself 'most out from underneath it. I filled in the hole he'd made, piled sand a foot deep all round the edges, and laid four or five big chunks of driftwood and pine stumps on top of the box. Then Eureka got up.

"There!" says she, "that'll keep him jailed for a spell, I shouldn't wonder, and McCarty can let him out himself by and by. He can breathe; there's holes enough in the box. You 'tend to your skiff and boat, Mr. Pratt, and then come right up to the house. I'll be waiting for you in the kitchen. Your luck, the tea leaf luck, has started; mind what I tell you."

I laughed for the first time in an hour.

"If the rest of it's like what's hit me already," says I, "I cal'late I'll finish afore it does."

Thirty or forty minutes later I knocked on the kitchen door of the Rest place. I looked around, as I walked acrost the lawn, for my old chum Apple-cart, or some others of the Right Livers, but there wa'n't none in sight.

Eureka was waiting for me, all on tiptoe with excitement.

"He expects you," says she. "He's in his office and you're to come right in. I've told him all about you. It's perfectly splendid. Don't you *dare* say anything but yes, Mr. Pratt."

Afore I could ask what I was to say yes to, she was piloting me through two or three big rooms, a whale of a dining-room amongst 'em, and knocking on a door.

"Come in," booms the big voice. Hitting a bass drum with a spoonful of sugared hasty-pudding might have sounded something like it; I can't think of any other soft-slick-loud-sweet noise that would fill the bill. Eureka opened the door.

"Here he is, Doctor Wool," says she.

And in I marched.

He was sitting at the other side of a big table, and the sun, streaming in at the window behind him, lit up the shiny top of his head like a glory.

"Be seated, sir," says he. "Be seated, I beg."

I set down in the chair he pointed out to me. He smiled and thanked me for doing it. I never thought afore that setting down was anything to be proud of 'special, but that smile and the thanks made me feel as if I'd done something wuth while. I told him he was welcome.

"Will you pardon me," says he, "if for a moment I continue with the little task upon which I was engaged. A mere business letter—a trifle only— and yet trifles neglected make the mountains upon which the ships of our lives are so often wrecked. You agree with me, I'm sure."

"Yes, indeed," says I, "I've noticed it often."

And yet now, as I come to think of it, I don't remember ever hearing of a ship being wrecked on a mountain.

So he went on with his letter writing and I looked around the room.

'Twa'n't a very big room—I learned afterwards that it had been the first floor bedroom of the old house—and there wa'n't much in it, in the furniture line. Two or three chairs, the desk, and a table with a vase full of posies on it, that was about all. The walls, though, was covered with pictures, mainly framed photographs and mottoes; there was a lot of letters framed amongst 'em, too. From where I set I could read a few of the letters.

One had "White House" printed at the top of it. The writing underneath went like this:

MR. PRATT'S PATIENTS

The President directs me to thank Doctor
Wool for his favor of the 19th.

So and So, Secretary,

Per R.

Another was headed "Office of J. P. Astorbilt &
Co., Wall Street, New York."

Mr. Astorbilt regrets that he will be unable
to see Doctor Wool on the date named in the
latter's letter.

There was a good many more, and the photographs was mainly of folks whose pictures I'd seen
in the newspapers, play-actors and congressmen and
such. Each one had a name on it, but whether they'd
been wrote by the folks themselves or not I wa'n't
able to say. The mottoes was generally good advice, like, "Man, Know Thyself," and "The Proper
Study for Mankind Is Man." In the middle place
of all was a crayon enlargement of Doctor Wool,
setting in a chair and beaming grand and good and
kind on all creation. He had a book open on his
knee, and you could see that he was thinking high
thoughts and enjoying 'em. Over this picture was a
big sign, "As We Think, We Are," which was what
he'd said to Miss Emeline on the beach, I recol-
lected.

94

I stared around at the decorations and the Doctor went on with his letter-writing. By and by he laid down the pen and turned to me.

"Ah!" says he, "you are observing my collection, I perceive. What do you think of it?"

"Seems to be—er—first rate," says I, not knowing just how to answer.

"Little tributes, little tributes, Mr. Pratt. Trifles in themselves, but gratifying in the mass, gratifying —yes. It is pleasant, although humbling, to feel that one is, even in a small way, a benefactor to one's fellow creatures. They flatter me."

"That one don't flatter you none," says I, waving my hand to the crayon enlargement. "It's as natural as can be. Joash Kenney, over to Wellmouth, never done a better enlargement than that; and he's the best enlarger we've got around here."

He bowed and thanked me again. I begun to fidget a little. Seemed to me 'twas time for whatever he wanted to see me about to get out from under hatches.

"You had something you wanted to say to me, I believe, Doctor Wool," I hove out, by way of suggestion.

He moved his big head up and down slow.

"I did," says he; "I did—er—yes."

"Then—then suppose you say it, if 'tain't too

95

much to ask. I ain't got none too much time, and——"

He stopped me with a wave of his hand. "Time," he purred, "is for slaves, as the wise man has said."

"It and the tide waits for no man; that's been said, too. And if I'm going to do any errand over to Wapatomac and get back to Wellmouth by night, I mustn't set here."

"I trust you will not go back to Wellmouth to-night, Mr. Pratt."

"I've got to."

"I trust not, Mr. Pratt. Eureka, our accomplished young friend in the kitchen, tells me that you are out of employment just now. Is that true?"

I fetched a long breath. The dog, and Miss Emeline, and all the rest of it, had made me forget my other troubles for a spell; now they come back onto me hard.

"It's true enough, all right," I said. "More's the pity, it's true enough."

"Yes—er—yes. I see, I see. Well—er—Mr. Pratt, I trust we may be able to change all that, to overcome that difficulty—er—yes."

I straightened up in my chair.

"What do you mean by that?" I wanted to know.

"I will explain presently. In the meantime will you be good enough to tell me something about yourself? What you have been doing, and the like. If you please."

I told him about everything I could think of; and what I couldn't think of he did. He asked about six questions during my yarn, but every question had a point to it. At the end he bowed and thanked me once more. As a thanker he was main-truck high; I never see anybody so polite.

"That will do," he said. "This bears out Eureka's story and what Miss Adams has said. She— and I, of course—are much indebted to you for your coolness this morning."

"There wasn't much coolness about it. I never was hotter in my life—my head, anyhow. My feet and legs was cool enough, when I was in that water."

I grinned, but he was sober as a deacon. Grins seemed to be scurce on those premises.

"How would you like," he says, "to remain with us; to become one of our little circle?"

"Here? At this—this place? Me?"

"Yes."

"But why? I ain't a Right Liver. There's nothing ails *me*."

"You misunderstand. I mean, how would you like to enter my employ? To become one of the staff of the Sea Breeze Bluff Sanitarium? To join

97

us in our great work for the uplift of humanity?"

I stared at him.

"Me?" says I, again. "You mean to give me a job? What kind of a job? What could I do here?"

"Various things. Superintend the grounds, attend to the livestock, cut the lawns——"

"Hold on! Hold on!" I broke in, forgetting my reverence in the shock of surprise. "What are you talking about, Mister? You've got Thoph Pease for that job."

He waved his hand as if he was brushing away a fly.

"Pease," he says, "is no longer with us. The society of the late lamented Theophilus is ours no more. He has departed."

"Fired?"

"One might call it that."

"You don't say! But there's McCarty. Him and me would never cruise together, not after this morning's doings."

For the first time since I'd met him he acted human and not like a plaster saint. His eyebrows pulled together and his eyes snapped.

"McCarty," says he, "will cease to trouble us, also."

"You'll fire him, too?"

He brushed off another fly. "Suppose we consider you and not McCarty," he said. "Will you accept my offer, Mr. Pratt?"

I shook my head.

"I don't know," says I. "I'd accept 'most anything, but it does seem to me that I'd be as much out of place here as a chunk of tar in a snowbank. What good would I be? I don't know anything about doctoring."

Then he commenced to talk, really talk, and inside of two flaps of a herring's fin he had me mesmerized, like Eben Holt's boy at the town hall show. He talked about the ills of humanity, and the glories of health and Nature and service and land knows what all. My brain was doing flip-flaps, but I managed to make out that the Sea Breeze Bluff Sanitarium for Right Livers and Rest was a branch station of Paradise, and to be connected with it was like being made an angel without going through the regular preparations. It was a chance he was offering me, a wonderful, eighteen carat, solid gold chance. I must take it, of course.

He run down, after a spell, and I got up off my chair.

"Well!" says I. "Well! I—I——"

"Say no more," says he. "I see that you accept.

The sanitarium has made an acquisition, Mr. Pratt. You may begin your new duties at once."

I was on my way to the door, but all at once, through the fog in my head, I begun to sight one reef that I hadn't paid any attention to afore.

"What—what wages do I get?" I asked.

He stood up and laid a hand on my shoulder.

"In a matter like this," he says, "I never permit expense to stand in the way. Salary is a secondary consideration. You will receive thirty dollars a month and your board. Good morning, Mr. Pratt. As you yourself might say, 'A happy voyage.' Good morning."

I went out and through the dining-room. At the kitchen door Eureka was waiting for me. She give one look at my face and then she grabbed me by both hands.

"You've said yes," she says. "He's hired you, ain't he?"

"Yes," says I, slow, "he's hired me, I cal'late. I didn't have to say yes; he said it all."

She was as tickled as a cat with a litter of six double-pawed kittens.

"I knew it!" she sung out. "I knew it! The luck's come! I told you 'twould! And the money, too!"

I leaned up against the door-jamb.

"Money!" I says slow. "Money!. . . . Humph! A dollar a day and board is money, I suppose, but I—well, I sha'n't declare no extry dividends right away, I can see that. He said salary was a second consideration. Well, I guess 'tis, Eureka! I guess 'tis."

CHAPTER V

AND so that's how I came to ship as fo'mast hand aboard the Right Livers' Rest. And 'twas a high old craft, I tell you. I went down to the beach once more and fixed up the *Dora Bassett* and the skiff. McCarty wa'n't nowhere in sight, though I judged he'd been there, for the big box was laying upside down and Pet wa'n't visible. I didn't feel bad on that account. I hoped he never would be visible to me again, nor his master neither.

Then I walked up to the kitchen.

"Here I be, Eureka," says I. "You can report me on board and ready for duty. What'll I do first."

"I'm to show you around first," she says, "so you'll be kind of familiar with the premises. The Doctor told me to. Don't you want to put your things in your room?"

"Ain't got any things with me," says I, "except those I've got on. The rest are in my chest over to Sophrony's. I'll write and have her send 'em by express to-morrow. Meantime you'll have to 'take me as I am,' as the hymn tune says."

"Oh, it won't make any difference," says she. "You'll have your uniform in a day or so, anyway."

"Uniform?"

"Of course. All the help here wear uniforms when they're on duty. I've got mine on now. Ain't you noticed it?"

She was wearing the same white rig she'd had on the night afore. 'Twas so clean and starchy it pretty nigh put a body's eyes out, but there was no uniform to it, fur's I could see. And I said so.

"But it is a uniform, just the same," she says. "See here."

She pointed to a big round thing, pretty nigh as big as the top of a teacup, that she wore fastened at her throat.

"Didn't you notice that?" she says.

"Couldn't very well help noticing it, unless I was struck blind. What is it?"

"Well, what did you think 'twas?"

"Why—why, it's a breast-pin, ain't it?"

"Breast-pin! The idea! Breast-pins ain't the style nowadays. It's my badge. See the initials: 'S. B. B. S.' They stand for Sea Breeze Bluff Sanitarium. We all wear one of those. You'll have one."

103

"Will, hey? You don't say! And have I got to rig up in white, too?"

"Of course. Oh, I'm just dying to see you!"

"Humph! Better wait till you do see me; then you may want to die. My red face sticking out of the top of a white jacket'll look fine, won't it! All I'll need is a black bow necktie to make me a reg· 'lar lighthouse. But there's something else on that badge, ain't there?"

"Yup. That's our motto, 'Think Right.' The Doctor's great on folks thinking right. He says a right thought is two-thirds of the battle. You can do almost anything if you only think you can."

"So? Well, I wish I'd known that this morning; maybe I'd have done that dog sooner. Somebody ought to teach *him* to think right, seems to me."

"Aw, you're just fooling. But it ain't any joke; it's so. It's helped me a lot. For instance, when you was here last night and told me how much you wanted a job, I made up my mind I'd think you into one. And I have; anyhow, you've got it."

"That's so. Well, I 'most wish you'd thought a little harder; maybe you'd have histed the wages some."

"No, you'll have to do that yourself. You must keep thinking, 'I want more money! I want more money!' That's what you must do."

"I will. 'Twon't be a mite of trouble for me to do that, Eureka. I'll think that in my sleep."

She put on her hat and we started off to look over the premises. There was consider'ble of 'em—big yards, and an acre or two of woodland, and a barn, and sheds, and I don't know what all. I met the rest of the kitchen help, the cook and the girl that done most of the waiting on table. The cook was a big woman about the size of Sophrony Gott, and her name turned out to be Olivia Gunnison. The girl's name was Annabelle Atterbury. They was both pleasant spoken enough to me, but I didn't take a big shine to 'em, somehow. I had an idea that Olivia could be pretty cross-grained if she took a notion, and Annabelle run strong to crimps and flounces and ribbon bows. She had bows at her neck and bows on her elbows and the biggest bow of all on top of her crimps.

"Say, look here, Eureka," says I, when we was under way once more, "our old chum Applecart, or Applegate, or whatever his name is, may live on raw steak and prunes, but that Gunnison woman don't, I'll bet high on that. *She* ain't taking no anti-fat remedies, I cal'late."

"Of course not. The servants don't take treatment, 'tain't likely. It's too expensive for them."

If that cook's appetite was corresponding to her

size, I should have figgered the treatment was the less expensive of the two, in the long run. But I didn't say nothing; 'twas comforting to me to know that I could eat what I wanted.

"What's Annabelle rigged up so gay for?" I wanted to know. "The way she's trimmed ship you'd think the Admiral was expected aboard. And it's the forenoon, too."

Eureka sniffed. "Um-hm," says she, "forenoon or afternoon don't make any difference, fur's that's concerned."

"She runs strong to bows, don't she."

"Yup. And you can spell bow more ways than one."

I thought this over. "I see," says I. "Yes, yes."

"You will see if you stay here long enough. Alpheus Parker, that drives the grocery order cart, is her latest."

We was in the woods by now and, to all appearances, ten miles from any other humans.

"Where's all the patients?" says I. "I ain't laid eyes on one of 'em yet."

"They're taking the sand bath, most of 'em. You'll see 'em pretty soon."

Sure enough, I did. And 'twas a sight I sha'n't forget in a hurry. We come out of the woods onto a sandy, shady beach in a little cove, something like the one where the *Dora Bassett* was moored, only more shut in and out of sight. Sticking up out of that beach was a parcel of mounds of sand, six foot long or thereabouts, each of 'em, and rounded on top, with what I thought was a bunch of seaweed at the end.

"Land sakes!" I sung out. "What's this—the graveyard?"

And I hadn't no more'n spoke when, if you'll believe it, the seaweed end of each of them mounds moved. 'Twa'n't seaweed at all, 'twas a head! Yes, sir, a head, laying on a little pillow. Them mounds was folks, living folks, buried up to their necks in sand and laying out on that beach. I don't know which upset me most, to see all them graves in the first place or to find they wa'n't graves, after all.

"These are some of the patients," says Eureka, cheerful. "They're taking the sand bath, same as I told you."

"But what for? What in the name of common sense——?"

"'Cause it's good for 'em."

"*Good* for 'em? Who said so?"

"The Doctor, of course. He ought to be around here somewheres, but I don't see him. Come on, I want to introduce you."

She led the way and I fell into her wake. When

I got close abreast of the cemetery I could see that
the remains—the patients, I mean—was wearing
bathing suits, just as if they was in swimming. Some
of 'em was buried plumb to the chin, and some had
one arm free so's they could turn the pages of the
books and magazines that was propped up in front
of 'em.

"That's something new," says Eureka, "those
books and things. Usually they ain't left alone like
this. The Doctor's generally here, or I am, and
we read to 'em out loud. Here's somebody you
know."

'Twas Miss Emeline. She was glad to see me
and real gracious and polite.

"I am sure the sanitarium has made a great acquisition," she says, beaming out of her tomb. "It
is needless, I am certain, for me to tell you how
grateful I am to you, Mr. Pratt."

"Don't say a word, ma'am," says I. "I'm only
thankful 'tain't no worse than it is. There was one
spell when I didn't know but we'd both be——"

I was going to say, "ready for the undertaker,"
but I hove short just in time. Considering where
she was, I thought maybe 'twould be too suggestive.
She didn't seem to notice I hadn't finished, but
smiled and bowed a good-by and went on reading
her book. The label on the cover of it was "Sun-

beams and Dewdrops, by Pansy Rush"; I could see the gilt letters plain, as I went past the foot of her grave.

"It's a love story," says Eureka, noticing what I was looking at. "She's always reading love stories, Miss Emeline is—when she ain't studying up her family tree."

"I should think she was 'most too antique for them kind of yarns," I whispered back.

"You don't understand. She's had a love story of her own, Miss Emeline has; a beautiful one, beautiful but sad. I'll tell it to you some time. Here's somebody else you know. How d'ye do, Colonel Applegate?"

'Twas the Colonel, sure enough, and his heap of sand was a boy's size Bunker Hill, as you might say. He hardly glanced at me—'twas dark when we met by the well, and I cal'late he couldn't have seen my face good—but the look he give Eureka was a combination of mad and scare.

"Say," he whispers, eager, "have you told Wool about—about last night?"

"No, not yet."

"Well, don't you do it. You keep a still tongue in your head and you won't lose anything by it; understand?"

Eureka winked at me on the off side.

"I don't know, Colonel," she says. "It's my duty to report any breaking of the rules, and you broke about all there was, if what Mr. Pratt here says is so."

He looked at me then. "Pratt!" he growls. "Who in blazes is Pratt?"

"This gentleman here. He's took Thoph Pease's place and is going to work for us regular."

"Colonel," says I, "how'd you like another ham sandwich?"

He started so that a bucketful of sand slid down off his hill. "Good Lord!" he sung out, under his breath, "are you that—— Was it you?"

"It sartin was."

"Good Lord! Have you told anybody?"

"Nobody but Eureka."

"Then don't you do it, there's a good chap. Heavens and earth! I've got troubles enough on your account; I don't need any more."

I cal'late Eureka didn't catch on to what he was driving at, but I did. I'd et some of them sandwiches myself.

"I told you they wa'n't fit for human fodder," says I. "Those sandwiches——"

"It wa'n't the sandwiches; it was that d——n doughnut. It weighed a pound, and it is right in the place it went when I swallowed it; hasn't moved nor digested one inch. Say, paw a ton or so of this sand off me, won't you, and give it a chance."

I laughed out loud, and Eureka's eyes were snapping with fun.

"All right," I says. "I'll keep mum, and I guess Eureka will, too. Won't you, Eureka?"

"Ye—es, I will, this time. But you mustn't do it again, Colonel Applegate. If Doctor Wool knew what you'd been up to you wouldn't have *anything* to eat for two days. He'd even take away your prunes and things."

"If he'd take away this doughnut, I'd be willing to risk it. What the brimstone blazes I ever came to this place for I don't know."

I laughed again. "It strikes me," says I, "that you ain't read your badge lately, Cap'n—Colonel, I should say. You ain't thinking right. As we think, we are, you know."

"Humph! I think I was a prize jackass, and I'm one yet. There! clear out; I'm going to try to get a nap if that doughnut don't object."

A little ways off from the Colonel, in a sort of private lot by themselves, was a big, red-faced, stout woman and a nice-looking young girl. The woman had a double chin and diamonds, and was reading through a pair of gold-band specs mounted on a gold handle. As we came nigher to her she turned her head and stared at us through the specs. If we'd been a couple of wooden posts she couldn't have stared any steadier or with any less regard for our feelings.

"Hortense," says she, not taking the trouble to lower her voice any to speak of, "who are these persons?"

The girl acted real embarrassed. She whispered something. It had about as much effect on the old lady as a teaspoonful of water might have on a bonfire.

"What?" she snaps. "I asked you who they were."

"Hush, Mother," says the girl. "It is the housekeeper. Good morning, Eureka."

"Good morning, Miss Hortense," answers Eureka, trying to look as if she hadn't heard any of the rest of it. "Good morning, Mrs. Todd."

The old lady did a little more of the wooden post business. Then she put down her gold spyglass.

"Umph," says she. "It's you, is it, Eureka! Mercy, what a name! Where on earth did you get it?"

"Don't know, ma'am. I've had it ever since I can remember. I cal'late it's one Pa dug up somewheres. He's great on names, Pa is. This is our new man, him that's going to take Th'ophilus's job, you know. Mr. Pratt, let me make you acquainted with Mrs. Cordova Todd and Miss Hortense Todd."

The girl smiled real sweet and pretty and bowed. All her ma said was "Umph!" What I said don't amount to nothing; 'twas the regulation lie about being pleased to know 'em.

"Mr. Pratt's an old friend of mine," explained Eureka. "He's a mighty nice man, too. And there ain't anybody on the Cape who can sail a boat better'n he can."

Miss Hortense acted interested. "Really?" she says. "Oh, I'm so glad. Perhaps Doctor Wool will let us go sailing sometimes. I'm ever so fond of the water, Mr. Pratt."

"Tickled to take you out any time, Miss," says I. "And the *Dora Bassett's* a good, able boat, if I do say it."

'Twas all I had a chance to say. Marm Todd ordered her daughter to be quiet.

"You know the sand bath is an hour of complete relaxation," says she. "Avoid unnecessary conversation, daughter."

She didn't avoid it a whole lot herself. Her voice was one of the kind that carry a good ways. We hadn't gone fur afore I heard her say:

"Hortense, how many times must I caution you against familiarity with servants? You will ruin that girl with the extraordinary name if you are not careful. I don't care if she is Miss Adams's pet fad at present. Other people's fads are not necessarily ours. And *did* you notice that creature with her? A salt-water barbarian! Why couldn't the Doctor have engaged a civilized being? Another yokel! As if there were not enough already."

Eureka's temper's about as smooth and hard to stir up as the average, but she was hopping now.

"Extraordinary name, hey!" she snaps. "Well, if I was labeled Evangeline Cordova Todd, I'd keep still when names was mentioned. What's a yokel, I'd like to know?"

"You've got me," says I. "I cal'lated I'd been called about everything during my going to sea, but yokel's bran' new. However, whatever 'tis, I judge I'm it. Sweet old gal, ain't she? The young one seems to be nice enough, though. And good-looking, too."

Eureka said the Todds was, next to Miss Emeline and Applegate, the star boarders at the Right Livers' Rest. Mrs. Evangeline Cordova was being treated for something or other, she nor nobody knew exactly what. Hortense, the daughter, was there because her mother was. The old lady never let her out of reach of her apron-strings.

"Scared she'll fall in love with somebody that ain't a walking money-bag, I guess likely," said Eureka. "All right, maybe she'll be surprised some day. True love always wins in the end."

"Does, hey?" says I. "How do you know so much about it? You ain't in love, are you, Eureka?"

She reddened up like a cooked lobster.

"Course not!" says she. "But I've read enough stories to know it always turns out that way. Why, in 'Madeline, the Shirtwaist Maker'—that's a story in the *Home Comforter,* Mr. Pratt—nobody thought the Duke of Lowescraft would marry Madeline, but he did; not till the very last number, though. Afore that they had the most awful times. You'd hardly believe such things could happen."

"Shouldn't wonder if I couldn't, that's a fact. But there ain't any dukes after the Todd girl, is there?"

"There's—but there! I'm forgetting what Miss Emeline's always saying about talking too much. I sha'n't say another word. But I know what I know, and, if you keep your eyes open, maybe you'll know, too, pretty soon."

My eyes was fairly well open already. Of all the

queer collections of humans outside of a crazy asylum, it seemed to me this sanitarium was the cup winner. But, after all, I shouldn't have expected nothing different. When you're well enough off so's you don't have to fret about anything but your heft or your diseases you begin to get queer, I suppose. And the queerer the cures for those ailings the bigger the attraction. A place like the Right Livers' Rest was bound to draw freaks, same as molasses draws flies.

I met the balance of the draft that forenoon. Doctor Wool showed up in a little while with some of 'em in tow. They'd been for a walk, it turned out. There was the three fat men that I'd seen cruising across the lawn in company with Applecart and McCarty that first night. They was mainly short of breath and long on perspiration, and their names was Smith, and Greenbaum, and Hendricks. Smith and Hendricks left the Rest works a month or so afterwards, and Greenbaum didn't amount to much, so there's no use describing 'em. But along with 'em was Clayton Saunders and Professor Quill, and they, as things turned out, amounted to a good deal.

Saunders was a nice-looking, pleasant-spoken young chap, about twenty-four, I should say. He was a Right Liver on account of his having been through a siege of sickness and not getting his strength fast enough. Doctor Wool was "building him up," though, to look at him, you'd say he was built a plenty, being six foot over all and broad in the beam besides. He had a twinkle in his eye when he talked to you, and him and I were friends from the first go-off.

Professor Quill was just as long and thin in the daytime as he'd looked in the lamplight. He had a kind, dreamy sort of face, and a gentle, absent-minded way of speaking. He'd been a teacher in a little one-horse college somewhere and was educated way up to his hair. He was an inventor, too, though none of his inventions had amounted to much, fur's money-making went. Between the inventions and the college boys, his nerves had had a breakdown and he'd come to the sanitarium. A rich cousin of his had sent him there; that was the story, according to Doctor Wool's tell. The Doc seemed anxious that everyone should know about that rich cousin.

I found out all these particulars later, of course. Just then 'twas just "Howdy do" and not much more. And yet, considering what happened afterwards, there was two little items that are worth mentioning, though they didn't seem much at the time.

Doctor Wool purred a word or two to Eureka and me and then led Professor Quill around, introducing him to the graveyard. When he got to Miss Emeline I heard the Professor give a little "Oh!" in that meek voice of his.

"Why—why, dear me!" he said. "Is it possible? Miss Adams! Bless me, I didn't expect——"

"Why, Professor!" broke in Miss Emeline. "Is it you? How strange! Doctor Wool told me a gentleman named Quill was expected here, but I didn't once think it could be you. How do you do?"

That was one of the happenings. The other was that, as Eureka was leading me away toward the house, I happened to look back. Clayton Saunders, the young fellow I was telling you about, had wandered over alongside the Todd lot and was standing there talking with Miss Hortense. The girl seemed to like it first rate, but you should have seen the look on her ma's face.

And now, being acquainted with the Right Livers and their boss, I started in taking up Thoph Pease's job where he dropped it. And he'd dropped consider'ble of it, now I tell you. There was a shipload of things that needed to be done right off and I was busy catching up. I cut grass and milked a cow and cleaned out her stall and the horse's, and tidied up the barn, and took care of the hens, and

helped Eureka, and done errands to the village, and
dug clams—for the help, of course; the Livers didn't
get anything so common and tasty as clams—and,
between jobs, I took over some of McCarty's "physical directing." Not much, of course—I wa'n't quali-
fied for "special exercise"—but I piloted the heavy-
weight brigade on some of their walks and runs
and got to know 'em pretty well, especially Colonel
Applegate, who put in the most of his spare time
cussing the Rest shop and himself for coming there.

They was grown men, those fat folks, but they
was as hard to handle as young ones in school.
They'd come there to be cured, and they'd paid
money—lots of it—for just that; consequently
you'd cal'late they would want to do what the Doctor ordered. But not much; they mustn't drink cold
water, so they would drink it every chance they got.
They mustn't eat sweet stuff, so if I didn't keep an
eye on 'em they'd buy a pie off the bake cart and
bolt it down as fast as they could. The Colonel
wa'n't quite as bad; his sandwich and doughnut
experience had warned him, I cal'late, but the others
was trials. They knew 'twas bad for their extry
flesh and that they'd have dyspepsy and repentance
afterwards, but that didn't make any difference.
Why, they'd even buy striped stick candy and crunch
that; and I bet they hadn't any one of 'em tasted

candy since they was boys. If there ever was a proof of the contrary streak in human nature, that fleshy quartette was it. As for liquor, that was forbid especial, so they talked about it most of the time. They found out that Pease and McCarty had been given clearance papers for getting tight, and that set 'em going at a great rate.

"Fired for taking a drink!" says Hendricks. "Think of it! Why, a chap ought to be promoted for being able to locate one in this Sahara."

"Say, Pratt," says Applegate, "would they fire me, think, if I got loaded? Let's try it and see. 'Twill be an interesting experiment. I'll give you ten dollars for a Scotch high ball."

"Better keep your ten," says I. "If you'd kept the five hundred you paid to get in here you could have bought enough Scotch to swim in, if that's what you want."

That always shut 'em up. The mention of that five hundred was better'n the "gold cure" for breaking the alcohol craving. They'd put in the next half-hour swearing because they'd been such idiots as to pay it. And yet everyone of 'em was well-off, and the five hundred wa'n't no more to them than a nickel was to me. They'd always had their own way afore, that was it; now they couldn't have it and they began to appreciate what they'd lost.

But they could have walked out of that sanitarium any minute; 'twas up to them. They didn't walk, and they'd have raised hob if they'd been told to go afore they was thinned down. Just young-uns, same as I've said.

Applecart—Applegate, I mean; sometimes I called him one name and sometimes 'tother—was a big man in stocks and corporations. The Consolidated Porcelain Brick Company was his pet; he was president of it. The Boston and New York morning papers came to the Right Livers' Rest and he always cabbaged the financial pages and read 'em through. In that way he reminded me of the Heavenly Twins—Hartley and Van Brunt—when I had 'em on Ozone Island. But the Heavenlies was just speculators; old Colonel Applecart was more'n that; he was what they call a magnet, a financial magnet, and his own name, and how he was getting on at the sanitarium, was in those papers pretty frequently. Once in a while reporters would come from the city on purpose to see him and get his views on the market.

I wrote to Sophrony and had her send my dunnage over from Wellmouth, and the first time I had an errand at Wapatomac I went in and saw Nate Scudder about that bill. Nate was surprisingly decent about it, for him. He wouldn't admit that I'd paid cash when I bought the stuff, but he did say that he didn't want to be unreasonable nor nothing, and—er—well, him and me would talk it over some more and he didn't doubt but we'd come to some sort of settlement agreeable to us both. He was so sweet and syrupy that I couldn't understand; there was a darkey in the kindling pile somewheres, knowing Nate as I did, I was willing to bet on it, but I hadn't located him yet.

Just as I was leaving, though, I began to get on his trail. Scudder came as fur as the store platform with me.

"You're over to the sanitarium for good now, ain't you, Sol?" says he.

"I hope it's for good," says I; "anyhow I've taken the job for better or worse."

"Yes," says he. "Well, you and me have always been pretty good friends, you know. Friends ought to do little favors for one another; don't you think that's a good Christian spirit?"

"I think it's better Christianity than trying to *do* one another, if that's what you mean."

"That's what I mean. Yes, yes; sartin. Well—er—I don't know as you know it, but when that place was first started I happened to be passing by and I dropped in to see if I couldn't get the grocery orders. That Sparrow girl—she's about as sassy and pert as they make—she put in her oar and kind of prejudiced Miss Adams and Doctor Wool against me, seemed so. Anyhow, I ain't got any orders to speak of. Now you're there, and, you and me being friends, as I said, why—why——"

"Why what?"

"Why, it runs acrost my mind that maybe we could make a little dicker for the good of both of us. You might put a few trades in my way and—er—well, I might give you—er—say, a little commission on 'em, and we'd take the commissions off that bill you owe. Understand? He, he, he! See, don't you?"

I looked at him. "Yes," says I, prompt. "I see first rate. It was a little foggy for a spell, but now I see fine."

He acted kind of doubtful. "He, he!" he chuckled again, but more feeble. "Well, what do you think?"

"Nate," said I, "do you know the motto over to the Right Livers' Rest? It's 'Think Right.'"

"What's that got to do with it?"

"Everything. I think that bill of yours was paid long ago, and I'm right. Good-bye."

He fairly hopped up and down.

"You—you——" he stuttered. "Am I a dum fool?"

"As we think, we are—some of us," says I, and walked off.

I heard afterwards that he was going around threatening to have me took up for what he called "deforming" his character. What little character he had left was a hopeless cripple long afore I knew him, so I didn't worry about that.

None of us at the Rest shop heard or saw McCarty again. I shouldn't wonder if he and Doctor Wool had a final session, but, if so, nobody else was present at the exercises. McCarty and his dog departed our life and, so fur as I could learn, there was no mourners. For a spell of a week or two we got along without any physical directors except the doctor himself and what little I could do to help. Then Eureka told me what Miss Emeline had told her, which was that a new director had been advertised for and that answers were coming every mail.

Meanwhile I settled down, doing my work—which was enough to keep me out of mischief, land knows!—and getting more and more broken in to Sea Breeze Bluff and the queer folks there.

"Mr. Pratt," says Eureka, "you're getting real used to your new job, ain't you?"

"Well," I says, "I cal'late a body could get used to Tophet if he stayed there long enough."

She flared up; the least mite of a slam at Doctor Wool was enough to set her going.

"Humph!" she snapped. "Most of the jobs there are permanent, from what I hear. You'd better learn to be contented where you are, first. 'Twill be good practice for you, if nothing more."

I laughed. She was as sharp as a fish-knife, that girl. We was getting better friends all the time.

CHAPTER VI

"EUREKA," says I one morning, "I have a notion that I've got track of the love story you hinted at that time."

She and I was having breakfast together. We ate by ourselves, generally speaking. She was housekeeper and sort of superior to Mrs. Gunnison, the cook, and Annabelle, the chambermaid; at any rate she figgered that she was and kept them under her thumb pretty constant. They'd had their breakfast and were out of the kitchen. Eureka and me was alone.

She looked up from her fried potatoes and codfish balls—the help wa'n't enough consequence for "treatment," which was a mercy, the way I looked at it; we ate what we wanted to—she looked up, as I say, and says she:

"What love story?"

"Miss Emeline's," says I. "I think I know who she's in love with."

She put down her knife and fork.

"You do, hey?" she says. "Who is it?"

"That Quill man; the Professor one; the thin

126

man with the long hair, that you're so sartin is mixed up in my 'fortune.' "

She acted awful surprised.

"For mercy sakes," she said, "what made you think that?"

"Oh, just for instance, I guess. You gave me to understand there was somebody she'd been in love with, and, if you'll recollect, that morning when they first met out there in the sand bath graveyard, they was astonished enough to see each other. Astonished and glad, too. And ever since then they've been thick as can be, setting on the piazza together, and walking together, and being buried alive right alongside of each other, and———"

"Rubbish!" she interrupted; "that's nothing."

"Maybe 'tain't, but it looks as if 'twas going to be something. You've noticed it yourself, you know you have."

"I've noticed they was friendly and sociable, but that's to be expected. She used to know the Professor in Brockton. He was a reg'lar caller at our house there. You see, Mr. Quill taught at the Edgewater Academy; he was one of the faculty."

"Yes, and now he's got a faculty of being right around where she is. Oh, I'm an old bach, Eureka, but I've got eyes."

"You ought to have 'em seen to, then. There's

something wrong with your sight if you think there's anything more'n friendship between Miss Emeline and the Professor. There ain't, and I know it."

"But, Eureka, look here. They're just made for each other, them two. He's old-familied and quiet and moony and respectable, just the same as she is. And they talk just the same kind of stuff—as if they'd swallowed dictionaries instead of prunes. And, more'n that, they——"

"Nonsense! It ain't so, I tell you. Miss Emeline's love story hasn't got a thing to do with Professor Quill. I tell you, I *know* it ain't."

She spoke as if she did know, that was a fact. I begun to cast around for other possibilities.

"Who has it got to do with, then?" says I. "Doctor Wool?"

She kind of started and looked at me sharp.

"What makes you say that?" she asked.

"Oh, just for instance, maybe."

"You ain't seen anything to make you think the Doctor is in love with her, have you?"

I laughed. "Not exactly," says I. "Fact is, I've always cal'lated the Doc to be too much in love with himself to waste much affection on anybody else."

I expected she'd flare up, but she didn't. Instead she kept looking at me hard.

"Then what made you mention him?" she says.

"Why, nothing 'special. Only I've noticed he keeps an eye on her pretty constant. And, as for her, she just worships the ground he treads on. That's plain enough for anybody to see."

"Rubbish! Is that all? Course she thinks an awful lot of the Doctor, and respects him and—and all that. Course she does! So do the rest of us, fur's that goes. But she ain't in love with him. He ain't the one—no, sir-ee!"

"Then who is?"

Afore she could answer Miss Emeline herself came into the kitchen. She was dressed to go out, and, or so it seemed to me, there was a kind of troubled look on her face. I cal'late Eureka noticed it, too, for she says:

"What is it, Miss Emeline? Is anything wrong?"

Miss Emeline answered quick and uneasy.

"No, no," she said. "I am going for a walk and I wished to tell you so in case there was anything you cared to consult me about. Is there?"

"No, ma'am. No. But—but are you sure you're feeling all right? You look sort of peaked and——"

"I—I did not sleep well, that is all. I shall return in one hour."

She left the room. Eureka stared after her, kind of worried like. All at once she slapped her hands together and swung around to me.

"Mr. Pratt," she sung out, "what day is this?"

"Friday," says I.

"No, no, the day of the month."

"Eighth."

She clapped her hands together again.

"I knew it!" she says. "She's been dreaming about him again. She 'most always dreams about him on the eighth or seventh or ninth or so. 'Twas the eighth it happened on. Poor thing! no wonder she looks peaked. I declare, you'd think eighteen years was enough to make anybody forget, but not her. And the way them dreams keep coming is enough to frighten anybody. I wonder if he will come back! If he should! My soul! if he should. Why, 'twould be just like a story in the *Comforter!*"

I shook my head. "Eureka," says I, "your talk is awful interesting—to yourself, maybe. It's a little mite foggy to outsiders, though. Why does she dream about him on the eighth or tenth, or whatever 'tis? And what's he and she got to do with eighteen years and the *Home Comforter?* And who is he, anyhow?"

For just a second she hesitated. Then she come over alongside of me and bent down to my ear.

"You promise not to tell anybody?" she whispered. "Not a living soul?"

"Not one, living or dead."

"Well, then, I'll tell you. She's been dreaming about Lot Deacon. There!"

She give this out as though it settled everything. It didn't settle me, though; I was more riled than ever.

"Sho!" says I. "You don't say! That's the most paralyzing notion ever I heard of. There's only one or two p'ints that ain't clear. Who in the name of goodness is Lot Deacon, and where does he live when he's to home?"

I was a little mite sarcastic, but she was too excited to notice. She straightened up and then bent down again.

"He is her young man," she says. "The one she's engaged to. There! that surprises you, anyhow!"

It did. I set up in my chair.

"Her young man!" I sung out. "Her *young* man! And she's engaged to him! Why—why—where?"

"Eighteen years ago, in New Bedford. They was keeping company—engaged, you know. Then they had some foolish squabble or other—something she wanted for the new house they was going to live in when they was married. She thought he ought to buy it, and he said he couldn't afford it.

Anyhow, they quarreled and he went off and left her. Next day, she had to go to Boston and stay for a fortni't. When she come back she found he'd skipped aboard a whaler. He'd left her a note saying he was going to make his fortune. *When* he made it he'd come back. He loved her much as ever and if she cared for him she'd wait. And— and she's been waiting ever since."

"Eighteen years?" says I.

"Yes."

"Heaven and airth! That was some v'yage he went on, wa'n't it!"

"Oh, he hasn't been whaling all this time. The ship was wrecked and the crew separated. Lot's part drifted around in a boat and was picked up by a bark bound to Rio Janeiro. He landed there, so much we know. And he ain't been heard of since."

"Tut! tut! tut! Well, I snum! Is this the love story you've been hinting about all this time?"

"Yes. Ain't it wonderful?"

"It sartin is. Do you mean to tell me that Miss Emeline has been setting back waiting all this time for a feller that cleared out aboard a whaler eighteen years ago?"

"Yes."

"Humph! Ten chances to one he's dead and buried."

"She don't think so. Over and over again she's told me that she's got a presentiment that he's alive and will come back to her some day. She was a poor girl when he went away; now she's well off, but that don't make any difference. In his letter he begged her to be true to him and she's done it."

"You don't say! Well, does she think—providing he is living—that he's been true to her?"

"Of course! He said in his letter that he would be. What are you grinning like that for?"

"Oh, nothing. Only I've run afoul of consider-'ble many whalers in my time and they. . . . Humph! Well, I must say I admire Miss Emeline's faith, that's all."

"Ain't you ashamed! I should think you'd be, to talk so. Why shouldn't he be true to her? I tell you she's been true to him."

"Ye-es, but maybe he's had more chances in South America than she has in Brockton and Boston. Land sakes, Eureka, be sensible! If this Lot man ain't dead, which is the most likely thing, he's practically sartin to be married long ago. He'll never show up, mark my words."

"Why not? And if he's dead, or married, why

should she keep dreaming of him? Answer me that."

"Well, I should say the answer was that he was the only one she's had so fur to dream about. I should want a signed contract from him that his dreams was confined to New Bedford, afore I bet high on his coming back to her. Sailors are sailors and eighteen years is a long time."

She was so mad she wouldn't speak to me for quite a spell, but at last I coaxed her into going up to Miss Emeline's room and fetching down a tintype of the missing Deacon man. Eureka said that Miss Emeline kept it on her bureau and wouldn't part with it for no money. If it had been mine I'd have sold it cheap. The long-lost wouldn't ever been hung for his beauty. He was wholesome and pleasant looking enough, but his clothes was old-fashioned and queer, of course, and his hair, which was thick and black, was plastered down in a couple of curls on his forehead. Likewise he was slim, not to say skinny.

"Don't wonder the old lady is unhappy after she dreams of him," says I. "Look at that hair! for all the world like a barber's on Sunday!"

" 'Twas the fashion then," snaps Eureka. "And Miss Emeline's always talking about his lovely curls. See the writing on the back."

I turned the picture over and there, wrote in faded ink, was "Emeline, from Lot. May 6th, 18———."

"Just two days afore he went away," says Eureka. "Think of it! It's the most romantic thing ever I heard of in my life. Oh, I *wish* he'd come back. Sometimes it seems as if I could see him; thin, and dressed poor, you know, but with the love-light shining in his eyes. Oh, I *wish* he'd come!"

"Humph!" says I. "He may wear specs by this time. Well, if I was he, I'd hurry up and come. There's too much Quill and Wool around here to keep love-lights burning for whalers. He'd better hustle or 'twill be too late."

When I got by myself I laughed over the whole business. Of course 'twas plain enough why Miss Emeline was possessed with the idea of her Deacon feller's coming back to her, and why she dreamed about him, and all. He was the one real, genuine *big* happening in her precise, prim little life and she just *wouldn't* give him up. Besides, she was a female and, in spite of her primness, had consider'ble of Eureka's hankering for the story book kind of thing, the romantic thing, the tender, sweet, sad, mushy thing. As I say, I laughed when I got by myself, but I didn't mention the subject again. What was the use? If she and Eureka got comfort out

of their pet fairy tale, why should I spile their fun
by telling 'em how ridiculous it was.

Besides, I had other things to think about. Doctor Wool and me had some words about the "physical directing" business. Of course most of the
words come from him; that was to be expected.
And they were sweet and buttery and uplifting as
usual. Every time I had a talk with that doctor
man I felt as if I was in church and that the only
things lacking was a hymn tune and a collection.
He preached the sermon, of course, but I did manage to speak up enough to do a little testifying. I
said I simply couldn't keep up the physical directing.
For one reason I didn't know nothing about the job,
and, for another, I was too busy with my regular
work to attend to anything else if I had known. He
must get somebody in McCarty's place and get 'em
right away, I told him.

"Otherwise," says I, "you'll have a new sufferer
on your hands, and his name'll be Sol Pratt."

He bowed and smiled, serene and condescending.

"I trust not," says he; "I trust not that—no. I
sympathize with you, my dear Pratt, I assure you.
But patience—patience, and in a very little while we
shall overcome this trifling difficulty. As you know,
I am advertising for a physical director."

He had been, of course, but so far the ads hadn't dredged up nothing worth having. There'd been answers sartin, but only one of 'em had been promising enough for him to ask the candidate to come down for inspection. Then it turned out that this one, who'd wrote large and lengthy about his "experience" and fitness for the job, had been trainer for prize fighters and was an "ex" one himself. One look at him was enough, and, if more was needed, his remarks when he run afoul of the clothes line was plenty and to spare. You see, he come down on the night train and walked over from the village in the dark. 'Twas a Monday and the line was stretched acrost the back yard. He didn't know it was there until it reminded him by catching him under the chin. 'Twas awful still, without a breath of wind, and what he said would have carried half a mile even if there'd been a gale blowing. Most of the Right Livers was setting on the front piazza when the exercises commenced, but nobody but Colonel Applegate and a few more of the male patients was there when they finished. The Colonel said afterward that them few remarks did him more good than anything he'd heard since he struck the sanitarium; they expressed his own feelings almost as well as he could have done it himself. But the applause was limited to him and his chums, and the new hand was shipped back to Boston in the morning.

Well, I reminded the doctor of this, but he just kept on smiling and purring and waving his hands till he got me mesmerized, as usual, and I left that office feeling that everything was all settled. 'Twa'n't till I got alone by myself that I realized I was just where I started and that nothing was settled at all.

That evening, after the Right Livers had turned in, I went for a walk, not that I needed exercise, but because I wanted to be clear of that Wool shop for a little while, anyhow. It had rained all day, but now it had cleared off, and I tramped and smoked for quite a spell. When I got back to the sanitarium 'twas after ten o'clock. The house was all dark except for a light in the kitchen. I judged that Eureka was setting up reading some of her *Home Comforter* yarns, such being her custom.

But when I stepped up on the back porch I heard voices inside. One of 'em was Eureka's, all right enough, but 'tother was a man's voice. I wondered if she'd got a beau and had never told me about him. In one way 'twouldn't have been surprising, for she'd grown to be such a nice-looking young woman; but, in another, 'twould have been surprising enough, for she and me were mighty chummy, and, if she'd had a steady company, I did think she'd mention him to me.

However, I cleared my throat loud, so's to give 'em warning, and started to open the door. But I hadn't no more than got it half open when I heard Eureka sing out and come running to meet me. Her eyes were shining, and she was as bubbling over with excitement as she'd been that night when I told her about my "fortune."

"Oh, Mr. Pratt!" says she, clapping her hands together; "oh, Mr. Pratt! what do you s'pose has happened now?"

"Land knows!" says I. "House got afire, has it?"

"No, no! Of course not! Do you think I'd be setting here if it had? But something has happened, something wonderful! Guess what it is! Guess the most wonderful thing you can think of."

I wa'n't so terrible upset. Eureka was always seeing wonders where nobody else could, and I didn't take a great deal of stock in this one.

"Humph!" says I. "Want me to guess, hey? Well, let's see. I guess Doctor Lysander has given somebody back their five hundred. That would be about as wonderful as anything I can think of off-hand."

I said it to tease her, but she was too excited even to notice a slap at Lysander the Great.

"No, no!" she says. "Don't be foolish. Somebody's come; come here to-night. Somebody you nor I never expected to see. Guess who 'tis."

I tried to think. Then a crazy notion got hold of me. "Good land!" I sung out all at once. "You don't mean—Eureka Sparrow; you don't mean that long-lost feller of Miss Emeline's has turned up? You don't mean *that?*"

She shook her head. "No," she says, kind of regretful. "It's wonderful, but it ain't so wonderful as all that. It's somebody you used to know, and so did I. But there! you come right into the kitchen and see for yourself. I guess you'll be some surprised!"

So into the kitchen we both went. Alongside the table was sitting a tall, straight-up-and-down feller, who got up as I came in. I blinked at him, for I'd been in the dark and the lamplight sort of dazzled me, and he stood looking at me. Then he put out his hand.

"Good evening, Mr. Pratt, sir," says he. "Very 'appy to see you again, sir, I'm sure."

For a second longer I stood blinking and staring. The voice was one I remembered, sartin; but who——

"I 'ave no doubt you don't remember me, sir," he says. "I 'ave changed a bit, sir, owing to 'ard luck which I've 'ad recent. But I should 'ave known you anywhere. When Eureka told me you were 'ere I was astonished. 'My word!' I said, 'I——' "

That was enough. The "my word" settled it. I stepped forward and looked him straight in the face.

"Well, I swan to man!" I gasped. "It's Lord James Hopper, by all that's miraculous! I swan to man! Hopper, how are you?"

And Eureka clapped her hands together and danced around the pair of us.

"I told you you'd be surprised," she cried. "I told you!"

I hadn't seen him since the Ozone Island days. He'd been Van Brunt's valet then, and was mixed up in all the Natural Life ridiculousness. I remembered him as tall and thin and dreadful neat and precise and dignified. He was tall and thin enough now, land knows; but the neatness and dignity had kind of gone to seed, seemed so. He wore the same prim little mutton-chop whiskers half mast on his cheeks, but there was a little gray in amongst the red of 'em, and the rest of his face had a two days' growth of beard on it. When I'd known him afore, his clothes always looked as if they'd just come out of the spare-room bureau drawer; now they was wrinkled and all splashed with mud; as for his shoes, they wa'n't nothing *but* mud. Take him by and large, he sartin did look as if he'd had a rough v'yage. Him and I shook hands, and then he went back and set down by the table, where he'd been when I come in. There was bread and butter and cookies on the table and a bottle and glass.

"I told you you'd be surprised, Mr. Pratt," crowed Eureka again. "You *are* surprised, ain't you?"

"Surprised!" I says; "surprised! Well, I guess you might call it as much as a surprise without straining the truth. Wonders'll never cease, will they! Hopper, where in the world did you drop from?"

His mouth was full of bread and butter, and he couldn't talk through the cargo, but he managed to groan. 'Twas a doleful groan, too. I looked at Eureka.

"Come, Eureka," says I, "you say something. What's he doing here? And where did he come from? Tell a body, can't you?"

She nodded. "You set down, Mr. Pratt," says she. "Set down and I'll tell you. Keep right on eating, Mr. Hopper," she says to him. "I know you're hungry, poor soul. And take a little more of that cherry bounce; 'twill do you good and keep you from getting cold. Just think, Mr. Pratt! he's walked miles and miles through the rain and all, and he ain't had a bite to eat since yesterday. Think of it!"

I thought. I cal'late Hopper thought, too, for he groaned again and poured himself out another glass of the "bounce." 'Twas some that Olivia Gunnison, the cook, had fetched over from her brother's at South Ostable, for "emergencies," she said; I judged Lord James—that's what we always used to call him on account of his high and mighty ways and his Englishness—figgered that he was an emergency.

"Just think!" went on Eureka, when I'd come to anchor in a chair. "I can hardly believe he's here. But he is! He is! You can see him yourself."

I could, and he could see the food and the bounce bottle, especially the bottle. He never let go of it for a minute. Eureka's tongue kept on running full speed ahead.

Seemed that His Lordship had dropped in on her unexpected, after all hands but she and me had turned in. He was weak and tired and faint from hunger and wet and thirst; she didn't mention the thirst, but 'twa'n't necessary. He'd started from Boston the day afore, but his money give out, or he'd lost it or something—his yarn was pretty foggy right here—but, anyhow, he'd got off the train at Tremont and walked the rest of the way. She'd pumped him pretty hard and had found out already that he hadn't worked for the Van Brunts for ever so long, had had a good many jobs since, but none of 'em real satisfying. One of the last he'd had was at what he called a "country club."

"And what," goes on Eureka, "what do you suppose fetched him down here to Wapatomac?"

I was filling my pipe, and now I reached under hatches for a match.

"What do you suppose fetched him here?" says Eureka, getting impatient.

"Well," says I, lighting up, "I judge 'twas his feet. You say he walked from Tremont."

She bounced on her chair. "If that's a joke," she snaps, "it's a pretty mean one. Of course his feet fetched him, poor thing! But what started 'em heading for here?"

"Don't know."

"Well, I'll tell you. He saw Doctor Wool's advertisement for a physical director, and he's come to apply for the place."

I guess likely she expected me to act astonished when she said this; if that's so, I cal'late I lived up to her expectations.

"Physical director! *Him?*" I sung out. "Go 'long! How you talk!"

But she was talking serious. She meant it. And,

it turned out, so did he. He'd had consider'ble experience in the gymnasium of that country club; 'twas a sort of young sanitarium, that club was, and he'd handled a good many critters like some of our Right Livers. Between bread and butter attacks and bounce relapses, he spun some yarns about his experiences that made me believe his applying for McCarty's job might not be such a joke as it seemed. I was willing to believe it; I wanted somebody to take the job off my hands, and if he would do it so much the better. Besides, knowing what he used to be, and seeing what he was now, I couldn't help feeling sorry for him. He looked like a family cat that had been locked out in a snowstorm all night.

"You'll help him get the place, won't you, Mr. Pratt?" asks Eureka.

"Ye-es," says I, kind of doubtful. "I'll be glad to help him get a trial at it. But what on earth, Hopper, has brought you down so that you have to hoof it thirty miles to get work. You? Good land! what are you doing; *crying?*"

If he wa'n't, I'd never see anybody do it, that's all. He had one hand on the bounce bottle—he'd never let go of that since he got back to the table—but he had a handkerchief in the other and was swabbing his deadlights with it. I'd never had anything set me back more; I felt like a man that had robbed an orphan asylum. To think that I'd been poking fun at a poor critter so wore out by his troubles that he cried!

"There! there!" says I; "don't do that. It's all right now. I'll do my best to help you with the Doctor. It's all right, I tell you. Stop it! What *is* the matter?"

He wouldn't stop, but kept on swabbing and talking.

"Don't mind me, sir," he says. "Don't mind me. It's—it's the thoughts of—of what I've lost that—that——"

"Lost!" says I. "Oh, you mean your money. Never mind that. You're amongst friends now and——"

"My wife," he sniffs. "My—my poor wife!"

Here was news, bran' new news. Eureka and I stared at each other. She spoke first.

"Your *wife!*" she says. "Why, we didn't know you was married!"

He didn't seem to pay much attention.

"My wife," says he. "My poor wife! Wife of my bosom. She's a 'ummer. Saving your presence, ma'am, she's a 'ummer."

"A which! Eureka, what's a 'ummer?"

"I don't know. He means a hummer, I guess,

146

but what—Mr. Hopper, don't take on so! What
——"

"A 'ummer," says Lord James again. "She—
she's a 'ummer, my wife is."

"Is! I thought you said you'd lost her. Is she
alive?"

He kind of perked up and looked at us over the
handkerchief.

"I don't know," says he. "I don't know. 'Er
name's Christina"—he pronounced it "Chrishtina,"
—"and she's a Swede. I married 'er at—at a place
in Philadelphia where we both was in service. She's
a Swede, and 'er English is—is a bit off, but she's
all right; she's a 'ummer. That's what I say, a
'ummer. Oh," says he, acting kind of queer and
vacant-like, "oh, 'ow 'eavenly 'appy we was! When
I think of it—I—I——"

He was going to cry again; I could see it coming, and so could Eureka.

She hove out a life preserver, as you might
say.

"But where is she now?" she wanted to know,
quick.

"Eh? I don't know. I don't know. Lost!
That's all I know. Lost. We come to Boston—I
mean New York—together. Left 'er at the rail-
way station—went to get a drink—of water. Come

back—she was gone. Wife gone! Everything gone. What's the use? What's the use?"

He collapsed into the handkerchief again. Eureka was ready to cry herself. Maybe I'd have been, too, only for one thing. I reached over when he wa'n't looking, got a clove hitch on that bounce bottle and put it under my chair, out of the way.

Eureka was all upset. "The poor man! the poor man!" she says. "Just think what he's been through! What will we do?"

"Well," says I, whispering, "I guess likely the first thing is to get him up to bed."

She looked over at him. He appeared to be asleep, or next door to it.

"Yes," says she, "I wouldn't wonder if you was right. He needs rest."

"He does," says I, "bad. Come on, Hopper. Let's go aloft and turn in. You can have the room next to me for to-night. Come on! Tumble up!"

He obeyed orders, obeyed 'em too well, 'cording to my way of thinking; he tumbled most of the way upstairs. But when he got there he was all right enough and seemed anxious to get to bed. I lent him one of my nightshirts—he didn't have any of his own along—and when I left him he was sleeping like a lamb. I went down again to the kitchen.

Eureka was waiting for me, all lit up with excitement.

"Oh!" says she. "Did you ever in your born days! Think of him wandering around under all that burden of sorrow. Ain't it splendid he come here, where his friends are!"

I didn't say nothing; I was thinking hard.

"I'm sure he'll make a fine director," says she. "And now I've got another job on my hands."

"On *your* hands?" says I, surprised. "What do you mean?"

"I mean I'm going to locate that lost wife of his, that's what I mean. Oh, I *do* think this sanitarium is the most romantic place in the world. There's two romances here already—Miss Emeline's and his. And your fortune, Mr. Pratt; that's another. I'm so glad I'm mixed up in 'em, ain't you?"

I wa'n't bubbling over with joy. There was altogether too much "mix" to suit a steady-going seafaring man like me. I went to bed myself, but afore I went I hid that bounce bottle where no more bereaved husbands could get at it.

CHAPTER VII

I DIDN'T sleep much that night. I put in most of it listening for sounds from the next room. But there wa'n't any. Lord James slept peaceful as could be, in spite of his sorrows. In the morning he called to me and asked for the loan of my razor. Then he wanted to know if Eureka wouldn't send him up a hot flatiron and the shoe brush.

When he came downstairs I wouldn't scarcely have known him, he'd changed so since the night afore. He was shaved, his clothes was cleaned and pressed, and his boots was shined. I declare! he was the old Lord James back again, just as he used to be.

And his dignity was back, too. He ate an astonishing amount of breakfast, considering; and his talk was as smooth and high and mighty as it was in the "Natural Life" days. Olivia Gunnison and Annabelle was ever so took with him; they thought —or so Annabelle said—that he was a "perfect gentleman." There was only one thing he wouldn't talk about, that was his wife, the one he'd lost, or had lost him. Eureka happened to throw out a hint about her and he shut up like a clam. And every time she mentioned the subject he changed it. No, 'twas plain he didn't care to speak of the " 'ummer"; seemed to be sorry he'd spoke of her in the first place.

Eureka said she guessed he thought his heart story—that was what she called it, his "heart story" —was too sacred a thing to be gossiped about by everybody. As for her, she wa'n't going to mention it again, and she hoped I wouldn't. I was willing to keep mum, and I told her so.

"We'll forget it," says I.

She flared up right off. "Indeed, we won't forget it!" says she. "We won't talk about it on account of his feelings, poor suffering soul! but I want you to understand, Mr. Pratt, that I believe his coming here and telling us that story wa'n't any accident. No sir-ee! He was *sent* here; that's what I believe —he was sent. And some day that lost wife of his will be sent here, too. You see."

I thought I was used to her story-book ways by this time, but every once in a while she gave me a fresh jolt.

"You don't really believe that, do you, Eureka?" I wanted to know.

"Of course I do."

"Humph! And you believe that New Bedford Deacon of Miss Emeline's will come, too?"

"Yes."

"And that my tea-leaf fortune, money and all, is coming true?"

"Sartin."

"Well, all right. As a believer, Eureka, you've got the rest of the human race hull down. You didn't use to be this way; you was more or less skeptic, if I recollect right. What's changed you so?"

The answer was ready on her tongue.

"Doctor Lysander P. Wool," says she, emphatic and reverent. "He's taught me to think right. As we think, we are. You think right, and keep on thinking, and everything'll *be* right. Mark my words."

"They're marked," says I. "But tell me this: Do you think that Lysander the Gr—that is, Doctor Wool, will hire His Lordship to be physical director here?"

"Of course I do. If not, why was Mr. Hopper sent?"

I didn't know, so I didn't try to answer. If my judgment was correct, he'd be sent away full as quick as he come.

But he wa'n't, and he did get the job. After breakfast was over he marched straight into Lysander's office. He was in there for half an hour. When he come out the Doctor was with him. By and by he hunted me up—His Lordship did, I mean—and says he:

"Pratt," he says, "the 'ead says you're to fit me to a livery immediate."

"Fit you to a what?" says I.

"A livery. I'm in service 'ere now."

I dropped the rake I was using and stared at him.

"Heavens to Betsy!" I sung out. "You don't mean he's hired you."

He drawed himself up, dignified as a Sunday School superintendent.

"Why wouldn't 'e 'ire me?" says he. "'E's a good judge of character, the 'ead, and a perfect gentleman. A man like me don't come 'is way every day and 'e knew it. 'Im and me'll get on fine. And you're to 'ave me fitted to the livery immediate."

"Meaning——"

"Meaning a livery, of course. A suit of white, like you and the rest of the 'elp wear."

I picked up the rake again. 'Twas all I could do to keep from welting him over the main truck with the handle of it.

"Look here, Hopper," says I, "I don't know how you and the 'head,' as you call him, will get on, but I do know that if you call my duds a 'livery' again there'll be trouble. It's bad enough to go around togged out like a life saver on drill day, but I can stand that 'cause I'm paid for it. What I won't stand is to have them togs called a livery. They may be one, but I don't want to know it. Understand?"

He came right down off his high horse and begged my pardon. Said of course he could see they wa'n't really livery at all. That being all settled satisfactory, I took him to the supply closet, off the kitchen, and sorted out some white duds for him to put on. The coats was all right, but every pair of pants we had on hand was a foot too short for his lower yards. However, Eureka said she cal'-lated she could piece onto the legs of a couple of pairs, so they'd do for the present, and we let it go at that. Inside of twenty minutes he was rigged up, white and regardless, same as me, but there was this difference betwixt us—he seemed to like the uniform and be proud of it, whereas I felt all the time like a hand-organ monkey. And he kept his "Think Right" badge in the most prominent place on his chest, while I hid mine under the lapel of my jacket. It's all in the bringing up, I presume likely; he was used to monkey clothes and I wa'n't.

But, so fur as his job went, he filled it fine. Doctor Wool was tickled to death with him, said he was a "genuine discovery"—whatever that might be.

"A most superior person, Pratt," purrs the Wool man. "Very adequate and superior, indeed—yes."

Well, he was superior, too everlasting superior to suit me. But he learned to keep his superiority for the Right Livers and the Doctor; he didn't try much of it in my latitude, now I tell you. Course he drapped the "sirs" and "Misters" that he soft-soaped me with the first night, and hailed me as "Pratt," same as he used to. But that was all right; it gave me the chance to call him whatever name come handiest. First along I was sort of afraid he'd show a hankering for the bounce bottle, but he never did, and, after a while, I forgot to expect it; begun to think maybe I was mistook about that, after all. But he never mentioned his lost wife from that night, and we never mentioned her to him.

He handled the patients tiptop, took 'em on walks, and exercised 'em, and saw that they was buried proper when "sand-bath" time come. Miss Emeline Adams thought he was lovely, and Mrs. Cordova Todd fairly raved over him. She said he reminded her of an old family servant she had once. "A treasure, Miss Adams, a veritable treasure, I assure you; and English, of course, just as James is. There are no good servants but the English:

we never have any other kind at home. Hortense, my dear, do you remember . . . Who was that you bowed to? Haven't I warned you not to be so familiar with that person?"

The "person" was Clayton Saunders, the young feller I'd met among the sand tombs that morning, in company with Professor Quill and Wool. He was Marm Todd's special horror, though the only horrible thing about him, so fur as I could make out, was that he didn't have much money. He had a little, 'cause he told me so himself, but I judged from his talk that he was pretty toler'ble hard up, though a likely boy of good character. Mrs. Todd wa'n't looking for character, and her daughter being labeled "For Sale—All Bidders but Millionaires Barred," she made up her mind to keep Clayton off the premises. Miss Hortense wa'n't nigh so particular, judging by appearances; she seemed to like young Saunders mighty well. A one-eyed man could have seen how dead gone he was on her, and, consequently, the old lady was as fidgety and nervous as a hen with a brood of ducks.

Clayton and I were pretty chummy by now. His ailments—the ones that had fetched him to the Rest shop—was about all gone, and he might have left if he'd wanted to; but he didn't want to. The reason for his not wanting to was so plain that even

1 didn't mention it. Now that Lord James was on deck, I had a little more time to myself, and I got a chance to go sailing or power-boating once in a while. Clayton was my shipmate on a good many of these v'yages. He knew a little something about sailing a boat, and I learned him a lot more. Afore long he could handle a catboat under power or canvas in any sort of everyday weather.

Sometimes old Applecart—Applegate, I mean, went along, too. A couple of the fleshy patients— Smith and Hendricks they was—had graduated from the sanitarium, and the Colonel and Greenbaum didn't hitch up any too well. So Applegate fell back on me and young Saunders for sociableness. We three cruised consider'ble. The Colonel was neck deep in his stock doings just at present. There was what he called a "hen on" in Consolidated Brick, and he, being president of the concern, got telegrams and letters by the barrel. First along Doctor Wool was fearful of all this; said the worry and responsibility would be too much for the patient, and the telegrams and things must stop. Then the Colonel made proclamations—he was cranky as all get out by this time; lost two pounds of temper with every one of flesh—he made proclamation that if they stopped coming he'd start going; he'd leave the rippetty-rip sanitarium that minute. So Lysander thought it over and changed his mind; said he guessed long as the Colonel thought 'twas right, why, doubtless 'twas; thought was all; as we thought, we was; etcetery and so forth.

Applegate and young Saunders had some lively arguments on those sailing trips. I remember one particular. I was at the helm, of course, and them two was sprawled around in the cockpit, taking life easy. The talk had drifted from one thing to another till it run afoul of business and opportunity and such.

"Don't talk to me about chances and opportunities," says the Colonel. "That sort of stuff makes me tired. There's opportunities laying around loose everywhere; the trouble is that you young chaps don't know an opportunity when you see it. Or, if you do know it, you are afraid to risk the chance of grabbing it. I tell you right now that if I hadn't taken risks I wouldn't be what I am to-day. I don't know as you know it, but I'm what they call a self-made man."

Clayton winked over his shoulder at me. If we didn't know it, 'twa'n't because we hadn't been told often enough. Colonel Applegate's self-madeness was the one thing he talked about more'n anything else, except, maybe, the stuff they gave him to eat at the Rest shop.

"Now that you remind me, Colonel," says Saunders, serious as could be, "I believe you have mentioned that fact. Yes, I distinctly recall your mentioning it. You remember Colonel Applegate's hinting that he was self-made, don't you, Pratt?"

I had to get over a hard coughing fit afore I could trust myself to answer.

"Yes," says I, choking, "seems to me I do."

"Yes," says Clayton, not a smile on his face anywheres, "we both remember it, Colonel."

"Well, I am, whether you remember it or not. Now, look here, Saunders, I'm old enough to be your father and I'm going to talk to you as if I was just that. I've had my eye on you for some time. You're a nice young feller, and smart enough in some things, but, unless I'm mightily mistaken, you haven't got what I call the business sense."

"So?" says Clayton.

"Yes, it's so. See here, you've got some money of your own, haven't you?"

Clayton kind of hesitated. I cal'late he was debating whether to tell Applegate to mind his own concerns or not. I guess likely the Colonel knew what was in his mind, for says he:

"Of course," he says, "I'm not butting in. You needn't answer unless you want to. My idea was to hand you a little advice that might be worth something to you some day, but it's no compulsory dose; you don't have to take it unless you want to."

"Quite willing to take it, Colonel, and obliged, besides. Yes, I have a little money."

"How much?"

"Well, thirty thousand dollars, perhaps."

I pretty nigh fell off the stern thwart.

"Thirty thousand *dollars!*" I sung out. "Thirty thousand! Great land of love! How you talk! Thought you told me you only had a little."

He hunched his shoulders. "That's little enough, when it's all you've got, isn't it?" says he.

"Little! My godfrey's domino! Thirty thousand! Why——"

"Shut up, Pratt," cuts in Applegate. "You haven't any business sense, either."

"Maybe not, but if I had thirty thousand dollars I wouldn't worry about the sense—no, nor the cents, nuther."

"Shut up, I tell you. Saunders, what are you doing with that money? Is it earning anything?"

"It's bringing me a fair rate of interest, if that's what you mean. Now that I'm knocked out of working I manage to live on my income, after a fashion."

"Bah! Why, see here, young man; if you had the business sense I'm talking about you would have doubled that money before now. When I was your age I didn't have thirty thousand by a whole lot, but what I did have was making more fast. You don't take advantage of your opportunities, that's what's the matter with you."

He went on to tell about "opportunities" he'd taken advantage of in his day. They had different names and lived in different parts of the country, but he'd took advantage of 'em, all right. If I was an opportunity and owned a ten cent piece I'd bury it when I heard he was anywheres in the neighborhood. And even then I'd sit on the grave.

Saunders listened, smiling and calm. Applegate finished up something like this:

"I've got an opportunity right now," he says. "One of my little jobs happens to be the presidency of the Consolidated Porcelain Brick Company; the fact is, if you asked me, I should say I was pretty near the whole works. Possibly you've noticed that the papers are giving some space to the company just now. There's a question of a dividend; perhaps you've noticed that. Some people think we're making money and will declare that dividend. Others think we've been losing money during the past year and will pass it. Whichever way the cat jumps, there's going to be a big difference in the price of the stock. Now I'm the only one that really knows what is going to happen. It's up to me. That's what I call an opportunity."

I should have called it one, myself. Clayton Saunders laughed.

"When is the guileless outsider to be informed as to the cat's jumping?" he asked.

"At the annual meeting in Boston. That's next Friday, four days off. I shall be at that meeting, my boy, and——"

But I interrupted. "You will?" I sung out. *"You will?* Why, Colonel, look a-here! How are you going to get away from the sanitarium? Doctor Wool won't let you off, will he?"

He winked. "There are some things he can't help," he says, "and that's one of 'em. I'll be at that meeting. If I wasn't, there'd be the dickens to pay in the stock market."

This was of a Monday. 'Twas Wednesday evening that the big happenings commenced. I was down at the cove, digging some clams for the help's breakfast. Colonel Applegate was setting on a sand heap, watching me and making guesses as to who owned a steam yacht that was laying to four or five mile out in the bay. She'd been there all day long and nobody in our latitude knew who owned her.

After a spell Lord James happened along, and him and the Colonel got to talking. I didn't pay much attention to their jabber, being busy, and pretty soon they went away together.

I filled my dreener with clams and started for the house. 'Twas a gloomy, overcast kind of an afternoon and now 'twas getting dark fast. I looked around, when I got to the edge of the woods, for Applegate and His Lordship, but I didn't see nothing of 'em. I was moving on again, when I heard a yell.

"Help!"

I stopped and turned quick. The yell seemed to come from somewheres out on the bay, I thought. I looked and looked. The yell come again.

"Help, Pratt! Help!"

And then another voice.

"'Elp! 'Elp!"

I give another long look and then I saw 'em.

Out about a hundred yards or so beyond where the *Dora Bassett* lay at her moorings was a dark spot on the water; a boat, 'twas, and in it was two people waving their arms and yelling. I couldn't see 'em plain, 'twas getting too dark for that, but I didn't need to. That last "'elp!" proved that one was Lord James; and the other must be Colonel Applecart. But what was they doing out there? And what ailed 'em? And whose boat was they in?

The last question answered itself first. I looked down the beach to where my skiff ought to be. She wa'n't there. She was gone.

The yells kept coming all the time, and more desperate every second. What on earth could be the matter? I dropped my dreener and run up the beach towards the point.

"What ails you?" I hollered.

"He-lp! 'Elp! Help! 'Elp!"

That was the only answer I got. There must be something desperate. I was getting scared. Were they sinking, or what?

"Come quick, Pratt! For 'eaven's sake, come! 'Elp!"

If I'd had time to think, I might not have acted like a fool, maybe. It generally takes time to keep the average man from acting that way, and I'm only average. What I should have done, of course, was to swim to the *Dora Bassett* and go after 'em in her. But I didn't. I was scared, and my one idee was to get to them two landlubbers as soon as possible. So I run out to the end of the point ahead of where they was drifting and started wading towards 'em.

"I'm coming, I whooped, "I'm a-coming."

"Help! 'Elp!"

Well, I started wading, as I said, but pretty soon

I got where I couldn't wade no more. The shore's
pretty bold off that point, and the water deepens
quick. I got up to my waist; then to my shoulders.
I couldn't wade, and, if I didn't do something in a
hurry, that skiff would drift by me. Don't tell me
I'd ought to have let it drift and gone back for
the motor boat. Don't tell me nothing. Land
knows I've thought enough about it since.

"'Elp! 'Elp! We're drowning!"

That settled it. In I splashed, heaɑ, neck and
heels, and commenced to swim out to meet that
skiff.

'Twould have been a pretty good swim if there
hadn't been any tide; but there was a tide—I hadn't
took twenty strokes afore I realized it, but 'twas
too late to back out. On I went, fighting for all
there was in me. Once I thought I wa'n't going to
make it, and then I remembered I'd got to. 'Twa'n't
a question now of just saving them two idiots; 'twas
one of saving me. I'd got to make that skiff or go
under, one or t'other.

Well, I made it, but just barely. She was 'most
past me afore I got alongside.

"Hand me an oar," I managed to pant out.
"Reach me—oar—so's I—can get a holt."

But nothing doing. Old Applegate, in the stern,
just set and looked at me, and Lord James, amid-

ship, waved both arms and kept hollering for help. I took a couple of everlasting big strokes and managed to grab hold of the skiff's rail, close to the stern. Then, for a jiffy, I hung on and fought for breath.

"Get in, get in," orders Applegate. "What are you waiting for?"

Getting in wa'n't such an easy matter. I thought sartin the craft would upset afore I swung over the rail. Course if I hadn't hitched along up towards the bow she would have capsized. But get in I did, though a bucketful of salt water got in with me.

"Why in tunket," I gasped, soon's I could gasp anything, "didn't you reach me that oar? Couldn't you see I was next door to foundering?"

The answer I got wa'n't what you'd call satisfying. The Colonel bu'st out into a perfect hailstorm of cuss words; they seemed to be hove at Lord James, nigh as I could make out.

"Here!" I ordered finally. "Stow that, will you? What ails you two, anyway? Show me where the leak is, so's I can stop it."

His Lordship answered, if you call it an answer. "Leak!" says he. "Is there a leak? My word! Oh, it's awful. We're lost! 'Elp! 'Elp!"

I grabbed him by the neck. I was mad, and some scared, besides.

"Dry up!" I ordered, "or I'll choke you. Colonel, where's the leak?"

"There's no leak that I know of."

"No leak! Then what in time is the matter with you? I thought you said you was drowning."

"*I* didn't. 'Twas that jackass there. He——"

"Stop! I want to know what's the matter? What were you yelling help and blue murder for? I thought you were sinking sure. And there ain't any leak. Except for what she shipped when I got in, she's dry as a contribution box. Well, never mind it now; you can tell me later. Give me the oars and let's get ashore."

They looked at each other.

"Oars!" gasps Hopper. "There—there—— Why, Pratt, it's awful! There——"

"Blast it!" roars Applegate. "That's what's the matter. There ain't any oars."

Well, it sounds silly enough, but 'twas a fact; there wa'n't any oars. There had been one—one that I'd left in the skiff to use when I went off to the motor boat—but that one His Lordship had managed to lose overboard. Seemed that the Colonel had taken a notion into his fat head to go to the *Dora Bassett* and get a memorandum book he'd left there the day afore; 'twas one he'd kept a record of his stock doings in and he'd been looking it

over and had left it on the locker around the cockpit.
If he'd asked me to pilot him 'twould have been
all right; but he didn't; he ordered Lord James to
do it.

'Twas shoal water between the *Dora* and the
shore, and His Lordship used the one oar to
reach down to the bottom and shove. They got
the book, but when they started in again the oar
got stuck in the mud and wouldn't come out, pulled
loose from Hopper's hands and stayed where 'twas.
The skiff didn't stay, though; it commenced to drift
out to sea. Even then if one had jumped in and
waded 'twould have been all serene, but neither
hankered to get wet, so they set still. Pretty soon
they was out where 'twas over their heads and they
couldn't wade if they wanted to. Then they commenced to yell.

'Twas a fine mess to be in, and the more I thought
of it the finer it looked. The wind was breezing
up, 'twas getting darker all the time, and we was
getting further and further away from home and
ma, as the saying is. There wa'n't a blessed thing
to do but drift—and we drifted.

'Twa'n't a silent drift, the first part of it, anyhow. Applecart asked more'n a million questions,
and when he found out I was going to set still and
do nothing, he commenced to call me about every

name he could think of. I stood it for awhile and then I spoke my mind.

"That'll be enough of that," says I. "I'll admit there is a dum fool aboard this craft, but we might not agree as to his location. If you've got to talk, talk to yourself, and not to me. 'Twas my oar you lost, and it's my skiff you run off in. If I don't call names, you needn't. Keep still."

But he didn't keep still; he commenced to lay into Lord James. He had an easier victim there, for His Lordship was scart pretty nigh to death and expected to drown every other second. He wouldn't talk back, so, after a spell, the Colonel let up on him, and whatever proclamation he had to make was mainly hove at the sanitarium and Wool. I'd heard him do that so often that I judged his barometer was getting back to "cloudy and lowering" instead of "high temperature and wind squalls."

We drifted and drifted, afore the breeze, which wa'n't directly off shore, but kind of quartering. It carried us up the beach, but further out all the time. 'Twas black night by now, and it got to be nine, and ten, and then eleven o'clock. By and by, off on the port bow, I see a little twinkle of a light. It got brighter and brighter as we drifted nigher to it, and at last I made out that it must be a lamp in the window of some house on a point making out from the main.

I wa'n't used to these latitudes much; most of my cruising had been done further down the Cape a good ways; but I did know that the beach along here was as lonesome as a graveyard, and I'd never heard of anybody's living on it. However, somebody must live there, or else what was the light?

We drifted and drifted. I could see that we was likely to drift by and I was figgering on jumping overboard and making a try for land by towing the skiff. But pretty soon there came a little shift of wind that carried us in nigher.

Colonel Applecart hadn't spoke a word for a long time; he was asleep, I cal'late. I'll say this for the old chap, except for the first few minutes after he found we was liable to drift to Jericho he hadn't whimpered nor acted scared. Mad—yes, but not frightened a hair. And now he was asleep. As for Lord James, he hadn't talked much nuther, but he wa'n't asleep. He sat all huddled up on the thwart amidship and every once in a while he'd shiver and groan. 'Twas plain enough that he figgered on making a port a good deal further off than Jericho, and he wa'n't happy at the prospect.

As I say, that shift of wind carried us nigher to the point and the light on it. And now, above the splash of the water and the whistling of the breeze in the pines ashore, I begun to hear a queer kind of noise; heard it and lost it and then heard it again.

"What in the nation," says I, "is that? Music, ain't it?"

Hopper groaned. "I've 'eard it a long while," says he. "It's 'arps, spirit 'arps a-wailing. It's a warning for us. It's our death knell. We're gone! We're gone! Oh, why did I come 'ere?"

I could have told him why he come, but 'twould have taken too long to do the subject justice. Besides, I begun to get a glimmer of hope.

"Harps nothing!" says I. "It's a concertina and it's playing 'Old Dan Tucker.' Here, you! You done consider'ble yelling a spell ago when 'twa'n't any use. See if you can yell now, when it may amount to something. There's somebody awake in that house, or shanty, or whatever 'tis. Help me roust him out."

I made a speaking trumpet of my hands and commenced to whoop "Ahoy!" and "Hello!" at the top of my lungs. His Lordship joined in, hollering " 'Elp!" and "Save us!" The Colonel woke up, and, after asking what in brimstone was the matter, opened his mouth and roared "Hi!" and "Hello!" like the bull of Bashan.

For a spell our screeching didn't do a mite of good. Old Dan Tucker kept on being a nice old man that washed his face in a frying-pan, and that was all. Fur's that goes, the tune sounded as if 'twas made with a frying-pan, being squeaky and scratchy and tooth-gritting. But, at last, just as I was giving up hope and about ready to make a try at the swimming, it stopped.

"Now, then," I sung out; "all together. Hel-lo!"

And the Colonel and Hopper joined in with "Hi-I!" and " 'Elp!"

Then the door of the building swung open and we could see a man's figger, a black shadow against the lamplight.

"Ahoy!" he yelled. "Who are you? What's the matter?"

" 'E-elp!" bellers Lord James. I had to tell him three times to shut up afore he'd do it.

"We're adrift in a skiff without any oars," I whooped. "Come off and pick us up, won't ye?"

I had to say *that* three times afore the feller in the doorway seemed to sense it. But then he come to life in a hurry. Inside of ten minutes he was alongside in a dory and had us in tow. We would have made a first rate landing only for one thing; the Colonel was so anxious to get on dry land that he jumped heavy on a rotten board in the skiff's

172

bottom—I didn't know 'twas rotten or I'd have had it fixed afore this—and went through, both feet. The water wa'n't more'n ten inches deep at the time, which was a mercy, and all the harm it done was for him to trip and fall overboard with a splash like an elephant taking a bath. But I couldn't help thinking, suppose it had happened when we was off there in the bay?

We fished him out—that is, the feller who had picked us up and I did; Lord James was half-way up the beach when it happened—and started him on a run for the house. Then I turned to our life-saver, and says I:

"Well," I says, "I sartin am obliged to you, Mister—Mister——"

"My name's Doane," he drawls; "Philander Doane. I know you, don't I? You're Sol Pratt, from over to Wapatomac. Have you broke old Scudder's neck yet?"

'Twas the long-legged loafer I'd met on the wharf that morning when I fetched Miss Emeline back in the *Dora Bassett.*

CHAPTER VIII

WELL, whoever he was, I was awful glad to see him just then, and I told him so. Together we hauled my skiff and his dory up on the sand. There was a sailboat moored a little further out and it tickled me to see her. She looked to me like a way of getting home again.

"That's too bad about your skiff, ain't it," says he. "She's liable to take in water some now, ain't she?"

I couldn't help laughing. "She can't take in much more'n she's got already," I told him.

"No," says he, solemn, "not till the tide's come up. I was cal'lating to haul my dory up and caulk her. She leaks so she ain't fit to use on any longish trip. Say, if I had hauled her up I'd have had some trouble getting alongside of you, wouldn't I."

I told him I presumed likely he would, and we started for the house. 'Twa'n't much of a house, nothing but a two-room shanty downstairs, with a loft overhead. I found out afterwards that this Philander Doane was what the summer folks label a hermit, meaning somebody that ain't loony, but is next door to it, being odd and queer and independent as a hog on ice. Loony was the only thing he was next door to; for he lived alone in that shanty, fishing and clamming and gunning, and there wa'n't a neighbor nigher than eight miles.

Afore we got to the shanty Colonel Applegate stuck his head out of the door. His temper had been getting raggeder all the time, and the sousing he got when he fell overboard had just about ripped what was left of it to ravellings.

"For heaven's sakes!" says he. "Pratt, are you going to stay out there and talk all night? Come in here, will you? I'm freezing to death."

I started to hurry, but the Philander Doane man didn't. I cal'late you couldn't have hurried him with a red-hot poker.

"Say," says he, as if he'd made some kind of discovery, "he's sort of fretty, ain't he? What got him tittered up that way?"

"Nothing got him," says I. "He was born 'tittered up,' as you call it, and having his own way all his life has kept him so. Come on, come on."

He come on, but he come so deliberate you had to watch the things he went by to make sure he was moving.

The setting-room or dining-room or kitchen, or all three together, of the shanty wa'n't much bigger'n a dry goods box. There was a table in it, and a couple of crippled chairs, and a big, rusty cook-stove with a wood fire. Applegate, in his wet clothes, was hugging the stove as if he loved it. As for Lord James, he was roosting on one of the chairs, looking happier than ever I'd seen him in my life.

"Come, come, come!" snaps the Colonel, his teeth rattling, "put some more wood on this fire, will you? Can't you see I'm half frozen?"

If Philander saw it, it didn't appear to jar him none to speak of. He hauled his feet over to the stove and took off one of the covers.

"'Tis sort of feeble, ain't it," he says, referring to the fire. "I snum! I never noticed it. I was setting here, a-playing to myself, when I heard you folks a-hollering. Thinks I, 'Who's that a-hailing this time of night?' Generally speaking, there ain't nobody comes by here more'n once a week and——"

"For heaven's sakes!" roars the Colonel again. "Are you going to get that wood, or ain't you?"

Philander looked him over. "Why, yes," says he, as deliberate as ever, "I'll get it, maybe, if I feel like it. I most always cal'late to do about what I feel like."

I judged 'twas time for me to take a hand. I

didn't want a row the first ten minutes after I got ashore.

"Never you mind, Doane," says I, "I'll get the wood."

But he wouldn't let me. "It's my wood," he says, "and I'll get it—when I get ready."

However, I went with him when he went out back of the shanty to fetch the wood.

"You mustn't mind the Colonel," I says.

"I wa'n't cal'lating to," says he, amazing prompt, for him.

"I mean you mustn't mind his talking sharp like that. His digestion ain't very good, and he ain't used to roughing it. He's one of Doctor Wool's patients over to the sanitarium."

He turned around with his arms full of pine sticks, and stared at me.

"You mean he's one of *them* crazy critters?" he says. "One of them lives on raw meat and cow feed? Humph! I always wanted to see one of them durn fools."

"Well, you'll see one now, for a spell, anyhow. But you mustn't think he's a fool."

"He can't get no cow feed here. I don't keep a beef critter. Who's the other one?"

"He belongs to the sanitarium, too. One of the help, he is."

"What makes him talk so funny? Calls help, 'elp. What ails him—got a split palate, has he? My cousin Nate's second oldest boy's got one of them and he talks like a sponge."

"No, no. His palate's all right. He talks that way 'cause he's an Englishman. He ain't been in this country more'n a dozen year."

He pretty nigh dropped the wood. "Sho!" he drawls. "How you talk! You don't say! A Britisher, hey? Well, I suppose I'll have to keep him here—over night, anyhow."

"Why wouldn't you keep him, for the land sakes?"

"Why would I? Dum foreigners! fighting against our folks, and all."

"Fighting against 'em! *He* never fought against our folks. We ain't fought with England for a hundred year."

"Don't make no difference; his great granddad done it, I bet you! And so'd he, if he dared. Well, I'm American, by Judas, and he better not say nothing against the Stars and Stripes while I'm around. Say, he dresses just like real folks, don't he?"

I didn't answer. I judged he figgered that Englishmen wore bead necklaces and calico, like South Sea Islanders. He was a specimen, that Doane man. How he'd escaped being caught and caged for a ten-cent museum was more'n I could make out.

We toted in the wood and got the fire going nice and comfortable. Lord James still set in one of the chairs and Applegate had cabbaged the other and was hugging the stove. Doane kept staring at Hopper as if he was some kind of animal.

"Say," says I, after a spell, "ain't got nothing to eat aboard this craft, have you, Philander?"

His Lordship spoke up.

"If I might 'ave something 'ot," he says. "A bit of 'ot toast now. And some tea, some 'ot tea."

Doane had started to haul the table into the middle of the room. He stopped hauling.

"Tea!" says he. "Tea! What do you want tea for?"

"Why—why, to drink, of course," says Lord James. "Upon me word, I believe the man thinks I want to bathe in it."

"Bathe! What do you want to bathe for? Tea! and a bath! Did you ever hear such talk? I'll give you coffee, if that'll do. If you want a bath you'll have to go down to the shore. Salt water's good enough bathing for me, and *I'm* an American."

"The coffee'll be tip-top," I says in a hurry. "Can I help you, Philander?"

But Colonel Applegate had a sermon to preach first.

"In the name of common sense, Pratt," he snapped, "what are you thinking of? Can't you see I'm soaked to the skin? Let the fellow get me some dry clothes first. How much longer must I sit here like a drowned rat?"

Doane was pawing 'round on a shelf after the coffee pot. For a second I thought he was going to heave it at the Colonel, but he didn't; he just set it down on the table with a bang.

"Well—by Judas!" says he, fervent.

"See here, you," says Applegate, not noticing the danger signals, "have you got any clothes in this shack that'll fit me?"

"No, I ain't."

"You haven't? Well, this *is* a devil of a mess!"

"Colonel," says I, "suppose you take this coat of mine. It's only white duck, and it's damp yet, but it's dryer than yours."

"What in blazes do I want to take your clothes for? You've been overboard, too, and you need 'em as much as I do."

"Maybe Lord Ja—Hopper here'll lend you some of his rigout. He's the only one of us that ain't been ducked so fur."

His Lordship didn't look real enthusiastic.

"I'm afraid they'll be a bit small, Colonel Apple-gate, sir," he says. " 'Owever, if you say so, I'll——"

But Philander interfered.

"There's my Sunday suit up aloft there," says he, with a jerk of his thumb towards the hatch over-head. "Maybe you could squeeze into the coat; and the pants, too, if you reef the bottoms of the legs. Anyhow, you can try."

Applegate grunted out a "Thanks" and got up off the chair. Then he looked at the ladder.

"Think I'm going to climb that thing?" he wanted to know.

Philander was lighting a hand lamp. He climbed the ladder a little ways and set the lamp on the floor of the loft. The Colonel watched him; the ladder shook consider'ble.

"Think I'm going to climb that thing?" says he, again.

Philander didn't seem to understand.

"What thing?" says he. "Oh, that ladder? H'm, I cal'late you'll have to, unless you figger on sleeping on the floor all night. All the bunks there is are up there."

"Sleep! you don't suppose I'm going to sleep in this hole to-night. I'll put on dry clothes and eat something, and then you can sail us over to the sanitarium."

Philander shook his head.

"I wouldn't sail to Wapatomac to-night for no man," he drawled. "It's a long stretch and a dead beat all the way. My catboat's got power in her, but the engine ain't working good; stops every now and then, so I can't use it. No, I'd have to sail, and I don't want to do that. There's too many shoals to risk in a sailboat in the dark. To-morror morning—or this morning, 'cause it's to-morror now —when it's daylight and after I've hauled my nets and cleaned my fish, I'll take you across, all right."

"After you've cleaned—— Why, confound you, do you realize I've got to get back? Pratt, for heaven's sakes tell him! There's that meeting in Boston Friday; I intend leaving on the noon train to-morrow. And there are a bushel of telegrams and letters waiting to be answered now. Tell him that."

"Colonel Applegate's got to get back, Doane," says I. "It's important."

I might as well have talked to a graven image. All the answer I got was: "Fish'll spile if they ain't cleaned right off."

"D——n your fish!" hollers Applegate. "I must

be at Wapatomac to-night. I ought to be there now."

"Can't afford to spile a day's catch. Squiteagues running pretty fair now, and I'm likely to have a good haul. Last week I got fifteen dollars' wuth one day."

"Maybe the Colonel'll pay you fifteen for taking him over," I suggested. 'Twas a poor suggestion just then. The old man's temper was gone and all his good nature with it. Besides, he always prided himself on not being took advantage of—by anybody except flesh-reducers like Doctor Wool.

"I will not," he snaps. "Fifteen dollars! Why, you robber, I can hire a boat and man all day for five."

That was true, he could. But he couldn't hire that hermit.

"I won't risk them fish," was all Philander would say.

Applegate growled and begged and ordered and swore, but it wa'n't no use. At last, being full of shivers, he decided to risk the ladder and hunt up the Sunday suit. His Lordship and I held the thing steady while he climbed to the loft. I thought sure the ladder would break, and after that I thought he'd get stuck in the hatchway, but he didn't; he got up safe, after consider'ble many groans and more language, and we could hear him pawing around after the duds.

Philander went into the next room, which was just a lean-to hitched on to the end of the shanty, and came back with a salt mackerel that dripped brine like a rainstorm. Then he put the coffee pot on the stove and rummaged out a loaf of dry bread and some hardtack. Next he put the mackerel in a fry-pan, and the shanty begun to smell like a Banks boat just in from a v'yage.

Lord James watched him, mouth open and eyes popping out. Philander went out after more wood and His Lordship tackled me.

"For 'eaven's sakes," he says, p'inting to the fry-pan, "what's that?"

"That's going to be supper, I cal'late. It smells mighty grateful to me."

"Supper! Supper for 'im?" He jerked his head towards the loft.

"I guess likely," says I, grinning.

"But—but 'e won't eat it. 'E can't. 'E's on strict diet."

"That's so, but this is Philander's diet, not his. If you asked me I should say 'twas salt mackerel and hardtack or nothing."

"My word!" says Lord James.

When Doane came in I got him to one side.

"Say," says I, "if you'll take us over to Wapa-tomac to-night I'll pay you fifteen dollars out of my own pocket."

I forgot I was standing right under the hatch. There was a roar from the loft that made us jump as if a thunder clap had gone off.

"You'll do nothing of the sort, Pratt. You mind your own business. Here, you, whatever your name is, help me down this condemned ladder."

Philander never even looked up. "You better help yourself, I cal'late," he drawled. "I'm busy."

Well, helping that fleshy man down that ladder was worse than helping him up. Hopper and I done it finally, and then I stepped outdoors. If I'd stayed in I'd have laughed sure, and that would have been mighty poor judgment.

That Colonel man in those hermit Sunday clothes was the funniest outrage I'd seen since I quit going to sea. How he'd ever squeezed into them pants I don't know. The coat was bad enough—it didn't come within a fathom of buttoning and there was a wrinkle from yardarm to yardarm in the back; but them pants! Oh, my! Oh, my! They was too short on top and too long at the lower ends, and—— But there! I better stop, I shouldn't wonder.

"Kind of scant, ain't they?" I heard Doane drawl. "I told you they would be."

When I got through with my laugh, and had swabbed the tears out of my eyes, I went in again. Philander was just putting supper on the table. You ought to have seen Applegate glare at it. When he found 'twas all he was going to get to eat he fairly b'iled over. But bile was all he could do. He didn't dast to touch the mackerel or the coffee— the memory of Sophrony's sandwiches and dough- nuts was too fresh in his mind, I guess—so he done the best he could on dry bread and hardtack. Water he drank by the pailful. After the third flood I put in my oar.

"See here, Colonel," says I, "I wouldn't overdo it. Doctor Wool says one glass of cold water is as bad as an extry pound for you."

He pretty nigh cried. "Blast you!" he roared, "would you take bread and water away from me? Why, they give that to jailbirds."

If he needed water, Lord James needed it more. 'Cording to his tell, he'd waited on the British no- bility a good deal in his time, and they don't run strong to salt mackerel, I judge. He was so hungry he had to eat it, and he drowned every mouthful with water. The pump was going most of the time.

After the refreshments was served I helped Phi- lander wash dishes. Afore I started on the job Applegate beckoned to me to come out of the shanty. I done it and he put his mouth close to my ear.

"Pratt," he says, "you can sail a boat. Let's take that one there," pointing in the direction where Doane's cat lay at her moorings, "and start her home. If we're quiet we can get a good start before that long-legged savage knows anything about it."

I shook my head.

"Not me, Colonel," says I. "I never stole nobody's boat yet, and I ain't going to begin this late along."

"But it ain't stealing," he whispered again. "You can pay him for borrowing it when you bring it back. I'll send the money by you. We'll leave that—that cockney physical director behind, as hostage."

I shook my head again. "No," says I, "I won't, for two or three reasons. He's right when he says there's too many shoals to risk sailing over in the dark."

"But it's a power boat; he said so himself. You can run a power boat; so can I, for that matter."

I'd let him handle the *Dora Bassett* when she was under gasoline half a dozen times, and it had made him so stuck up he thought he was admiral of a fleet. I didn't have nigh the confidence in his navigation that he did, but that wa'n't my reason for saying no.

"No use, Colonel," says I; "I won't steal that boat—nor borrow it, either, that way. I've tried 'most every kind of salt-water job, but I've never been a pirate. You take my advice and offer him fifteen dollars in the morning. That won't be but a little while to wait; it's one now."

Be hanged if he would! It was a holdup, and no living man could hold him up.

While the dish-washing was going on I noticed that he and Lord James were mighty confidential. I didn't pay much attention at the time, but later I did.

About a quarter to two he made proclamation that he was going to bed. Lord James said he believed he'd go, too. I was willing to turn in myself, but Philander said there wa'n't but two bunks in the loft, and him and me would have to rig up shakedowns on the main deck. So, after the two passengers had shinned the ladder, we commenced bed-making.

I happened to ask that hermit what 'twas he was playing when we first drifted abreast of the point. I asked it without thinking; I ought to have known better, for that concertina, so it seemed, was his hobby, and it having been mentioned, he didn't want to talk about nothing else—nor quit talking nuther.

"She's a wonder," says he, getting the thing out of a locker in the wall. "Fourteen year old, and just look at her."

I looked. That concertina was a wonder in its way. The handles that was on it first had wore out long ago, and he'd made new ones of braided rope yarn. And the bellows was patched in more places than a cranberry picker's overalls.

"She's a wonder," he says again. "You ought to hear her when she gets going good. Kind of wheezy at the start, afore she fetches her breath, but after that there ain't nothing can stop her. Here; you listen."

I had to listen, 'cause he wouldn't let me do anything else. He and the concertina bust loose in "Sweet By and By," and I give you my word it made you wish you was there, and the sooner the quicker.

"Now she's struck her gait," he says, vainglorious. *"Ain't* she going some, hey?"

She was. There came a perfect howl from the loft, Applegate's voice 'twas.

"What kind of a devilish noise is that?" roars the Colonel. "For the Lord sakes, cut it out! *Shut up!*"

Philander shut up. It's surprising, but he did. I

cal'late the shock of anybody's not liking that concertina kind of numbed his faculties. He acted as
if he'd had a stroke of paralysis, and him and I
turned in without another word scarcely. I wa'n't
long in getting to sleep, now I tell you.

And I wa'n't long sleeping nuther. What woke
me up was the Colonel, just tiptoeing out of the
door. 'Twas gray light of a cloudy morning. I
looked around for Lord James, but I didn't see
him. Philander was sound asleep on the floor side
of me.

"Hello, Colonel," says I; "where you bound?"

He started and turned his head. "S-sh!" says
he, quick. "Don't make such a racket. Bound?
I'm bound outside, where I can smell something besides fish."

And out he went. Doane turned over and
wanted to know what was up.

"The Colonel's up," says I. "I guess likely that's
all."

He settled himself to snooze again, and I tried to,
but 'twas no go. I got to wondering what that fat
man had turned out so early for. Over at the Rest
shop he got up early, but then 'twas 'cause he had
to. Here he didn't.

So I laid there, betwixt sleeping and waking. All
at once, though, I was wide awake. I'd heard

something; it came from outside the shanty, and 'twas the "chug-chug" of a motor engine.

I give one jump from the shakedown to the door. My eyes was wide open enough now, and they saw a sight.

In front of the hermit's shanty, there on the point, the beach curved in to make a little cove, or harbor, like. Out in the middle of this cove was a catboat—Philander Doane's catboat—with the propeller churning up the water under her stern, and two men aboard of her. One of these men was in the bow, hauling up anchor; he was Lord James. 'Tother was aft by the steering wheel; he was Colonel Applegate. The catboat was beginning to move.

I took this in at one gulp of my eyes, as you might say. Then I whizzed out of that door like a sky-rocket.

"Hi!" I yelled. "Hi, Colonel Applegate, what are you doing in that boat? Where are you going?"

From astern of me in the shanty I heard a whoop from Philander.

"Boat?" he sung out, his voice jumping high and shrill. "What boat?"

From his seat by the helm the Colonel waved his hand, serene and patronizing and calm.

"It's all right, Pratt," he hollered. "I know what I'm about. I'll send somebody back after you by and by. Just now I'm going to see that I catch that noon train to Boston. All right with that anchor, are you, Hopper?"

Afore I could answer something bust past me. 'Twas Philander, and if I've said he moved slow when he moved, I'll take some of it back. He wa'n't moving that way now.

"You—you——" he screamed, dancing up and down at the edge of the water. "Come out of that boat! What do you mean?"

The Colonel grinned, expansive.

"You're there, are you," he hailed. "Well, you see that you can't rob me, don't you. I'll pay you five dollars for the use of—— What! What's the matter?"

The matter was that the engine had stopped. It give a cough or two and then petered out altogether. Philander had said 'twa'n't working right, and here was proof.

Applegate begun to swear. Lord James yelled. Philander yelled, too, but there was a reason for his yelling.

"Keep her off!" he bellered. "Keep her off! Look where you're going! There's a rock there! Keep her *off!* Put your hellum hard down! Oh, by Judas, *there you go!*"

You see, that catboat had just got under way

enough to keep moving at a fair clip, even though the power had give out. Applegate had forgot all about steering, and was bending down trying to crank up. Consequently, the boat went sliding along straight ahead for, maybe, thirty feet. Then there was a bump and a scrape and a ripping, grinding smash. The boat stopped with a jerk, heeled down to port and begun to sink. She had reason to, for there was a two-foot hole in her bottom.

" 'Elp!" screeched Lord James. "We're drowning."

It looked to me as if he might be right this time. I jumped to Philander's dory and started to push her off. But afore I could much more'n start, 'twas all over. The catboat sunk more swift and then her stern went under. It sunk only a little ways, hung on the rock that had knocked the bottom out of her, and then capsized. Applegate and His Lordship went out of sight in a lather of foam.

But they was up again in a jiffy. The water was only to their shoulders. The first thing Hopper said when he got the salt out of his mouth was " 'Elp!" but he said it fervent.

I was still shoving at the dory. Philander jumped up and down on the sand.

" 'Elp!" screams Lord James.

" 'Elp!" mocked Philander back at him. " 'Elp yourself, you thundering fool! Wade ashore!"

Hopper and Applegate begun to wade toward the nighest dry spot, and every step the Doane hermit called 'em a different name. The Colonel started to say something, but he was shut up quick.

"You—you everlasting old fat fool!" screams Philander. "You—you sculpin head. Now you've done it, ain't you! Want to go to Wapatomac right off, hey? Well, you won't! Your rotten old skiff's out of commission, my dory leaks, and now, by Judas, you've ruined my catboat. Want to go to Wapatomac? Then you can swim there. I'd like nothing better than to see you try. O-oh, you *cussed* fool!"

I didn't interrupt him. Fact is, my sentiments and his had a strong family likeness.

If I should undertake to tell all that happened the rest of that day, I'd be kept busy. And yet I can't think of it now without laughing. If ever a man had the conceit took out of him 'twas Applegate. It didn't come back nuther. Philander saw to that. He bully-ragged that fleshy Right Liver something terrible. He never let him open his head scarcely. No, from then on there was only one skipper of that hermit shanty, and his last name begun with a D.

It commenced to rain and thicken up pretty soon, and you couldn't see more'n a hundred yards from shore in any direction. I cooked what breakfast there was; the hermit said he wa'n't going to get het up over that cookstove fixing grub for a passel of dum fools. There was nothing in the shanty that the Colonel could eat, and he done the best he could with more dry bread and water; seemed to be thankful to get that. He put in the heft of his time pacing up and down the shore and looking out into the drizzle for a boat or something to pick him up.

I thought myself that we'd be picked up pretty soon. I knew my turning up missing wouldn't raise such a dreadful row at the sanitarium, but his would. Not only Cape Cod, but Boston and Providence and the stock market would be anxious to know what had become of *him*. I mentioned it to him once, trying to encourage him, but he only waved his hands and groaned.

"It's that annual meeting, Pratt," he said. "If I'm not at that meeting there'll be the Old Harry to pay. Why—why, they'll think I've skipped out! The papers'll be full of it. Consolidated Brick Common will drop to perdition."

Yes, I was sorry for him, but I couldn't do nothing to help. Walking home was out of the question; there was five miles of half-flooded salt marsh to cross afore you struck solid ground. Our only hope was they'd send out searching parties in boats and they'd locate us. If the weather had only been clear!

It got clear along about eight at night. By that time Applegate had about give up hope and had turned in. Lord James had turned in afore. He and the hermit had had a high old rumpus about the Revolutionary war, or some such foolishness. I couldn't make out just what 'twas about or who started it, but I heard Philander hollering and His Lordship dropping H's, and went out to see what was the trouble.

"Don't you talk to me," Doane was saying. "Don't you dare to talk to me. You can't come round here cal'lating to make us folks slaves, 'cause we won't have it. We don't have no kings and queens, we don't. King! by Judas! I wouldn't have a king on my premises no more'n I would a—a tramp. If one of 'em come lording it around me, I'd—I'd take and bang him over the head with a clam hoe."

Hopper was pretty excited, too, but more disgusted than anything else.

"King!" says he. "A King around this awful 'ole! My word! If 'Is Majesty could only see, same as me, what a crowd of 'orrible blighters there is in this Gawd-forsaken country, 'e'd be thankful we dropped you when we did. Of all the ignorant——"

"There! there!" says I, nosing in; "cut it short. Send it to the Peace Congress. Come on, Doane; let's you and me see what we can do with that cat-boat of yours."

When the tide rose we got the boat off the rock and in on the beach. Then we worked over her together, and while we was working that hermit asked me more'n a barrel of questions, about Nate Scudder mainly, when I was going to break his neck, same as I said I would. Him and Scudder had squabbled over a bill and Philander was down on him and Huldy Ann like a keg of nails on a sore toe.

That evening, when the other two had gone to bed, he got out his concertina and tuned up. A day's rest hadn't done that agony box any good; 'twas worse'n ever, if such a thing's possible. I never heard such a noise; like the wailing of something dying and dying hard, it was. But he fairly gloried in it.

I asked him who learned him to play. I *had* to ask something; thought maybe he'd stop cruelizing "Rock of Ages" long enough to answer, anyhow, and I'd have that much recess.

"Nobody l'arned me," says he. "It come to me natural. Seems as if 'twas born in me, as you might say."

If it had been born in *me,* I'd have took ether and had it out. I wished I could take some right then.

"You know what I want?" he asks. "What do you cal'late I've got a hankering for?"

"Land knows! A shotgun, maybe."

"Shotgun? How you talk! What made you think 'twas a shotgun?"

"Oh, I don't know. Maybe I got your longings and my own mixed up."

"Well, 'twan't a shotgun. I've got one shotgun already."

"All right. Don't tell me where you keep it, that's all; I don't dast to know. There! There! What is it you're hankering for?"

"A violin," says he, "an A Number One violin."

"A fiddle."

"No, no, a violin. A fiddle's easy enough to get. I want a real violin, same as Adeline Patty and the rest of the high-tuned music folks you read about play onto. A fiddle's cheap; but a good violin costs money, they tell me. I sent for a catalog, and some of 'em was high as a hundred dollars. A hundred dollars—Judas, think of it!"

"You wouldn't know how to play one if you had it, would you?"

"I could l'arn. I bet you 'twould come natural to me, same as the concertina. If I ever get one I'll send you word and you can come hear me play."

"All right; be sure you send it—don't fetch it yourself. Better stick a special delivery stamp on the letter, too. If ever you get that violin, Philander, I want to know it quick."

'Twould be one of them things a man ought to be prepared for, 'cording to my notion.

About half past nine I took a good-bye look out over the water, hoping there might be some craft in sight. No such luck, though; so I turned in on my shakedown. Philander said he'd be in pretty soon, and I left him on the bench outdoor.

I woke up about an hour later. I heard something, just as I had that morning, and 'twas the same sound, too—the "chug-chug" of a motor boat.

Thinks I, "They're coming at last. We'll be able to get away from that concertina now." And outdoor I put, dressed mainly in nothing particular.

There wa'n't nobody in sight, but the "chug-chug" sounded from the end of the point beyond the pines. I run barefoot through the beach grass and over the pine needles until I got 'most to the shore on that side. And there I met Philander coming back. He started and kind of jumped when he saw me.

"Doane!" says I, "Doane! Where's that boat? Quick!"

He took an awful long time to answer.

"Boat?" says he. "What boat?"

"That motor boat. There's one around here somewheres. Don't you hear her?"

You could hear her—yes, and, more'n that, you could see her, too. Her light was a good ways off shore and heading away from us.

"Oh, *that* boat?" says he. "Yes, I did hear her. She ain't coming this way."

Of course she wa'n't, and 'twa'n't likely she would unless we done something to make her. I yelled and hollered "Boat ahoy!" and the like of that, till I couldn't scarcely speak. No use, the boat kept going away, and pretty soon her light was just a speck in the distance.

Philander kept fidgeting back of me.

"It's too bad, ain't it," says he. "She can't hear you, I'm afraid."

"Course she can't now. But she might have heard you if you'd hailed afore I got here. When did you first make her out?"

Well, he didn't know exactly. Fact is, he wa'n't sure. You see, he—— Well, consarn him, he didn't seem to be sure of nothing. I never see a person act queerer. I couldn't get much sense out of him about that boat. And yet he seemed to be mighty tickled about something; so absent-minded he wouldn't answer my question, hardly.

I went back to my shakedown, mad and disgusted enough. And suspicious, too. Yet I couldn't locate any reasonableness in my suspicions. There was no reason why, if that boat—whoever she was —had come close in to the point, he shouldn't have hailed her and told the folks aboard about us. Yet I couldn't help believing she had come close in. 'Twas odd, and queer. I fell asleep wondering about it.

CHAPTER IX

'TWA'N'T until two o'clock the follering afternoon that we got away from that point and that shanty and that hermit and that concertina. Then a boat, with an auxiliary, came chugging along. When she was nigher in, I see she was the *Dora Bassett,* and she certainly looked good to me. A feller from Wapatomac was running her and Doctor Wool was aboard; so was two young chaps, reporters from Boston papers.

The Doctor looked pretty anxious and worried —for him, but when he found that Applegate was safe and sound he chirked up consider'ble. The reporters chirked up, too. They was the first ones to jump ashore, and they put on speed for the shanty. Here was what they called a "scoop." They'd located the missing president of the Consolidated Porcelain Brick Company, and for a day and a half all creation had been divided as to whether that president had run away, on account of the company's being worse than bankrupt, as was common talk, or was dead, which would be pretty nigh as bad.

But if they was glad to see the Colonel, the Colonel was gladder still to see them. It didn't take him nor Lord James long to get aboard, now I tell you. Philander didn't shed any tears over our leaving, nuther, but he got one surprise all right.

The Colonel turned to him. "Doane," says he, "I've called you a robber and a few other pet names, haven't I. Well, I'll take some of 'em back. You tried to hold me up for a big price when I wanted you to take me home that first night, but——"

" 'Twas on account of my fish, I told you," interrupts the hermit. "I——"

"There! there! wait till I get through. You tried to hold me up, but I wouldn't be held. I don't blame you for trying; that's business; you thought you saw your opportunity and you did your best to take advantage of it. That's all right; if you had had *some* easy marks to deal with, you'd have won. You lost because you didn't have an easy mark. I'm not going to pay you for that, but I am sorry about that boat of yours, and—here, take this; perhaps it will pay damages."

He handed over a wad of bills. Philander looked at the one on top, and his eyes stuck out.

"My—my Judas!" says he. "Why—why, this is enough to *buy* the boat. I hadn't ought to take this."

The Colonel didn't pay no attention; just turned

and stepped aboard the leaky dory. Doane turned
to me.

"Why, Sol," he says, "I—I——"

"Keep it," says I, "and say nothing. He's got
plenty more."

"Well, I swan! If I'd known he was going to
act like this I cal'late I'd have done different last
night. But when that young feller said . . .
Humph! Well, I swan!"

"What young feller? Last night? What do you
mean?"

"Hey? Oh, nothing, nothing."

"Come on, Pratt," says Doctor Wool. "Don't
keep us waiting."

On the way home the *Dora Bassett* fairly flew.
She couldn't go too fast to suit Applegate or those
reporters. Seems there'd been the Old Harry to
pay in the stock market. 'Twas the general feeling
that the Colonel had skipped and that affairs in
the Brick Company was a good sight worse than
anybody had suspected. The stock had gone down,
down, down. It had "dropped thirty points," so the
reporters said. The annual meeting had been post-
poned until night, and the other directors had given
out a statement that, barring the president's absence,
everything was fine; but nobody paid any attention
to it.

"But why," roars Applegate, pounding the weather rail, "should you think I'd skipped out? Do I look like an embezzler? By the great and everlasting," or something like that, "I'll start a few libel suits. Somebody'll pay for this."

Doctor Wool purred explanations. Of course, *he* didn't think any such thing, no, indeed. But, as the Colonel was aware, the papers had been stirring up rumors—no doubt utterly false and malicious—concerning the Brick Company; and its president's unexplained absence, just at this time. You see—er—well——

"But why 'skip out'?" shouted Applegate. "I might have been dead or drowned. By George! I came near enough to both. Why in perdition didn't you give me the benefit of the doubt?"

One of the reporters answered. "It was that steam yacht, Colonel," he said. "There was a steam yacht lying off here about the time that you—er—disappeared. No one knew who she belonged to. Naturally, when it was found that she had gone, and you had gone, too—— Why—well, the coincidence attracted attention."

"But how about me?" I wanted to know. "And Lord James—Hopper, I mean? Did they think *we'd* gone steam-yachting? Has the stock market price of clams dropped any?"

It appeared that they hadn't thought much about us. When they did they cal'lated maybe we'd seen the Colonel clearing out and he'd taken us along to keep the secret safe. 'Twas a fool notion, the whole of it.

"How'd you happen to come cruising after us, then?" I asked. "What put you on the track?"

Wool would have liked to take the credit himself, that was plain. But the reporters knew, and so he couldn't.

"Our clever young friend, Saunders, is responsible," purrs the Doctor. "He has been very active in your behalf—er—Pratt. Has taken quite a fancy to you, I believe. He was the one who discovered that your skiff was missing. Yesterday he endeavored to persuade us to send out searching expeditions up the shore. In fact, last evening, on his own responsibility, he went out alone in this very boat and was gone for hours. I—er—chided him for it when he returned. In his state of health it was an unjustifiable risk."

I never said nothing. But I was thinking hard. I remembered what happened on the point last night; likewise I remembered how queer Philander had acted then and when we left this morning. The more I thought of it the more I wanted to. I'd have smelt a rat sure, if I could raise any respectable reason for there being one on the premises.

The minute we struck the sanitarium the Colonel sent a half peck of telegrams to Boston. Then he set to work hiring a special train to take him up there. 'Twas arranged for, finally, and he hurried off. Said he'd be back when he could, probably early the following week. Doctor Wool went with him to the station; the Doc was purring directions as to diet and right thinking when they drove out of the yard.

Eureka was glad to see me and Lord James, especially me. I judged that she and Miss Emeline were the only ones at the Rest shop who had wasted much worry on my being lost. The Doctor was too much interested in Applegate, and the cook and Annabelle were feeling sorry about Lord James, the "perfect gentleman."

"But I wa'n't so awful worried, Mr. Pratt," Eureka said; "I knew if I kept thinking right 'twould be right in the end."

"Yes," says I, "but 'twas getting to that end troubled me."

"And besides," she says, "I knew nothing dreadful had happened—terrible dreadful, I mean. Your fortune said you'd meet trouble, but you'd come out fine."

I drawed a long breath. "That fortune'll be the death of me yet, Eureka," I told her. "If I fell into the hay cutter I presume likely you wouldn't fret; you'd know I'd come out 'fine.' "

"Oh, you silly!" says she, and laughed. Lord James had come in, and he heard the last part of this. He rubbed his chin.

"Why did she laugh?" he wanted to know. "My word! there's nothing funny about falling into the 'ay cutter."

"Don't you see?" says Eureka, trying to explain. "He means he'd come out fine—chopped fine. He's joking, as usual."

"But—but that wouldn't be a joke; that would be 'orrible! Chopped in a 'ay cutter! My word!"

He said Americans were "blooming red Indians; they 'adn't no 'uman feelings at all." We didn't try to explain any more. What was the use?

All the rest of that day I tried to get a chance to talk to Clayton Saunders, but I didn't get it. *He'd* disappeared now, it looked like. I asked Doctor Wool where he was, and the Doctor didn't seem to know much more'n I did. Clayton had gone away and left a note saying he'd had a hurried business call that might detain him for a while, but that he'd be back soon. He didn't come back that night, though. I grabbed a chance when Miss Hortense Todd was away from her ma's apron strings, and I asked her if she knew where Saunders was.

'Twas a simple question, but it had an astonishing effect. She kind of caught her breath and, it seemed to me, turned pale under the tan on her pretty face.

"Why—why, what do you mean?" she asked. "Has—has—— Nothing has happened to—to Mr. Saunders, has it?"

"Not that I know of," says I.

"Then why did you ask that question?"

"I don't know; no reason special. He's gone somewheres or other, so the Doctor says, and I wondered when he was coming home, that's all. I wanted to talk to him."

She looked at me, and her big brown eyes looked as if they'd look me through.

"Then you had no real reason for asking—me?" she says, slow.

"No, no more'n I've told you. Do you know where he's gone?"

The color was all back in her cheeks now. She smiled.

"Why should I know where he has gone?" she said, and walked off. If I'd been a betting man I'd have risked as much as a lead quarter that she did know, just the same.

Neither young Saunders nor Applegate showed up on Saturday or Sunday. The Boston newspapers was full of the doings in Consolidated Brick stock. Seems that when no news of the missing president arrived on the morning of Friday, the day of the annual meeting, there was pretty nigh a panic in the stock. The price went slumping down, five points at a lick. And then, just after the exchange had closed, come the telegrams saying he was all right and was on his way to the meeting. At that meeting the company voted to pay its regular dividend and give out a statement showing that its affairs was in fine shape. Consequently, when the market opened on Saturday, Consolidated Porcelain Brick Common was hitched to a balloon, so to speak, and went up faster than it had gone down. All hands wanted to buy, of course, and such a hurrah you never saw. At twelve o'clock, when the broker works shut down, the price of a share was higher than it had ever been since the company was formed.

During Monday forenoon one little thing happened. I was the only one that saw it happen, and, if I'd told that I saw it, the other things that happened later might not have happened at all. I didn't tell; 'twas none of my business, anyway, and, even if it had been, I don't know as I—but there, it wa'n't.

I was cutting grass down nigh the edge of the pines at the back of the sanitarium grounds. As I finished the course I was on and swung my lawn mower about on the back tack, I noticed a cap bob up out of the bushes off to the port of me, and a hand wave as if 'twas beckoning.

Afore I could much more than wonder who 'twas that was hid in them bushes, I noticed something else. Off to the starboard, the Right Livers, a part of 'em, was taking their sand baths. Mrs. Cordova Todd was planted amongst 'em, but Miss Hortense wa'n't. She had a headache, so His Lordship had told me; and was laying down in her room. Which might have been all straight enough at the time, only now she wa'n't laying down, for, from where I was, I could see her window. 'Twas open and she was looking out of it at that cap and hand in the bushes. And she waved her own hand back.

Thinks I to myself, "Sol, you never made a mistake yet by sticking to your job. Your job just now is cutting grass."

So I cut, and I looked every way but at them bushes or that house. Maybe 'twas five minutes later or perhaps 'twas more, but, anyhow, the next time I turned around Miss Hortense was coming out of those very bushes. She had a piece of white paper in her hand. She looked up from it and saw me staring in her direction. That paper went out of sight in a second. I kept on shoving the lawn mower.

She walked over towards me.

"Good morning, Mr. Pratt," says she. She was trying awful hard to keep her voice steady, but it shook just a little.

"Oh, good morning, Miss Hortense," says I, jumping as if she'd come on me unexpected. "Well, I'm surprised to see you out here in this sunshine. Thought you was on the sick list."

"My head is much better, thank you. It's—it's a beautiful day, isn't it."

I said 'twas, and she went on back to the house. I done some more thinking. I wondered who that note was from and why it made her look as if she'd been washed in a glory bath, as you might say. She acted a little scared, seemed to me, and yet her face was fairly shining. She was sweet enough to eat, Ah, hum! Right Livers wa'n't the only ones whose diet was limited; being an antique old bach, poorer'n Job's cat's grandchild, has its drawbacks.

Dinner, or lunch—you called it one thing or t'other according to your bringing up—was put on table at the sanitarium at one o'clock. Eureka and I was eating ours in the kitchen when Doctor Wool come running out, his big, round face blazing. I'd never seen him excited afore, but now he was.

"Pratt! Pratt!" he snapped—no purring this time; "Pratt, come! I want you."

He actually grabbed me by the coat sleeve and dragged me out of that kitchen.

"Come!" he orders; "foller me. No, stop. You have a glass, haven't you?"

"A glass?" says I. "Glass of what?"

"A spyglass—a telescope. Where is it? Aboard your boat?"

I stopped to think. "Why, no," says I, " 'tain't. It's up aloft in my room. I fetched it there so's to——"

"Get it," he ordered. "Quick!"

When I come downstairs with the spyglass he grabbed my arm again.

"Come," he said. "Foller me."

I follered him, across the lawn, through the pines, and down to the knoll overlooking the beach abreast of which the *Dora Bassett* was moored. There, all ashake with excitement, and looking anything except an invalid, was Mrs. Evangeline Cordova Todd.

"Where have you been?" she wanted to know.

"Didn't I tell you to hurry? They will be out of sight in a minute. Hurry!"

Doctor Wool done his best to be his own smooth, serene self, but even his best wa'n't very good just then. He snatched the spyglass from under my arm, pulled out the joints, and put it to his eye. I looked where he was pointing it. Away out on the water and moving toler'ble fast was a boat, a power boat; I could just hear her engine cough.

The Doctor looked and looked. Mrs. Todd was fidgeting all over.

"Is it?" she says. "Is it? I *know* it is. Don't waste so much time! *Hurry! Is* it?"

Wool lowered the glass. "I think so," says he. "My eyes are not used to—— Here, Pratt; look through this glass and tell us who is in that boat off there."

I give one look. My eyes are pretty good, and they *was* used to the glass.

"Why," says I, "I swan if it ain't Miss Hortense! Your daughter, ma'am."

"Who is with her?" She and the Doctor both asked it at once.

"It looks to me," I says, "as if—— Yes, 'tis. It's young Saunders. Humph! That's surprising. Thought he'd gone away."

I didn't have a chance to say any more. Mrs.

Evangeline Cordova was ploughing through the sand for the shore. Doctor Wool yanked me after her.

"Your boat," he says. "The—the *Bassett,* or whatever her name is—— Is she ready to start at once?"

"Why—why, yes. I cal'late she is. But what ——"

"Then start her. Put me aboard at once and start. We must catch that other boat. Hurry up."

Well, I was consider'ble flustered; couldn't make head nor tail of the business, but I hurried fast as I could down to the shore. My skiff was there. I'd gone over to Philander's shanty on Sunday, mended her bottom with new boards and pitch and paint and rags, and towed her home.

The Doc was aboard of her afore I was.

"Get in," says he, "and shove off quick."

But Marm Todd had a word to say.

"Wait," she orders. "Wait. I'm not in yet."

"But, madam, you are not going. It is not necessary, believe me. I can——"

"Going! Of course I'm going! Do you suppose I shall stay here when my daughter is eloping with a pauper? You—Pratt—help me into that boat."

She didn't need much help. She got in, same as a hippopotamus might have got into a bathtub, and

she took up pretty nigh as much room. I had no
light job shoving that skiff off, and, after 'twas off,
I had another to find a place to set and row. However, we made the *Dora Bassett,* more by good luck
than anything else, and Doctor Lysander and I
dumped that Evangeline over the rail like a bag
of potatoes. Then we got in and I started up the
engine. Down inside me I was hoping she wouldn't
start, but she did; never worked better since I
owned her; that's the contrariness of things in
this world.

"Now," orders the Doctor, "catch that boat.
Catch it, do you hear."

I give you my word I didn't want to catch it.
What Mrs. Todd had said had give me an idee of
what was happening. Them two young folks had
made up their minds to be human and sensible and
get married, same as people that care for each other
ought to. I found out afterward that it had been
planned afore Clayton left the sanitarium to go on
that mysterious business errand of his. The note
which that boy in the bushes brought to Hortense
was just the final clincher, that was all.

I didn't want to catch 'em, and I did hope they'd
get clear; but Doctor Wool was my boss; he paid
my wages, and, as long as he was skipper, 'twas up
to me to obey orders. So I set the *Dora Bassett's*

nose on the stern of that other launch and we hiked along at a fast clip.

'Twa'n't a silent v'yage, by a consider'ble sight. I never see a madder woman than that Todd specimen. She kept clinching her fists and unclinching 'em, and her mouth above her double chin was set tight as a crack in a locked door. But what came out through the crack was all pepper, I tell you.

"The hussy!" she breathed. "The ungrateful, wicked hussy! After all I've done for her, and the care I've taken that she should meet only eligible men—men of position and money. And now——— Oh, but there! I might have expected it. Last summer at Florence she might have married a Count, a real Count, if she had had sense. He was completely infatuated with her; she might have had a title by merely turning her hand. But no, she wouldn't listen to me. Persisted in going her own gait. Said he was too old! Old! And now——— She is just like her father, for all the world He was a perfect fool in practical matters."

The late Todd was lucky to be late, 'cording to my way of thinking. I could see what had made him late so early.

She swung around on the Doctor and handed him some of the seasoning.

"*You* are to blame for this," says she. "Didn't

you tell me that this ridiculous sanitarium of yours was absolutely free from—from creatures like that Saunders? Didn't you promise to keep an eye on my daughter and notify me if you noticed the least hint of anything wrong? Oh! *Oh!* If this is *not* prevented—if we *don't* get to land before that boat does, you shall pay for it. I'll give your sanitarium *one* advertisement that it won't get over. I have some influence with society, thank heaven, even if I have none with my own child."

Lysander the Great wa'n't nigh so great just then. He tried to explain that it wa'n't his fault, he'd done his best, and so on, but the explanations didn't count for much.

"How about that note of yours which I hold?" she wanted to know. "The money you talked me into advancing you? You want that note indorsed, I believe. You——"

"Hush, hush, Mrs. Todd, please," begged Wool. "This is not the time to——"

"I shall not hush. Either you will make this—this Pratt catch that boat, or you and I will have a financial settlement as well as the other sort."

I was picking up information fast. I cal'late Lysander thought so, too, for he began to pitch into me for not hurrying.

"I'm doing the best I can," I answered, short.

"Talk like that won't help, and"—I put some emphasis right here—"it *may* do the other thing."

"But will you catch that other boat?"

"Yes, I presume likely I will. We're gaining on her all the time."

We were, too; worse luck! The other craft was the *Lily* and belonged to Samuel Snow over to Wapatomac. Sam made his brags about her speed, but she wa'n't in it with the *Dora Bassett*. We was overhauling her slow but sure. If, as it looked, Clayton was bound across the bay, we'd lay him aboard sartin, long afore he made port.

On we went. It got so we could see the pair of elopers without the glass. Clayton was at the helm and poor Miss Hortense was huddled up alongside of him. I did pity her. I hoped Saunders would have the spunk to hang onto her in spite of her ma.

All at once the *Lily* turned from the course she'd been making and set off at right angles.

"They've turned, haven't they?" asked Wool.

"Yes, they have turned. They're not going the same way. Why?"

"Well," says I, and sorrowful, too, I shouldn't wonder, "I cal'late he realizes we're overhauling him and he's going to try to land at Bayport or thereabouts."

"Don't you let him," orders Mrs. Todd. "Don't you dare let him. You follow him, do you hear?"

I never wanted to mutiny more in all my life. But, during that life, I never *had* mutinied. I swung off on the new course myself. And we kept on overhauling the *Lily*.

This course brought the shore closer all the time. We got in so we could see the Bayport church steeple and the buildings on the beach. In we went, further and further. We could see Clayton and his girl plain now. She was crying on his shoulder.

"We shall do it," says Wool, a trace of the purr coming back as his satisfaction grew. "We shall do it, madam. I told you to trust in me."

Mrs. Todd actually smiled; but it was a mighty ugly smile.

"I do believe we shall," she said. "And when I do——"

We got in amongst the flats and channels. At high tide they're all right; at any other time they're mighty bad navigating and the tide was on the ebb now.

The *Lily* swung in to the deepest channel. I set the helm over and started to foller, best I could.

"Why do you do that?" snapped Mrs. Todd, quick as a wink. "You are going out of your way."

" 'Tain't safe to go across there," I answered, sullen.

"But their boat went across."

"She don't draw within six inches of what we do, ma'am."

"Nonsense! If you go across there you can head them off. Why, you are going way around. You are going *back*. Stop! *Stop* it, I tell you!"

I was going back, in a manner of speaking. The flat ahead, between us and the *Lily,* was shoaling fast. I knew I'd got to go around the end of it. I didn't answer; kept on as I was.

"Stop it!" fairly shrieked that everlasting woman. "Stop, do you hear! Doctor Wool, make him go straight ahead. They are getting away from us."

"Pratt," says Wool, "I think you are over-cautious. Why not do as the lady wishes?"

"Because 'twould be a fool thing to do. They get over all right, but we can't. And——"

"Are you going to sit there and let him spoil everything? Make him go straight ahead, why don't you? Doctor Wool, if my daughter gets off with that man I will—I will ruin you; I will, I swear it."

Wool was fidgeting and getting red and white by turns.

"Can't you see what is the matter?" sung out the Todd critter. "He's doing it on purpose. He never meant to catch them; I saw it in his eye when he first started. He's been paid to let them get away. Bribed! that's what it is—bribed!"

Nobody had ever accused me of taking money that way afore. I was so mad I could hardly hold the wheel steady. I needed only one thing and that the Doc provided.

"Pratt," says he, "I must say your conduct is suspicious. Do as I tell you; foller that boat."

I looked at him. "Do I understand," I says, deliberate, "that you *order* me to go across that flat?"

"I order you to foller that other boat. Where it can go, you can."

"Of course he can, if he wants to. He's been bribed, I tell you. He was in it from the first."

For a second I hesitated. Then I shoved the helm over.

"Orders are orders," says I, and I never said anything more resigned and happy. "You take the responsibility, I don't."

And I headed straight across that flat. *Now* we gained, I tell you. Clayton was follering his channel, but we was cutting acrost lots. Only a hundred yards between us and the *Lily*. We could hear Saunders telling that poor Todd girl not to cry.

Doctor Wool grinned. Mrs. Todd leaned over the rail.

"Hortense," she screamed, "I order you to leave that person at once and come here to me."

'Twould have been a damp trip if Miss Hortense had tried it, but she didn't try. The *Lily* kept on and so did we, but we gained and gained.

I looked over our bow. The sand on the bottom was shining in the sunshine. The foam we was making was all riled up from the suction.

"She's shoaling fast, Doctor," says I. "If you take my advice you'll——"

"Be still," snaps Mrs. Todd.

"Be quiet, Pratt," orders Wool.

I obeyed orders. I kept still and I kept quiet, but now 'twas me that begun to grin.

Half a minute more. Then there was a bump. The *Dora Bassett* shook from stem to stern. Another bump; then a long, soft, scrapy noise. She stopped short. I looked over the side. We was hard and fast aground.

"What—what?" sputtered Wool.

"Go on! Go on!" ordered the Todd woman.

I leaned back against the stern rail.

"Well, ma'am," says I. "I'm obliged to tell you that we can't go on. We're hard and fast on this flat and here we'll stay till the tide goes out and comes in again. I warned you, remember. 'Tain't my fault. Doctor Wool ordered me to go ahead and I minded what he said. That's what he pays me for. Hey, Doc?"

The *Lily* was going ahead, lickity-cut. All at once, though, she swung around and came back a little ways. Clayton Saunders realized what had happened to us and figgered 'twas his chance to say something. He brought his boat up into the wind and hailed us.

"Mrs. Todd," says he, "your daughter and I made up our minds to be married some time ago. You could not have prevented it, no matter what you had done. We shall visit the minister here in Bayport and then take the train for the city. I think you are perfectly safe where you are. There is no danger, is there, Pratt?"

"Not a mite," says I, cheerful. "All we've got to do is to wait seven or eight hours for the tide. We're safe enough."

"Mother," says Miss Hortense, "I am sorry it had to be this way, but there was no other. Clayton and I will write you when we get to Boston. I shall be very happy; you must console yourself with that."

Mrs. Evangeline Cordova didn't look as if she hankered for consolation. She fairly choked, she was so mad.

"By the way, Pratt," says Saunders, "when you see Colonel Applegate, tell him that I have developed the business sense. I came down to that point, where you and Hopper and he were playing Robinson Crusoe, on Thursday night in your boat there. That chap who was your host—a peculiar genius, isn't he—told me that you were safe and sound and then it occurred to me here was one of the Colonel's 'opportunities.' Consolidated Porcelain Brick Common had fallen off tremendously in price owing to the rumor that its president had decamped. I wired my brokers to buy, buy on a margin and buy a lot. I sold out to-day. I am worth much more than thirty thousand now. I paid Doane—I think that was his name—not to tell any of you that my boat had called that night. Good-by. Good-by, Doctor Wool. Good-by, Mrs. Todd."

"Good-by, mother," called Miss Hortense. "Don't worry."

The *Lily* swung around and started full speed for Bayport. Mrs. Todd and Doc Lysander glared at each other. I, thinking of Colonel Applegate and what he'd say when he found out that he might have been took off that point twelve hours sooner than he was, grinned expansive.

But I was the only grinner aboard the *Dora Bassett* the rest of that day.

CHAPTER X

WE got off that flat enough sight quicker than we had any right to expect, that is, Doctor Wool and Mrs. Todd did. About an hour and a half later, and some time after the up-train for Boston had whistled at the Bayport depot, a feller come meandering down to the beach, got into a dory and pulled and poled out our way. Seems young Saunders had sent him, and a message along with him. The message was just a short note: 'Twas from Miss Hortense, only she wa'n't Miss Hortense any longer. It said that she and Clayton were married and were on their way to the train. "Mother, dear," must forgive her for what she had done. It was all for the best, "and some day, Mother, dear, you will realize it." She would write again that night and tell her ma where to come to meet her and her husband.

Maybe Mrs. Evangeline Cordova would realize 'twas for the best some day, as the note said, but the some day wa'n't that day, by a good deal. Doctor Wool done his best to purr her into some sort of a civilized state, but he had his hands full. She was more down on him than she was on anybody else, and they went off together in that dory, he arguing and she with her nose in the air. I told the feller who'd come to take us off that I'd stay where I was till the tide was high enough to float my boat. I wa'n't going to leave the old *Dora,* of course.

'Twas half-past nine at night afore I got clear and under way, and 'twas 'most eleven when I got back to the Rest shop. Eureka said there'd been all kinds of a time while I'd been gone. Doctor Wool and Mrs. Todd drove home from Bayport in a hired rig, and the old lady was talking when she came into the yard and hadn't stopped, scurcely, since. She wouldn't come down to supper, though Doctor Lysander had plead with her, through the door of her room, for ever so long.

"She's awful down on him," says Eureka. "I never saw anybody so down as she is on him. Keeps saying it's all his fault and she'll make him pay for it. How was it his fault, Mr. Pratt?"

"Don't know," says I.

"No, and I guess likely she don't, either. Crossgrained thing! I never could bear her."

I didn't say nothing about the "note" that Marm

Todd had flung at Wool's head in the boat. 'Twa'n't none of my affairs, anyhow, though the news was interesting and opened up all sorts of chances to guess. This much I was sartin of: I'd ruther owe 'most anybody money than that Todd woman.

The next morning she left Sea Breeze Bluff Sanitarium bag and baggage. She'd had a telegram from Hortense and Clayton and was going to where they was, I cal'late, though she wouldn't give in she was bound there. I drove her over to the depot and she was mum as a clam all the way.

At that depot who should we meet but Applegate. He'd just arrived from Boston.

"See here, Colonel," says I, "I've got a message for you." And I give him Clayton Saunders's parting remarks.

First he swore, and then he laughed.

"The young scamp!" he says. "I'd like to wring his neck. Keeping me starving to death on bread and water when he might have taken me home. So he wanted you to tell me he'd been developing business sense, did he? Ha, ha! the young robber!"

"How much do you suppose he made out of keeping you there?" I asked.

"Don't know. By Jove! now that I think of it, perhaps I do know a little, though. A broker friend of mine told me that a customer of his, a young chap, he said, must have had some sort of a tip on the situation, for he cleaned up over seventy thousand by buying heavy on Friday. I wonder—I believe it was Saunders he meant."

"Good land!" says I. "Seventy thousand in a day. That ain't a bad job, is it? Say, Colonel, you was his opportunity that time, wa'n't you? Why don't you tell Mrs. Todd how much her new son-in-law is worth? It might comfort her some; she needs comfort."

It did comfort her, too; you could see it. She said her daughter was an ungrateful, undutiful girl and the Saunders person was a "beast." But she asked twice afore she got aboard the cars if the Colonel was sartin 'twas seventy thousand the beast had made.

She went away and I ain't seen her since. And her leaving that sanitarium was the beginning of a regular exodus, so Miss Emeline said, though what she meant I ain't sure; I always thought an Exodus was some person in Scripture. If it means a general clearing out of all hands, she was right, for no less than six Right Livers left that Rest shop that week, and some more the next.

Clayton and Hortense and Marm Todd went, of course, and Greenbaum quit on Saturday. The Colonel quit, too, and so did three other patients.

Didn't seem to be no 'special reason for their going; just decided to go, and went, that's all.

I was sorry to say good-by to Applegate. He and I had got on well together, and though he'd called me a pile of names when his prunes and such quarreled with his digestion, he never meant nothing by it. I asked why he'd decided to give up his "treatment."

"You're thinner'n you was, Colonel," says I, "but you're a long ways on the weather side of being a dime show skeleton even yet."

He laughed. "I know it," says he, "but I'm tired of being a mark. I have been one for some time, and now that I know it, I'm going to quit."

"Know? What do you mean?"

"Oh, nothing," says he. "Pratt, how much do you know about the past history of our old friend Wool here?"

"Why, nothing much," says I, trying to guess what he was driving at. "I don't know much of anything. He's had a lot of experience curing folks, that's about all I know. And Miss Adams thinks he's a wonder."

"She does, that's a fact. But I wonder if she . . . However, that's not my funeral. Only I tell you this, Pratt, for your own good: I wouldn't bank too much on your job here being a permanent one. Good-by."

I thought he might have thanked me for all the favors I'd done for him, but he didn't. The only other thing he said to me was just as he was climbing into the wagon with the Doctor.

"You'll hear from me before long, Pratt," he says.

I wondered what he meant by my job not being permanent. And I wondered, too, what there was about Doctor Wool's "past history." Anyhow, I began to believe that, whatever it was, he'd dropped a flea in the ears of Greenbaum and the rest and that the said flea was responsible for their clearing out so sudden.

'Twas plain enough that Wool didn't like the "exodus." He never said nothing, of course, and went on his grand, purry, imposing way same as usual. He made proclamations—for Miss Emeline's benefit mainly, I judged—that the departing ones was cured and well and he'd told 'em to go. But I didn't believe it and even Eureka was suspicious.

The worst of it was that, though he kept putting advertisements in the papers, no new victims came to take the places of them that had gone. That looked queer to me; seemed almost as if somebody was quietly putting the kibosh on that sanitarium.

It was lonesome around the place now. Miss Emeline and Professor Quill was the only Right Livers left. There was more hired help than there was folks to wait on. If it had been my shebang I'd have discharged somebody, so as to save expenses, but the nighest that happened to that was when Annabelle, the waiter girl and chambermaid, left of her own accord to marry the grocer's cart driver, and Wool didn't hire no one in her place. Even Lord James Hopper was kept, though he had scurcely anything to do. He didn't complain; land, no! that suited him first rate; but if I'd been he, I'd have made believe be busy, for safety's sake.

I thought Eureka had forgotten all about that lost wife of his, the Swede one, the " 'ummer" that he and the cherry bounce had talked about the night of his making port at Sea Breeze Bluff. But it turned out she hadn't, not by a consider'ble sight. One night I found her in the kitchen, busy writing something on a piece of paper.

"How do you spell 'communicate,' Mr. Pratt?" says she. "With two m's or one?"

"I don't, unless I'm drove to it," I told her. "Then I take a chance on two. Why? What do you want to spell it for?"

"Oh, nothing," says she, and that was all I could

get out of her. But, later on, when she'd gone out, I picked up that piece of paper from the floor where she'd dropped it, having made a blot. What was wrote on that blotted piece read like this:

"Information wanted of the whereabouts of Mrs. Christina Hopper, who lost her husband in the New York depot. She is a Swede woman and cannot talk good English. Her husband is James Hopper, an Englishman. Communicate at once with E. H. Sparrow, Wapatomac, Mass."

"For mercy sakes!" I said to myself. "Has that girl been advertising for His Lordship's wife? This looks like it."

And, when I taxed her with it, she owned up. She had been putting advertisements in Boston and New York papers and paying for 'em out of her own pocket. She was dreadful fussed to think I'd found it out.

"But, Eureka," says I, "it's the most foolish thing ever I heard of. In the first place, I don't believe Lord James ever had a wife. 'Twas just talk, all that was."

"Talk! Why should he talk that way? What made him talk?"

"Well, when a man who ain't ate anything **for as** long as he had takes to pouring down——"

"Solomon Pratt, I'm ashamed of you! I don't believe you've got any heart."

She had one, and 'twas big enough to take in all outdoors. I did feel ashamed of myself, though I hadn't any reason in the world to feel so. I tried to tell her that, if she was set on putting in them ads, she better let me pay for half of 'em; but 'twas no go.

"No," says she, her eyes snapping. "I want to do it all myself. Then, if she *is* found, I shall feel *so* proud; just the way Evelyn, in the *Home Comforter* story, felt when she brought back her lover's old sweetheart to him. She sacrificed herself to do it, but 'twas noble and she didn't care."

What could a body say in answer to that kind of tomfoolishness?

"But *you* ain't sacrificing nothing, Eureka," I managed to put in. "*You* ain't in love with Lord James, are you?"

"Of course not! If I fall in love with anybody, I should *hope* 'twouldn't be a married man. No, I'm not sacrificing anything, but I'm just crazy to bring those two together again."

"Well, all right," says I, giving up. "I'll own up that you're just crazy, if that'll satisfy you. But do tell me this: Does Hopper know you're advertising for his 'ummer?"

"Of course he don't! And don't you breathe a word to him. I want it to be a surprise—if there *is* any it."

I changed the subject. "Have you seen the Professor to-day?" I asked her.

She looked at me. The same queer look was in her eyes and mine, I guess.

"Yes," she answered, "I've seen him, but only at meal times, that's all."

"Humph! I caught a glimpse of him then myself. Been up in that room of his all day, same as usual, has he?"

She nodded. "I guess he has," she says. "And the door's always locked. What do you suppose he does up there, Mr. Pratt?"

"I don't know. It's a curious thing, that is. Does Lysander—does Doctor Wool keep you and the cook away from the hall that room opens off of, same as he does me?"

"Yup. He found me there yesterday and he drove me out quick, I tell you. Told me not to come nigh there again. Mr. Pratt, Professor Quill is doing something in that room; he's making something that he and the Doctor don't want anybody else to know about. I'm sure of it. Did you smell anything when you was up in that hall?"

I had, but this was the first I knew that she'd smelled it, too.

"Like rubber burning, was it?" I asked.

"Yes, that's it exactly. Smelled as if somebody'd left their overshoes on top of the stove to dry, and then had forgot 'em."

"Perhaps that's it. The Professor's absent-minded enough to leave his head on a hot stove, fur's that goes."

"Nonsense! there's no stove *in* that room."

Well, 'twas a queer business and it had been going on now for a fortni't. First along the Professor stayed in that room only part of the mornings and took his exercise and his sand bath with the rest of the Livers. But now, when he was one of the only two Livers left, and you'd think he'd naturally get more attention and petting from Wool, he didn't take any, hardly; stayed up in that third-story room all the time, and sometimes even had his prunes and eggs and raw steak sent up to him. And when they was sent up 'twas the Doctor himself took 'em; no one else ever got that job.

Naturally, of course, all hands was curious to know what it meant. I asked Lord James if he knew. He swelled up with importance.

"It's a secret," says he. "Nobody's supposed to

know it, but the 'ead told me, in confidence like. The 'ead trusts me, of course, and 'e told me 'e knew I could keep a secret. My word! if you only knew 'alf of the secrets I've been trusted with in my time!"

"Sure," says I, drawing him out; "sartin! Don't doubt it a mite, Hopper. But this ain't so much of a secret as you think 'tis. You ain't the only one that's trusted. I know about what Professor Quill's doing, myself."

"Did the 'ead tell you?" he asked, eager.

"Oh, that's telling. I can keep things to myself when it's necessary."

"But did he tell you about the special exercises and all?"

"Oh, I ain't giving it away."

"No, no. But did 'e tell you all? I 'ave my doubts if 'e did. 'E trusts me, the 'ead does. Why, 'e told me the whole thing; 'ow the Professor was taking special exercises for putting on weight, and 'ow 'e 'ad to do it alone in that room. Oh, 'e told me all about it. It's a new treatment; a bit of an experiment, I mean to say; and until it's established as a success no one ain't to know it. The 'ead 'as charge of it, 'imself. 'E didn't tell you as much as that, I know."

"No," says I, "he didn't. I'll have to give in

that he didn't tell me as much as that. I don't believe he's told anyone that but you, Hopper."

"Of course not. 'E knows who to trust, the 'ead does."

I didn't say no more, but I grinned when I got away by myself. Lysander the Great was a wise old wizard, he was. He knew better than to fill me up with any such yarn as that, but he wanted the impression to get around that the Professor's being in that room was on account of "special exercising" and so he breathed the news into Lord James's ear as a "secret."

Special exercise, hey! Well, it must be a hot old exercise that makes the patient smell like a burnt rubber boot.

And if the idee was to put flesh on poor Quill's bones it wa'n't a success so fur. The poor critter looked thinner and more worried and tired every day. We hardly saw him at all; that is, Eureka and I didn't. And even Miss Emeline saw him only by fits and starts. She was troubled about it, that was plain. One afternoon, down on the beach, when we was alone, she whispered her troubles to me.

"I'm afraid Professor Quill is overtaxing his brain," she says. "He looks tired; don't you think he does, Solomon?"

She was the only one on the premises that ever called me by the whole of my for'ard name. "Solomon" had a nice, dignified, old-family, orthodox sound to it that kind of pleased her, I cal'late.

"Don't you think Professor Quill looks tired, Solomon?" she asked again.

"Yes, ma'am," says I.

"Don't you think he's overtaxing his brain?"

"Don't know, ma'am. He looks as if he was taxed about all he could stand, I must say. There ain't such a lot of him to tax, if you assessed him by the square foot."

She never paid any attention to the last part of this. The "don't know" was all she understood, I presume likely.

"You do think he is overtaxing his brain; I can see that you do. So do I. Of course you know what he is doing up there in his room?"

I mumbled something or other.

"Perhaps you don't really know," she says. "It is a secret, but I feel that I can trust you, and I do want to discuss it with some one. He is at work on a new system of mathematics for use in his college curriculum. You know what a curriculum is, Solomon."

If she thought I did there wa'n't any use contradicting her. Besides, if I said anything about the thing I might get out of soundings. I kept still and tried to look as all knowing as my namesake in Scriptur'.

"Yes," she went on, "it is a new system of mathematics. A wonderful system that he is perfecting all by himself. But I do wish it did not take up so much of his time and energy. I am worried about him."

She looked as if she was.

"Yes, ma'am," says I. "Did he—did the Professor tell you about his—about this curry—curry——"

I'd forgot it already. All I could think of was "curry-comb." But she didn't notice.

"No," she says. "Of course I don't mention the subject to him, or he to me. Doctor Wool told me not to. It was the Doctor who told me of the system."

I nodded. I expected that. The Doctor was telling a whole lot these days.

"He said—Doctor Wool, I mean—that Professor Quill had this on his mind when he came here and was so unhappy in idleness that the Doctor believed it best for him to continue to work at it. Here he could work by himself and under the Doctor's guidance as to diet and exercise. Doctor Wool is humoring him by permitting him to do it in secret; it helps him to think right. And as we think, so we are, you know, Solomon."

I knew, or I'd ought to have known by this time, having had the doctrine preached to me times enough. "Think right!" Well, it looked as if our old chum Wool was strong on thinking right and talking any way he pleased. Here was two "secrets" he'd started going and neither one of 'em was the real one, 'cording to my notion.

Miss Emeline hove a long sigh.

"I mustn't be selfish," she said. "I miss the Professor's society, of course. He and I were very congenial—old friends, you know—and I miss his companionship. However, it will be all right soon, I'm sure. It has seemed to me that he has avoided—— But there! I am permitting myself to become nervous and foolish. I have other anxieties and they. . . . What *am* I talking about? We'll think right, won't we, Solomon? Ah! here comes Doctor Wool himself. Now we shall get back into the proper uplifting atmosphere."

We did. That is, I presume likely we did. The Doctor came parading down to us, his big face shining, his smile working overtime, and the whole of him sticking up out of that desolation of sand and pines like a white-washed meeting-house back of a run-down cemetery. He was a wonder to look at, and to hear; and yet I was—well, I was getting hardened, I'm afraid. I didn't experience religion *every* time he got into the pulpit. Down in my hold was a doubt, a doubt that kept growing, like a toadstool in a dark cowshed.

Two things I felt fairly sure of: One was that Miss Emeline was right when she started to say that Professor Jonathan Quill avoided her. T'other was a downright sartinty that he didn't like that avoiding any better'n she did.

And now I've worked up to what was the most astonishing happening of all that lit on me while I was at that Rest shop. It's so astonishing, so ever-lasting ridiculous and unbelievable, that I swan to man I hate to tell about it. Yet I've got to, I'm going to, and you and me can argue as to whether Ananias and Saphiry or me was the biggest liars as much as you please.

It happened about a week after I had this talk with Miss Emeline. And it bust loose in the kitch-en and on Eureka and me, just as most of the sur-prises had bust. We was together there, Lord James having gone to his room to read a passel of English newspapers that Clayton Saunders had sent him from Boston. Clayton used to get a lot of fun out of His Lordship's ingrowing Britishness and he sent these papers with a note saying they might freshen up Mr. Hopper's acquaintance with the nobility and gentry, something that was too precious to lose. Olivia, the cook, had gone to her cousin's in the village. Eureka and I were alone, as I said, and it was just a quarter-past eight. I know, because I looked at the clock when the knock came at the back door.

I answered that knock, wondering who the knocker could be. I though it might be Annabelle, the ex-chambermaid, come to spend the evening, maybe. But it wa'n't; it was a man, and no man I'd ever seen afore, I was sartin. Men that I knew around Wapatomac didn't wear high, shiny plug hats, nor yeller spring overcoats, nor carry canes with ivory heads as big as a catboat's anchor, as you might say.

"Good evening," says the feller, brisk and polite. He had a big, hearty voice, and was big and husky and fleshy all over, and when he moved the hand that held the cane I noticed there was a yeller kid glove on it.

"Good evening," said I. My fust notion had been that he might be a peddler or a book agent. Yet he didn't look like either one of them nuisances.

"Good evening," says he again. And then, kind of hesitating: "Does—does a party—a lady, I mean, by the name of Adams live here?"

"Miss Emeline Adams, do you mean?" says I. It seemed to me that my saying the name sort of staggered him; and he didn't look like a chap that was easy staggered, nuther.

"Er-er—— Yes," says he. "Does she live here?"

"She does. Yes."

He fetched a long breath. "Is she in?" he wanted to know.

"Why, yes," says I, doubtful. "She's in, but——"

Afore I could say any more he pushed past me and walked into the kitchen. Eureka had been standing inside the door, listening, and he pretty nigh bumped into her. He started back and stared at her with all his eyes.

"This—you—this ain't her, is it?" he sung out. "No. No, course it ain't."

"Ain't who?" says Eureka, about as much surprised as I was to see him act so.

"This is Miss Sparrow," says I. "She's the housekeeper."

Him and Eureka shook hands. She was looking him over from head to foot, yeller overcoat and tall hat and cane and all. I could see her eyes begin to stick out. This feller, whoever he might be, was her idee of the real thing, that was plain. She said afterwards that she thought for a minute that Earl Somebody-or-other in the *Home Comforter* had come to life and come visiting.

He stared at her hard, and rather approving, too, I thought.

"Excuse my glove," says he, polite as a dancing teacher.

Eureka colored up, red as a peach in August. She was real pretty when she got that way.

"Won't—won't you set—I mean sit down, sir?" says she.

"He wants to see Miss Emeline," I put in, by way of explanation.

"Oh," says Eureka, trying not to look disappointed; I do believe she'd been hoping he'd come to see *her*. "Well, Miss Emeline is in her room. I don't know as she has gone to bed—I mean retired—yet, but it is pretty late."

The feller pulled out a gold watch as big and expensive and shiny as the rest of him, by comparison of course, and looked at it.

"Late!" he says. "Why, Good G—gracious! it ain't half-past eight yet. Does she go to bed with the chickens?"

"No, not exactly, but she goes awful early. She's under treatment, you know."

"Treatment?"

"Why, yes. This is Sea Breeze Bluff Sanitarium

for Right Living and Rest. Didn't you know that?"

He nodded. "Yes," he says, "I remember now they told me 'twas something like that. I should think there'd be rest enough, from the looks of the place outside. But see here, is Em—is Miss Adams sick?"

"Not exactly, but she is invalided—not strong, you know. Er—if you'll wait here, I'll go and see if she is up."

He stopped her. "No, no," says he, quick. "Don't do it yet. I—I—— Let me talk to you two a little first. That will be all right, Mister—Mister——"

"Pratt, Solomon Pratt," I told him. "Better set down, hadn't you? I can most generally talk better that way, myself."

He acted awful nervous for such a big, fleshy, sun-burned man. He threw back the yeller overcoat and I could see that the suit underneath was a check, and not a quiet, soothing-syrup kind of a check nuther. But it fitted him fine and must have cost a heap of money. Then he laid his cane on the floor and begun to peel off the kid gloves. There was a diamond ring on his finger that flared like Minot's light in Boston Harbor.

"Won't you take off your hat, sir?" says Eureka.

"Hey? Good Lord, I forgot it! I'm a regular

kid to-night—or an old woman, I ain't sure which. And no wonder, when you come to think of it. Excuse me, Miss, for keeping my hat on all this time. I know better."

He laid the hat on the floor side of the cane. Eureka grabbed it up as if 'twas solid gold and laid it reverent on the table. His head, in the lamplight, was balder than Doctor Wool's. All it needed was gilding to be a Boston State House dome.

He pulled up a chair and set down. I set down, too. Eureka didn't; she just stood and looked at him.

"Are you the new minister?" she says.

They'd hired a new parson at the Orthodox church in the village and we'd been expecting him to call; so, maybe, the question was natural enough. But if you'd kicked the chair this feller sat in he couldn't have got out of it quicker.

"Minister!" says he. "Minister!" Then he looked himself over. "Say, girl," he says, "what's the matter with me? Is my rigging snarled or has that fool tailor made a mistake? A parson! You'll be taking me for a missionary next."

We didn't neither of us know what to make of that. I begun to suspicion the feller was a lunatic. And yet he looked rational enough.

I guess he see we was puzzled, for he set dowr again, and says he:

"You'll have to excuse my language, Miss. I don't mean nothing by it. Parsons up here may be all right, but I've had experience with the foreign breed, and when you asked if I was one I blew up a little. Sit down, sit down. I want to talk to you about—about this Miss Adams. How is she?"

"Are you a relation of hers?" asked Eureka.

"Why, not a relation of hers, exactly—no. I'm a friend—that is, I'm a friend of a friend of hers. She lived in New Bedford one time and—and this friend of mine knew her there."

Eureka gasped out loud; I heard her. I don't know but I gasped, too.

"New Bedford!" she says. "Why! why! you don't tell me! What—what did you say your name was?"

"I didn't. It's—er—Jones. That's it—Jones; John Jones. What's the matter—anything?"

Eureka sighed. The wild expression faded off her face. "No, sir," says she, with a look at me. "No, sir, it's nothing. Only when you said New Bedford I thought for a second—I hoped—but it couldn't be, of course. It's all right."

The Jones man was looking at her hard. Now he reached into the hatch of his vest and fetched

ut a couple of cigars, everlasting big ones, with
gilt bands on 'em.

"Have one?" he says, reaching towards me.

I hesitated; them cigars looked tempting, but——

Eureka spoke what I was thinking.

"You—you're going to smoke, Mr. Jones?" she
says.

"Sure thing! I generally am smoking, though
where I came from we don't get cigars with jewelry
n 'em like these. They soaked me twenty cents
piece in Boston for these. I told the clerk that
old 'em to me he was a pirate, but I bought 'em
ust the same. Didn't mean for him to get the idea
hat I couldn't afford to smoke what I wanted.
Vell," to me, "why don't you light up? Want a
natch?"

Eureka was troubled in her mind. You could
ee she hated to disaccommodate a genuine member
f the nobility like this one, but she knew what
vould happen if him and me lit up.

"I don't know——" she stammered. "I'm afraid
Miss Emeline wouldn't like to have you smoke in
ere if she's coming down. She's turrible down on
obacco."

"Sho!" Mr. John Jones looked some put out.
Humph!" he says. "She must have changed since
—since my friend used to know her. Why, her

old man—her father, I mean—used to smoke like a
tin lantern. Well, never mind. I can wait."

He put the cigar back in his pocket. "So she's
down on tobacco, is she?" he says.

"Indeed she is. Mr. Pratt'll tell you so, too.
Mr. Jones, when this friend of yours and Miss
Emeline's used to live in New Bedford, did he
know a sailor man—a whaler man—named Lot
Deacon?"

The Jones feller started again. For a second
he didn't answer. Then:

"What? Who?" he stuttered.

"Lot Deacon. Oh, I hope he did and that he
told you something about him. Lot Deacon wa
Miss Emeline's young man; she was engaged to
him."

"She was, hey? Well, well!"

"Yes. That's why, afore you said what your
name was, I hoped you might be him. She's talked
about him to me so much. She dreams about him
too. You see, he promised to come back to he
some day and she just knows he will. She's neve
give up hope."

Jones mopped his forehead with a silk handker
chief.

"Is that so?" he says. "Well, well! Lot Dea
con? Lot? Why, seems to me I have heard m

friend speak of him. Big, fleshy feller, rather light-complected, and——"

"Oh, no! No, indeed! He was slim and dark and he had the loveliest curls."

"Curls? Gee! He must have been a sickly look-ing pill. However, that was years ago. Probably he's had a chance to improve since."

Eureka almost forgot her reverence for his clothes, she was so mad.

"Indeed, he wa'n't a pill!" she snaps. "I've seen his picture and *I* call him real handsome."

He didn't seem to be paying attention. Went on talking almost to himself, seemed so.

"That was years ago," he said. "Where's the time gone to? A man can get rid of curls and bones if he has time enough. I cal'late he was meek as Moses, too; meek and scared to say his soul was his own."

"Miss Emeline likes what you call meekness. She says it's the sign of a gentleman to be re-tiring. She likes that almost as much as she does slimness."

"She does? That's funny. I don't. I don't want a wife that's meek, not by a jugful. I used to say so to the boys on the plantation. 'Fellers,' I used to say, 'some of these days, when I've made my pile, I'm going back to God's country to be married.

And then I'm going to tog my wife out—whew! Sealskin sack down to her heels, thumbnail diamonds in her ears, bonnet with ostrich feathers on it. That's what! Give me,' I used to say, 'a woman that folks'll turn around in the street and look at when she passes 'em.' That's what I used to say."

Eureka was listening with all her ears. Now she sighed again.

"That would be lovely," she says, "wouldn't it? I know just how you feel. If I had a husband I'd want him to feel that way. But Miss Emeline wouldn't; no, *indeed* she wouldn't."

Jones went on thinking out loud.

"Queer," he says, "that Emeline Adams should like thin, bashful folks. She ain't that way herself. Plump, lively girl she was, something like you, only not quite so much of her. Dressed pretty and gay. Full of her tricks and cut-ups. Always dancing and——"

I was out of my chair by this time. He'd forgot to say 'twas his "friend" had told him this. Spoke as if he remembered it himself. My head was whirling; I was beginning to think all sorts of impossible thoughts.

But Eureka only thought of what he'd said. Afore I could speak she put in.

"Dancing!" she screamed. "Dancing! Miss Emeline! Miss Emeline full of cut-ups! And plump! Why, she's as thin—I mean slim as can be! And as for dancing—why, she thinks it's the invention of the Evil One himself. She always dresses in black, and——"

But Mr. Jones was on his feet now, and as much upset as she was.

"Hold on there!" he ordered. "There must be some mistake. This ain't the Emeline Adams I knew. It can't be. She——"

The door between the dining-room and the setting-room opened. It always stuck and opened hard; now we heard it open.

"Eureka," said Miss Emeline's voice, "what *is* all this noise? I heard it even in my room. If Doctor Wool——"

She was at our door now. I glanced at John Jones. His bald head was wet with perspiration and he'd turned white under his tan.

"Eureka," says Miss Emeline, coming into the kitchen, "I must say, I——"

She stopped. She and Jones looked at each other—looked and looked. And, slow but sure, what little color she had melted away.

"Oh!" she gasped, faint. "Oh! What? Who?"

John Jones held up his hands and dropped 'em
again.

"Lord A'mighty!" says he. "Emeline!"

"Oh! oh!" pants Miss Emeline. "Lot!"

And down she went in a heap on the kitchen floor.

CHAPTER XI

AND that's the way the miracle happened, just as I've told you. We got Miss Emeline up off that kitchen floor, and set her in a chair and sprinkled water on her; that is, the Jones—I mean the Deacon—man and I did; Eureka was pretty nigh as much upset as her boss, and kept flying around, saying: "Ain't it *wonderful?* Oh, I *never* believed it would really happen! I *told* you so, Mr. Pratt!" and so on, forever and ever, amen.

Miss Emeline came to after a while, and the first thing she said was: "Does Doctor Wool know?" And when Eureka said that he didn't, being upstairs in the room with Professor Quill, she said not to tell him.

"Don't tell him; don't tell anyone—yet," she stammered. "I—I can't—— Oh, Lot, is it really you?"

I don't wonder she asked. I remembered that tintype she kept on her bureau and 'twas pretty hard to realize that this was the fellow who had set for it nineteen years afore. Eureka tipped me

255

the wink and jerked her head towards the other room. She and I went out of that kitchen and left 'em together.

'Twas three-quarters of an hour later when Miss Emeline opened the door. I was glad to see her. My ears was tired listening to Eureka's whispering. Course she had to whisper, so's to keep Doctor Wool from hearing and coming down, and she whispered all the time. Wasn't it wonderful? Did I ever hear anything like it? Didn't I think Mr. Deacon was a splendid man? And dressed—— My soul! did I notice his clothes? And his jewelry? And so on, never stopping hardly to draw breath. I was pretty well shook up and stunned myself, and I *couldn't* talk much; but Eureka talked enough for two.

Miss Emeline was mighty weak and pale when she opened the door. When we started to speak to her she asked us not to.

"Please—please don't," she begged. "I—I must go to my room. This has been such a shock—such a surprise that—that—— Oh, *please* don't speak to me!"

"But Mr. Lot—Mr. Deacon, I mean," bust out Eureka. "Will he——"

"He is going back to the village to-night. To the hotel there. To-morrow he will come back, of

256

course. But in the meantime you must not breathe
a word to anyone. I—I—— He will explain.
Please don't ask me anything."

She went up the stairs, holding onto the balusters
with one hand and her head with the other. Eureka and I went out into the kitchen again.

Deacon was standing by the table. He looked
pretty nigh as shook up as Miss Emeline. He was
swabbing at his forehead with the silk handkerchief.

"Hello!" says he, pretty average trembly. "Say,
this beats cock-fighting, don't it. I—I guess I'd
better be getting back to town and hunt up sleeping
quarters."

"You're going *away!*" says Eureka. "Going
away—to-night?"

"Oh, I'll be back again in the morning. She—
that is, Emeline—thinks I'd better. We've fixed it
up. She wants me to pretend to be an old friend
of hers that has come here for treatment. Then
I can stay without all hands knowing—knowing how
it is between us. You two have got to promise to
keep mum. Will you?"

"Sartin," says I. Eureka looked awful disappointed.

"Keep mum?" she says. "Why, ain't you going
to tell everybody? I should think you would. It's
so wonderful! So lovely and romantic and splen-

did! Just like the most beautiful story that ever was! Are you going to keep it a *secret?*"

"Um-hm. For a while we are. She'd rather have it that way, and I guess it's about as well. Ye-es, I guess 'tis."

"But ain't you———"

"There, there!" I cut in. "I presume likely the parties interested know best what they want to do. It ain't for us to pass out advice, Eureka. Come on, Mr. Deacon; I'll hitch up the horse and drive you over to the hotel."

I took him by the arm and hustled him out to the barn. I knew if he stayed where he was Eureka'd be sartin to ask him a million questions about where he'd been all these years and so on; and 'twas plain enough he wa'n't in no condition to be pumped.

But, as it turned out, pumping wa'n't needed. While we was driving over he spun the whole yarn himself. Seems he'd been about everywhere in those nineteen years. Up to Behring Sea on that whaling voyage, and to Chiny, and England, and France, and Italy, and Turkey, and the South Seas. He'd set his heart on making money—a lot of money— same as he swore he was going to in that note he left Emeline when he went away. But 'twa'n't until he got back to South America for the third time that luck begun to come his way. Then he went up the Amazon River and him and two other fellers, another Yankee and an Englishman, got a rubber-growing grant from the government and settled down. They'd prospered, right from the start. He was worth all kinds of money now.

"But I never forgot the girl I left to home in New Bedford," he says, sort of warming up as he went along. "When I struck South America the first time, after that three years of whaling and ship-wrecks and so on, I was flat on my back in the sick bay for almost another year. Then, soon as I was well enough to hold a pen in my fist, I wrote to Emeline. She says she never got the letter; anyhow, I never got any answer. So I thought she was still mad at me and I didn't write again. But I never forgot her. No, sir! And I never got married, neither. Bill and George, my two partners, they took up with a couple of liver-colored native women and was happy. But not me—not Lot Deacon! The boys used to say to me, 'Lot, why in thunder don't you take a wife, same as we've done?' But I said, 'No, not much. I ain't saying nothing against halfbreeds; they make good enough wives; but some day, when I've made my lucky, I'm going back to the States and marry a *real* girl—one like this.' And then I'd show 'em this photograph."

He had the photograph in his inside pocket. He lit matches so's I could look at it. I never said nothing as I looked, but I thought a heap. Was this Miss Emeline Adams? This young, plump, lively-looking country girl, all crimps and ribbons and fol-de-rol? Whew! Nineteen year had made a difference in her as it had in him.

I guess he knew what I was thinking, for he put the photograph back in his pocket and hove a sigh that seemed to come from the foundations.

"That was a good likeness when 'twas took," he says. "I couldn't hardly believe that. . . . But there! I'm getting off my yarn. Four years ago I come back to the States and started to hunt her up. Course I supposed likely she was married and didn't want to see me, but I wanted to see her. I had no luck at all. I traced her to Boston and there I lost her. By and by I gave it up and went back to my partners and rubber. A month ago I tried it over. This time I put advertisements in the papers."

"Miss Emeline never reads the papers nowadays," says I. "She thinks they're coarse and vulgar. She takes the *Christian Herald*."

"Yes, I know; so she told me. Lord sakes! I never thought of advertising in *that*. However, nothing come of the ads and I was about ready to quit, thinking she'd snaffled another man and wanted to be rid of yours truly. Then, a few days ago, in New York, I run into a feller named Peters, her second cousin."

"Yes. I've heard Eureka mention him. He's about the only relation she's got now. Benjamin Peters, that's his name."

"Um-hm. Nosey Peters, we used to call him. And when old Nosey said she wa'n't married and told me where she was, I fetched a yell that scared the barkeep—I mean the hotel man—'most to death, bolted for the train, stopped in Boston just long enough to have a few extra duds made, and here I am."

He sighed again.

"Yes, sir," he says. "Here I am."

"Did you tell Miss Emeline about how you learned where she was?" I wanted to know.

"Yes. Say, what's the matter with Nosey; anything? She didn't seem to like to hear about him. Seemed to think he was a hard ticket. Acted like a nice enough chap to *me*. Little mite of a sport, maybe, but that's all."

I grinned to myself, in the dark. "He made a lot of money in the show business," says I. "Was a play-actor for a spell, and then run a little cheap theatre of his own, so Eureka says."

"Christmas! that's nothing. Why, one of the

best fellers I know runs a show and a dance hall at Para. A Britisher, he is, and a tip-top chap, square as a brick. He staked me more'n once, in the old days, when I was broke."

"Don't doubt it, but I wouldn't tell Miss Emeline so. She thinks play-acting is sinful. Cousin Ben is the family disgrace; she never speaks his name."

"The devil you say! Humph! Well, well!"

He didn't say any more until we made the hotel gate. Then he says:

"Say, Pratt, I'm to apply to your skipper over there—what's his name? Oh, yes, Wool—in the morning as a sufferer from something or other. Emeline wants it that way. Can you think of any disease that'll fit me? I don't look like a consumptive, do I?"

"Not worth mentioning, you don't, no. Disease? Let me see. Why, say: you might tell him your heart had troubled you for ever so long. That would be more or less true, wouldn't it?"

He laughed and said heart-disease would do first rate. So I said good-night and left him.

When I got back to the sanitarium and had put up the horse and buggy, I found Eureka, still setting up in the kitchen, waiting for me. She was too crazy excited to sleep.

"What did he say to you?" she wanted to know. "Tell me every word."

I told her as many words as I remembered. She was more excited and tickled than ever.

"It's lovely! lovely!" she says. "And he's such a fine man, a man of the world, same as you read about. He's been everywheres and seen everything. Oh, did you hear what he said about the way he'd dress his wife! Think of Miss Emeline walking down the Roo de Tivoly in Paris all rigged up in diamonds and sealskins! Think of it!"

"Yes," says I, kind of doubtful; "I've been thinking of it."

"Isn't it splendid? Isn't she lucky to get such a man? Oh, if somebody like that come after me I'd—I'd——"

She couldn't say any more; the joy of it was too much for her. She'd have set up all night, I cal'late, but I wouldn't. I went aloft and turned in. As I tiptoed past the door of the room where Professor Quill was supposed to be perfecting his mathematics or doing his special exercises, I heard Doctor Wool's voice purring soft and steady. And the burnt rubber smell was strong as ever.

Next morning the sufferer from heart-disease drove into the yard according to schedule. He had his dunnage with him—a trunk and a big bag all plastered over with foreign labels. Doctor Wool heard the wagon-wheels and come as nigh to hurrying as I'd ever seen him, except that time when he dragged me down to the beach to chase Clayton and Miss Hortense. When he found that the visitor was a candidate for right living he almost melted into butter, as you might say. He had Lord James and me look out for the dunnage and he helped the Deacon man out of the carriage himself. They went into the office together and the door was shut, prompt but careful.

Miss Emeline came down about noon. She looked as if she hadn't slept for a week. The discovery that she and Mr. Deacon were old acquaintances was made just as 'twas planned, and I must say that she carried it off enough sight better'n he did. He was pretty nervous, but she was calm and cool, outside. No use talking, Boston first-family training counts, a time like that. Doctor Wool watched 'em pretty close, but I don't think he suspicioned a thing.

And from then on Mr. Lot Deacon, the South American manufacturer, became star boarder, in Colonel Applecart's place, at the Right Livers' Rest. Doctor Lysander fairly poured ile over that ex-whaler. There was nothing too good for him. Being a heart-diseaser, he hadn't scarcely any exercises to take and his diet wa'n't cramped enough to notice. I judged that the price the new boarder was paying was a big rock in a thirsty land to Lysander the Great just then.

Deacon spent full as much time with Eureka and me as he done with Miss Emeline, though of course he spent a lot with her, too. Eureka heard some of their talk together and she told me every word.

"I can't understand Miss Emeline," she said to me. "She don't act half as glad and radiant and soul-satisfied as she'd ought to, seems to me. Why, he's fetched her the loveliest ring. It's as big as— as a bonfire, pretty near, and she don't wear it at all. Keeps it in her bureau drawer in a box. I know she don't like jewelry, but I don't see how she can help liking that. Mr. Deacon told me it cost fifteen hundred dollars. Fifteen hundred *dollars!* I didn't know all the rings in the world cost that much. Sometime, when I get the chance, I'll show it to you, Mr. Pratt."

She did show it to me and it was a bonfire, all right enough. The one Lot wore on his own finger wa'n't a circumstance to it. Blessed if it didn't pretty nigh put a body's eyes out to be in the room with it.

"I heard 'em talking about it yesterday," says

265

Eureka. "They was alone together and I tried not to hear, but I couldn't help it. He asked her why she didn't wear it. She kind of shivered like, seemed to me, and she says:

"'I can't, Lot. I can't—not now, if ever.'

"'But why not, Emeline?' he says. 'We're engaged, ain't we? Have been for nineteen year, and Lord knows that's long enough.'

"'Lot,' she says, 'how do you know I want to marry you, after all this long time?'

"'*Marry* me!' says Mr. Deacon—and no wonder! 'Why for God sakes, Emeline——'

"'Oh, don't, *don't* talk that way, Lot. I can't bear to hear you.'

"'All right, I won't. I'm trying not to, but it comes hard. I've been living kind of rough for a good while and I can't rub the roughness off all to once. But what do you mean by talking about wanting to marry me? Haven't you been waiting for me all this time? And saying you knew I was coming some day? And dreaming about me? That Sparrow girl says you have.'

"'Did she say that? Has she been talking to you of my affairs? She should know better. If she wasn't such a well-meaning, kind-hearted girl, I should discharge her this moment.'

"You better believe I felt pretty bad when I heard

266

that, Mr. Pratt. But what Mr. Deacon said made me feel so proud I didn't care.

" 'Discharge her!' he almost hollered. 'Discharge *her!* Why, Emeline, how you talk! She's a fine girl! A bully girl! I never saw a better, handsomer, nicer-behaved girl than she is. And I've seen some in my day, all colors and kinds.'

"I tell you I was proud when I heard that, but Miss Emeline only shivered again and asked him please not to speak of the dreadful creatures he'd met in the awful places he'd been in. He went on pleading with her.

" 'But, Emeline,' he says, 'how can you talk about marrying me that way? Ain't I been true to you all these years? Didn't I work for nothing but to make you happy some day? What in—I mean what do you think I hunted you up for if it wa'n't for just that? After I found you hadn't married anybody else, of course.'

"She bust out crying. 'Oh, I know it, Lot,' she says. 'I know it. You're a kind, good-hearted man. I know. But are you sure *you* want to marry—me?'

" 'Why—why, Emeline——' he stammered. imagine he couldn't find the words to answer her with. She spoke again afore he did find 'em.

'You must be patient,' she says. 'You **must**

bear with me. And, for my sake, you must learn to speak lower and not use such—such language and slang. Perhaps, if you do that, and never tell Doctor Wool or anyone else a word of this that is between us, I—I—perhaps—— But oh, I wish you wouldn't wear those clothes.'

"I give you my word, Mr. Pratt, I almost hollered out loud when she said that about his beautiful clothes. And he was as much surprised as I was.

" 'Clothes,' he says. 'Why, what's the matter with these clothes? I spent four days in Boston getting these clothes made. Paid the tailor extra to hurry. "Blame the expense!" I says to him. "Tog me up! Spread yourself! *I'm* game." That's what I said.'

"But she only cried again and went off to her room. I didn't hear any more, Mr. Pratt, and I wish I hadn't heard that much. What makes her act so? I can't understand. If he wasn't such a splendid man, just like a regular nobleman, I might; but I can't now. Can you?"

I just shook my head. It did seem to me that Eureka's and Miss Emeline's pet romance they'd built so much on wa'n't turning out to be all sugar; there was some vinegar in it.

I was coming to like the Deacon man first-rate. He and I and Eureka spent more and more time together. He seemed to enjoy being in the kitchen with us full as much as he did confabbing with Wool or Professor Quill. Yes, or even Miss Emeline. And he kept his eyes open; he was as sharp as a razor. There wa'n't much got by him, I tell you.

One day I was out in the barn and he drifted in. I was currying the horse and he set down on the wheelbarrow and begun to ask questions. They was questions about Wool and Quill and Miss Emeline, mainly. Especially about Wool.

"Who is he, anyway? Tell me what you know about him."

I told what I knew, which wa'n't so much. He listened, mighty attentive.

"So Emeline's money—part of it, anyhow—is in that feller's hands. She's backing this Breeze Bluff health factory, is she? I guessed as much. Now tell me something about the schoolmaster, old Long-shanks—Quill, I mean. What is he doing here?"

I said he was a patient, suffering from general breakdown.

"Humph! Does he dance his breakdowns in that room overhead there? He's shut up in that room most of the time, and no one but Wool is allowed to come near him. What is going on in that room?"

I hesitated. "Well," says I, "there's two explanations been given out so fur; that is, you can call 'em explanations if you want to."

I told him about the "mathematics" and the "exercises." He sniffed.

"Rats!" he says. "Tell that to the marines. You're no marine, Pratt. What do you think is up?"

For a minute I didn't answer. Then I spoke what I'd been thinking for some time.

"I believe," I told him, "that there's something else going on, something that's a dead secret between the Professor and the Doctor. Miss Emeline told Eureka once that Professor Quill was, besides being a schoolteacher, a sort of inventor, as you might say. He's invented half a dozen contraptions that have done pretty well for somebody else, though he ain't made much out of 'em. I——"

"Hold on there! Wait a minute. How did Emeline know all this?"

"Why, she and Quill are old friends. They knew each other up to Brockton. Didn't she tell you that?"

"No. No-o. Fact is, she don't seem to want to talk about this Quill feller at all. Hum! . . . Hum! . . . Well, never mind that. So you think he's working at some invention or other in that room, do you?"

"That's about the only thing I can think of. Don't it sound reasonable to you?"

"Why, yes. Only, if he's here for his health, he don't seem to be getting much of it. And why does Wool lie about it? And where does Wool come in, anyway? Pratt, what's your real inside opinion of this Doctor Lysander P. Wool anyway? Just between you and me—what is it?"

I spent a second or two deciding how to answer. He didn't wait for the decision.

"I see," he says. "Yes, yes. You think he's a blamed old fraud."

"Why—why, good land, Mr. Deacon! I never said nothing like that."

"I know you never said it. I said it and you thought it. All right. Now I'll say something else you've thought: You think there's some kind of crooked work going on here."

"There's nothing crooked about Professor Quill. I'll take my oath on that."

"So will I, from what I've seen of him; but it's here, just the same. You know what I'm going to do? I'm going to heave out a line or two baited with the name of Lysander P. I'm in hopes I may get a bite or two that'll lead to information."

When he said that I had an idee. I laid down my currycomb, got a pencil out of my pocket, and

271

wrote a name and address on the back of an old envelope.

"You might heave one of your lines in that direction," says I. "Perhaps you'll get a bite and perhaps you won't."

He read what I'd written. " 'Colonel William J. Applegate. Such and such Street, Providence, R. I.,' " says he. "Humph! So you think——"

"I don't think at all, Mr. Deacon; I can't afford to. But I guess sometimes, and, judging from the way the Right Livers cleared off these premises in a few days after the Colonel did, I *guess* maybe he'd come across something interesting and had spread the news, on the quiet. Anyhow, I'd chuck a line that way if I was you."

"Thanks. You're a cagey old bird, Pratt. All right, I'm another."

"Yes, and there's a third that's just as cagey, and some more, too, if I'm a judge. His name is Lysander P. Wool. That's what you mustn't forget."

"I won't. If I have a business call that takes me away from these latitudes for a week or so pretty soon, don't be surprised. And don't ask too many questions as to where I'm going, either."

For a week or so after this nothing special happened. He and Miss Emeline were together about as much as usual and no more. When they was together Doctor Wool most generally happened to be somewheres in the neighborhood. Once the Doctor spoke to me concerning 'em. Of course the questions he asked wa'n't really questions—just everyday talk, that's all—but it was him that led the talk in that direction.

"Miss Adams and our new friend, Mr. Deacon, are congenial spirits, are they not," he says, smiling as ever.

"Seem to be," says I.

"It would appear so. Yes. I am—er—delighted, of course. Delighted—yes. They are old acquaintances, I believe."

"So Eureka says Miss Emeline says."

"Yes. Old acquaintance should not be forgotten, the song tells us. Mr. Deacon is a gentleman of wide experience, I should say."

" 'Pears to be."

"No doubt he and Miss Adams knew each other —er—very well in years gone by."

"Think so?"

"Yes—er—— Why! Why! What's this?"

He forgot to purr when he said the "What's this?" The organ music stopped and his voice sounded human and pretty sharp, all to once. I looked up. What I saw was Professor Quill and Deacon walking across the lawn together. I looked at them and then I looked at Wool. His heavy eyebrows was drawn together and, until he noticed that I was watching him, he looked uglier'n ever I see him.

He started over to meet 'em. When he spoke the ugliness was all gone. He was smooth and beautiful as a taffy image in a candy store window. Oh, he was a cagey old bird, Lysander was, just as I told the Deacon man.

"Ah!" he purred. "Good morning, gentlemen. Good morning. You have been for a little stroll together? Yes?"

"Yes," says Deacon. "We've strolled some. Hey, Professor?"

Professor Quill acted pretty nervous. Yes, and scared, too, seemed to me. His thin face—thinner than ever, since he'd been doing the "mathematic exercise"—went sort of pale and he stammered when he spoke.

"I—I happened to meet Mr. Deacon and we—we walked together," he said.

"Of course, naturally. And talked, too, I presume. That is one of the charms of walking, according to—er—one of our great authors. A walk without the pleasant accompaniment of conversation is like—er—I forget the comparison, but it is immaterial. You have talked—yes."

"Guess I've done most of the talking," says Deacon. "The Professor's kind of tired, I judge. Acts pretty worn out, to me."

"Oh, not at all; not at all," put in Quill, in a hurry. "I—I am quite fresh, I assure you."

Wool shook his big head, same as a Sunday-school superintendent might shake it at a naughty little young-one in the front pew.

"Ah," says he, smiling, sugary but reproving, as you might say, "the Professor does not forget our motto, I see. He is thinking right—thinking right, yes. But we must not forget our rules, also, must we? I am sure it is time for your exercise, Professor Quill. If I might—in my capacity as father of this little—er—flock—offer a suggestion, it would be that you should not forget your exercise, Professor."

The Professor was already on his way to the house.

"I—I did forget," he stammered, walking fast. "I beg your pardon, Doctor Wool. Mr. Deacon, you—you will excuse me, won't you?"

"Sure thing," says Deacon. "Don't let me interfere with the exercises, Profess."

"Professor Quill *is* fatigued," purrs Wool, of-

'rering explanation. "His system was quite broken down when he came here, but we are gradually re· building it we—er—trust. Did he—er—tell you of—er—of his treatment, Mr. Deacon?"

"Not a thing. We just talked along, that's all. Guess it's time for *my* exercise, ain't it? Where's that long-legged director? Hi, King Edward! Looking for me, was you?"

He called Hopper "King Edward" or "Richard the Third" or "Queen Victoria" or any British name that come handiest. His Lordship didn't like it a mite, but he didn't dast to say anything.

Two days later he—Deacon, I mean—went off on that "business errand." He told Miss Emeline —so Eureka said; I got all that kind of news from her—that he'd be gone only a few days. He was going to look into a finance affair, that was his excuse to her and to Wool. She seemed resigned to have him go. Their secret had been kept first-rate. Eureka and I were the only outsiders that knew it.

So he told her he was going on the finance errand; but to me he said different.

"I'm off," he says. "When I come back I may bring a fish or two off those 'lines' you and I were talking about. I hope I shall."

"Mr. Deacon," I whispered, looking around to make sure nobody was listening, "have you located that—that thing that keeps the Professor in his room?"

He winked. "I am beginning to smell the rat," he says. "I rather guess I'm beginning to smell him."

"What's he smell like?"

"He smells like rubber."

"Humph! I smelt as much of him as that. You can't go through that upstairs hall without smelling that much."

He winked. "Maybe so," he says, "but I've been used to that smell for a good many years. It's my business. However, that ain't the smell I'm going after on this trip. I'm going to smell wool. So long, Pratt."

CHAPTER XII

MISS EMELINE don't seem to be mourning for her long-lost now he's gone as much as she did when she thought he never would come back," I says to Eureka.

Deacon had been away from the sanitarium five days, and, though I'd been hoping he might write and report, he hadn't at all.

"Course she don't!" snapped Eureka. She was awful touchy on the subject of Miss Emeline and Lot, seemed so. The touchiness was growing on her every day. "Why should she? She knows now he will come back."

"Has he wrote to her?"

"I don't know."

"Does she write to him?"

"I suppose likely she does. Engaged folks usually write to each other, don't they?"

"Does she talk about him?"

"No, not much."

"What does she talk about?"

"Why, not much of anything. Mr. Pratt, what

is the matter with Miss Emeline? There's something on her mind. She's awful troubled about something."

I noticed that myself. I should have thought 'twas on account of her "engagement"—I had my opinion as to the joy of that engagement by this time—if it hadn't been for her telling me, long afore the Deacon man showed up, about her "anxieties." No, it wa'n't that alone, nor another thing that I suspicioned strong, 'twas something else, some worry that was on her mind. 'Twas plain enough to see that 'twas there, but what it was I didn't know.

There wa'n't any use talking about it; there's never much use talking when talk don't do any good, at least that's my way of thinking. A pile of folks in this world think different, I know, but that's my way. So I changed the subject.

"This Deacon man is a tip-top chap, ain't he," says I.

"Yes," says Eureka.

"I like him fine. Don't you?"

"Yes."

"And he likes you. You heard what he said to Miss Emeline about you, and he's said the same to me a whole lot of times. Says you're a stunning good girl."

I thought that would please her, and I guess it did. But she didn't say nothing. I tried again.

"Say, some folks have all the luck, don't they?" says I. "And them that have it don't seem to appreciate it. Miss Emeline don't appear to hurrah over what's in store for her as much as a body'd think she would. Godfrey! Suppose you was going to marry a man—and a good man, too; a little rough, but that's nothing—just suppose *you* was going to be Mrs. Lot Deacon, sealskin sacks and diamonds and Roo de What-dye-call-its and—and all the rest of it. Just suppose you was going to be that, Eureka; hey? *You* wouldn't tell him not to wear thunder-and-lightning clothes, would you? I tell you, I—— Why, what's the matter?"

She whirled on me like a teetotum. Her eyes fairly flashed sparks. Acted as if she was fighting to keep from crying.

"You—you——" she sputtered. "How—how —what do you mean by talking to me that way? Just because I'm poor, and work out, and haven't got any family—I mean any that's more aristocratic than a mud-turtle's—you—you think you can say anything you want to to me. *I* haven't got any feelings. I—I——"

She choked right up then and turned away. I never felt worse in my life. I liked Eureka; I never saw a girl I liked more; and I wouldn't have hurt her feelings for no money. I couldn't see how I'd hurt 'em now, but I ain't lived fifty-odd year without learning that there's times when argument with a female is as bad policy as thumping a bull's nose with your fist to see which is the hardest. I walked over to her and put my hand on her shoulder.

"Land of love, Eureka!" says J. "I didn't mean to do any harm and I beg your pardon for it. As for heaving your poverty at you, that would be a smart thing for *me* to do, wouldn't it? I'm so scant of money myself that I welcome a shift in the weather, on account of the change in it."

That made her laugh and she cheered up a little.

"Oh, well," she says, "I am foolish, I suppose. Born that way, I guess. I don't know what ails me lately."

I changed the subject again.

"Any news from the other strayed-or-stolen?" I asked her. "Any answers from that missing wife of Lord James's?"

"No, not a thing. I shall begin to believe as you do, pretty soon, that there ain't any wife and never was."

If *she* was losing her faith in romance and the like of that there must something ail her sure, I thought. This was the fust time I'd ever heard her even hint that the Swede 'ummer wouldn't report on deck some time or other. And she'd quit talking about my "fortune," too; never mentioned it at all. She seemed absent-minded, sort of, and blue and more'n once during the next couple of days I caught her setting alone in the kitchen, staring at nothing in particular and sighing every little while. When I'd ask her what the trouble was, she'd just say, "Nothing," and get up and go away.

"I guess you're in love, after all, Eureka," I says, hoping to tease her into better spirits. "You act just the way the lovesick young women in your *Home Comforter* yarns do. Who's the lucky man? You told me 'twa'n't Lord James, he being married already. There's only me and Wool left on the premises, and I'm too bashful to ask you which of us 'tis."

"Oh, *don't* be such a punkinhead," was all the satisfaction I got out of that.

I was over to the village the next forenoon and stopped into the post-office, hoping there might be a note for me from Deacon. There wa'n't, though, but Nate Scudder come out from behind the letter-box rack and hailed me. Him and I hadn't had much to say to each other since he offered me the "commission" on whatever I'd help him sell the sanitarium. I was surprised when he called me by name and offered to shake hands. I answered pleasant enough, but I didn't shake.

"Got a minute or two to spare, Sol, have ye?" he says. "I—I want to talk with you a little mite."

"All right, Nate," says I. "If I wanted to talk with you 'twould be a little mite, too. You'd be surprised how little."

"Now, now," says he, "what's the use of quarreling? I ain't going to talk about that bill—not now, I ain't. It's something else. Here, come on inside here, where we can be comf'table. Come on, won't ye?"

First I wa'n't going to, and then I thought I would, just for the fun of it. I was curious to find out what he was up to now. So he took me into the back shop, amongst the kerosene barrels and empty boxes, and, after beating all around Robin Hood's barn by talking about the weather and so on, he finally commenced to work up into the latitude of his subject. And that subject surprised me; 'twas Lord James.

"This Hopper man over to your place," he says; "he's sort of manager there, ain't he?"

"Manager nothing!" says I. "He manages his own job, same as I manage mine, but that's all he manages."

"But it's a pretty good job he's got, ain't it?" says he. "Makes good money at it, don't he?"

"Why, fair to middling, I cal'late. Why? *He* don't owe you any 'bills,' does he, Nate?"

"No-o. No, he don't owe me nothing—not yet. Is he any relation to Eureka Sparrow?"

"Relation? Him? Why, he's from England and she hails from Wellmouth Neck. I can't think of any two places that's less liable to be relation to each other than that, not offhand. What in the world put that notion into your head, Nate?"

He hummed and hawed. "Oh, I don't know," he says. "They was so thick and friendly, you see."

"Thick and friendly! Nate, if 'twas hard cider season I'd begin to believe you had been sampling stock, even if 'tis pretty early in the day for that kind of exercise."

Course I knew better; the only time he ever sampled anything was when somebody else was paying for it; but I liked to stir him up.

"Look here, Sol Pratt," he snarled, "I want you to understand I don't drink liquor. I've got better sense."

"That so? Well, I always heard 'twas good sense not to drink your brand of cider, Nate. However, we won't argue about that. What do you mean by saying Eureka and His Lordship—Hopper, I mean—are thick and friendly?"

"Well, they was together over at Horsefoot Island that time and now they're together again and—and——"

"What are you driving at, Nate?"

"Oh, nothing much. Sol, you answer me this: If the Sparrow girl and that Englishman ain't awful friendly, what is she doing his advertising for him for?"

I whistled. "Oh, I see," says I. "Yes, yes, I see. How did you know she'd been advertising?"

He fidgeted a jiffy and then he says: "I know 'cause I've seen her advertisement in the Boston papers. Huldy Ann, my wife, and I both see it. That's how I know. Who's this wife of his? And how did he lose her? Funny thing to lose, a wife is, seems to me."

I laughed. "You can lose 'most anything in New York, so I've heard tell," I answered. "It's a pretty big place and there's lots of kidnappers around."

"Humph! Huldy and I went to New York thirteen year ago and she didn't get lost. Nobody kidnapped *her*. What are you grinning at?"

I could have told him, but I thought 'twas just as well not to.

"Nothing," says I. "My face itched, I guess. Hopper's wife is a foreigner; she can't speak hardly any English, and so 'twas easy for her to get lost. That's his story, anyhow."

"Humph! I cai'late there's a pretty good-sized reward for her, ain't there?"

"Not that I ever heard of."

"How you talk! Course there's a reward. There must be, else why would Eureka Sparrow be so interested? Seems natural enough if a man lost his wife he'd pay a reward to get her back. By cracky! he'd have to."

"Maybe so."

"No maybe about it. Oh, you can't fool me, Sol Pratt. That Sparrow girl sees a chance to make some money, and that's what she's advertising for. I know a thing or two, I do."

"Do you? Land sakes! I *am* surprised. Learn something every day, don't we."

"Quit your fooling. There's something queer about that English Hopper man and I always thought there was. He ain't a common person at all; anyhow, *I* never see anybody like him. You always call him 'Lord James' and so does Eureka. What makes you? Tell me now, honest."

I looked at him. He was serious as a meeting-house door. I was having a fairly good time and

I thought 'twas too bad to cut it short. I shook my head.

"You're asking a whole lot of questions, Nate," says I, trying my best to be mysterious. "What are you so anxious to know for?"

He answered averaging quick for him.

"Nothing, nothing," he says. "I read only t'other day about a Lord that had been play-acting on the stage in this country for years and years. Nobody knew he was one, nuther, till his dad died and left him a million or so. You can't always tell about them foreigners."

"That's so, you can't. You're a pretty smart feller, Nate, you are. But if I was you, I wouldn't talk much about Lord—I mean about Mr. Hopper, nor about Eureka's advertisements, neither. It's supposed to be a secret and you might get into trouble."

"My soul and body! *I* sha'n't tell. Huldy Ann nor I ain't mentioned it to a soul. I—I was just sort of curious, that's all, just curious. Understand, don't you, Sol? Say, don't tell Eureka I spoke to you about her advertising. She might not like it."

He made me promise I wouldn't tell Eureka nor His Lordship, and finally I said I wouldn't. But all the way home I wondered and wondered what in the world set him on that track. At last I came to the conclusion that he figgered Eureka must be in the thing for money and the least idee that some one was going to lay hands on a cent was enough to stir him all up. It was a joke, the whole business, and his notion that Hopper might be a real Lord was the funniest part of it.

Another couple of days went by, and I forgot it altogether. Then I was reminded in an odd way. 'Twas Eureka that reminded me.

"Mr. Pratt," says she, "what do you suppose Nate Scudder wants to see me about?"

She'd caught me unexpected, and I had to swallow afore I could answer.

"Wants to see you?" I says. "Why? Does he?"

"He says he does. His man—the poor thing that delivers his orders for six dollars a week—was in here just now and left me a note. Here 'tis; read it."

I took the note. It was wrote in pencil on a piece of brown paper and read like this:

Dear Eureka:

I wished you would come over to my house along about eight o'clock to-night. I got something important I want to talk to you about. It is business and you will not be sorry you came. Do not say anything about it to anybody but send word by Eli [Eli was his order man]

that you will be on hand. *Come sure.* You
will not lose anything by it. I always thought
a lot of you and your folks and so did Hulda.

Yours truly,

NATHAN T. SCUDDER.

"What do you make of that?" says she, watching
my face. "What do you suppose he wants to see
me about?"

I dodged that question. Asked one of my own
instead.

"Are you going?" says I.

"I told Eli I would. First I was mad, on account of that silliness about he and Huldy Ann
thinking a lot of me and my folks—that's enough
to make anybody mad. Then I got curious, wondering what it could be that I 'wouldn't lose anything by,' and I said I'd go. I thought maybe you'd
go with me."

"I'd be glad to. But—but you notice he says
you're not to say anything to anybody."

"I noticed it, but I don't have to mind Nate Scudder unless I want to, I should hope. I'd like to
have you come first rate, if you will. Pa always
said it took at least six average humans to keep
abreast of old Nate, and you're more'n average,
'cording to my thinking, so you'd be worth as much

as the extry five. I'd feel safer if you was along. Will you come?"

I didn't have to be asked again. Remembering Nate's talk to me, I should have hated to miss it. Maybe here was the answer to the conundrum.

"Yes," says I, "I'll go with you, Eureka. I'll drive you over to-night, if the Doctor don't say no."

He didn't and we arrived at Scudder's on time. All the way over Eureka was speculating and wondering what it meant and what Nate wanted to see her about. I had a kind of foggy guess, but I didn't guess out loud; kept pretending to be as puzzled as she was.

Nate met us at the front door of his house, which was out back of the store. He wa'n't any too glad to lay eyes on me.

"I was kind of expecting you'd come alone, Eureka," he says. "However, I suppose likely you didn't like to make the trip by yourself. You can wait out in the store, Sol. Some of the fellers from the village and around are there, and they'll be awful tickled to see you."

"They'll have to tickle themselves then," says Eureka, decided. "Mr. Pratt's going to stay with me. I fetched him for just that."

He backed and filled, said 'twas kind of private and so on, but she never budged.

"You can see us both or neither," she told him. "*I* ain't particular which it is, myself."

So, after a spell, he decided to make the best of it and shoved us into the front parlor. 'Twas a dismal sort of a place, with hair wreaths, and wax fruit, and tin lambrekins over the windows, and land knows what all. It looked like a tomb and smelt pretty nigh as musty and dead-and-gone.

We sat down on the hair-cloth sofa, holding hands to keep from sliding off onto the floor, and he walked around trying the doors to see if they was latched. He acted awful fidgety and excited.

"Where's Huldy Ann?" says I, by the way of starting things going.

"She's—she's busy," he says. "Eureka, I—I wrote you I had something to say to you, didn't I?"

"Yes," snaps Eureka, who was pretty fidgety herself, "you did. Why don't you say it?"

"I'm going to, I'm going to. I—I—— Well, you see, Eureka, it's such a sort of private thing that I—— Sol, don't you think you'd better see the fellers in the store? They'll be disappointed if they know you're here and they don't get a chance to say hullo."

"Then they'll have to bear up best they can," says Eureka. "Mr. Pratt don't think any such thing.

He's going to stay right here. Go on and tell what the private thing is. I can't stay all night."

He took a couple of turns up and down the floor, and then he begun, really begun this time.

"Eureka," he says, "you've been advertising for a wife—not for yourself; course I don't mean that. Ha! ha! No, I don't mean that. But you've been advertising for a wife for your Mr. Hopper man. You have, ain't you?"

At the mention of these ads Eureka had stiffened up like a wooden image. Now she flew at him.

"What if I have," she says. "What business is that of yours, Nate Scudder? How did you know about it?"

"There, there, don't get mad. I see it in the papers, of course. I—I—— Say, look here; what reward is there for that wife?"

"Reward?"

"Yes, yes, reward. What will this Mr. Hopper pay for his wife, suppose a body fetched her to him? What'll he pay?"

"Pay? Nathan Scudder, what are you talking about? Do you mean to tell me that you know ——"

"I don't mean to tell you nothing. I'm just asking about that reward. See here, Eureka; suppose a—a sartin party had got track of that wife, that Swede woman, and could fetch her to her husband any time—would you be willing to divide the reward with that party?"

Eureka looked at him, and then at me, and then at him again. She was so set back she didn't know what to do.

"Reward!" she stammered. "There ain't any reward. What——"

But Nate was excited, too.

"I know better," he sung out. "Course there's a reward. Would anybody be fool enough to take all that trouble and pay for them ads for nothing? There is a reward, and I want half of it. I'm reasonable; I might have took the whole. Huldy Ann says I ought to; but I'm reasonable, I want to do the fair thing and save trouble. When that postal card came saying that the people she was working for thought likely she was the one that had been advertised for, I——"

"Postal card! What postal card! Whose postal card?"

"Why, yours, of course. It had 'E. W. Sparrow, Wapatomac, Mass.,' on it and I——"

"When did it come?"

"It come four days ago, that's when. And I took all the trouble to go clear up to Boston and see those people, and pay my fare and hers and—and——"

He stopped. Eureka was standing right in front of him, and her fingers were twitching. He didn't have much hair left, but if I was him I'd have been scared of losing the remainders.

"A postal card!" she snapped. "A postal card for me! Come four days ago! And you—and you—— Where *is* that postal card?"

Nate turned pale. I guess he'd said more'n he meant to.

"It's—it's in your box this minute," he stammered. "I—I was going to put it there afore, but it got—er—er—mislaid somehow, and—and——"

"Mislaid! I know who mislaid it. And who kept it and read it, too. Oh, you—you—— I'll put you in jail for this. I can. I can put him in jail, can't I, Mr. Pratt."

I didn't know, but I hated to disappoint her. Besides, she had all of my sympathy.

"Seems to me I've read of folks getting about ten years for stealing other people's mail," I said, cheerful.

"Stealing!" Nate fairly jumped up and down. "I never stole it. I—I——"

The door from the hall opened, and Huldy Ann put in her head.

"He's come," says she. "He's here now, ahead of time. What'll I do with him?"

I guessed who 'twas right off, and afore Nate could answer I stepped over to that door and sang out:

"Hopper!" I hailed. "Hopper, here we are! Come ahead in."

And in he came, afore either Huldy or her husband could make a move. He looked surprised enough to see us.

" 'Ello," says he. " 'Ello, Pratt. 'Ello, Eureka. What's all this? What's up? Did 'e send for you, too?"

"He did," says I. "I'm glad to see you, Hopper. You're right where you belong, even if you are ahead of time. The———"

"Huldy!" hollered Nate, "don't go. Stay here. I——I need you."

"But I can't stay, Nathan. I mustn't. I can't leave———"

"Stay here, I tell you! And shut that door."

She shut it and stayed. Lord James looked as if he cal'lated he'd struck a crazy asylum on the loonies' busy evening.

"What? For 'eaven sakes," says he, "what———"

"He's got your———" began Eureka. Scudder shut her off.

"No, you don't!" he yelled. "No, you don't! I want my half of that reward. It was me that got her. I've took time and spent money, and, by cracky, I'm going to be paid for it! You, Lord Hopper, or whatever your name is, I expect you to pay me a hundred dollars or else I'll ship her back where she came from. I will, by cracky! and then I'll sue you for the cash I've spent. I——"

"Shut up!" Somebody had to say it, for Eureka and Lord James and he and Huldy Ann were all going at once. "Shut up!" I shouted. "Let's have some common sense here. Nate Scudder, do you really mean you've got a hold of Hopper's wife— Christina—the one he lost?"

"None of your affairs what I've got a hold of, Sol Pratt. You keep out of this. I'm going to get that hundred dollars, or——"

He stopped. 'Twas Lord James that stopped him. That physical director had grabbed him by the neck. I never see a man so white and wild as that Englishman.

"What—what are you saying?" he panted, betwixt his teeth. *"What?"*

Eureka was half way to crying.

"He's got your wife," she sobbed. "The wife you lost in that New York depot. I've been advertising for her, to help you, and now he—— Oh, you *poor* thing! Mr. Pratt, quick! He's going to faint"

But he wa'n't going to faint. He looked at us all, and then he made a flying jump for the door. Huldy Ann—I cal'late that woman ain't afraid of nothing if there's a dollar tied to it—she got in his way and hung onto the knob. He see 'twas no use there and made a jump to the other door, the one that led into the next room. That he flung open and bolted headfirst through it. Nate started to foller, but he run into the centre table, with the lamp and photograph album on it, and tumbled flat with the album on top of him. It struck his head and made a holler sound, like thumping an empty barrel—but I didn't remember this till afterward.

I hadn't time to remember anything. From that next room came a scream, two screams—one was from Lord James and t'other was a woman's voice —and *such* a voice. Then there was noises like of things falling and banging around and more screams. Afore we could any of us get our wits together, out of that door come His Lordship again, running for dear life, and right astern of him, with one hand in his shirt collar and pounding him like a pile-driver with the other, come a woman about six foot tall and broad in proportion and with a face on her like a wild cat let loose. He was hollering for mercy, and she was screeching in some sort of foreign lingo. For just about a half a minute they was in that room with us. Then they shot out through the door that Huldy Ann had been holding shut, slam-banged through the hall and outdoor. The yells and thumps moved around the corner of the house and died away in the distance. From the direction of the store and post office sounded a tremendous hubbub. I judged the gang of loafers there had been some surprised and scared.

Of course they all hands come piling into the house to know what was up. Two or three of 'em had water buckets and one had an axe. You see, they figgered the house must be afire. I was laughing so I couldn't say nothing. Eureka was halfway betwixt laughing and crying; and Nate was rubbing the place where the album hit him and calling his wife names for letting the free-for-all get by her and outdoor. She might as well have tried to stop a train of cars, but that didn't make no difference.

While the powwow was going on the big woman came back again. She was consider'ble rumpled and scratched up, but there was fire in her eye. She had Lord James's collar in one big fist and she pounded the table with the other and talked a blue streak. Nobody could make out plain what she said, for she was mainly jabbering Swede lingo, but there was English enough, of a kind, to give us some idee.

Afterward we learned more, and the sense of it was about this:

Her husband—His Lordship *was* her husband, all right enough—had run off and left her that time in the depot. He'd done it on purpose, and I don't know as I blame him much. She was a holy terror. I never see such a female. Ever since she'd been working around in different folks' houses, in different places, but she never stayed long in one of 'em, and there wa'n't any tears shed when she quit, nigh's I could find out. The people she was with at the last place had heard her yarn, as much as they could understand of it, and when they read the advertisement in the paper had wrote the postal to Eureka, the one that Scudder had got hold of. He'd read it, seen a chance to grab some money, and had gone up there, found she *was* Mrs. Hopper, and had brought her down with him on the cars. He hadn't told her that he had her husband—fear the reward wouldn't be paid, I cal'late—but had give her to understand she was going to have a surprise, something fine, for coming to Wapatomac with him.

That's the yarn. The only part I couldn't understand was why the folks she was working for hadn't told Nate that she wanted to find her husband only to break his back for him. I cal'late they was too glad to have her took off their hands to take any chances.

Well, Eureka and I left the whole crowd trying to pacify her and came away. At the door I called back a parting word.

"Say, Nate," says I, "Eureka says you can have all the reward. She don't want none of it."

On the way home Eureka was pretty nigh hystericy. First she'd cry and then she'd laugh. I laughed till I ached all over.

"But why—*why*," says she, "did he talk about her so loving that first night? Cry about her? And call her a hummer, and all that?"

"Well," I said, "I've give you my explanation a good many times. A pint of cherry bounce'll make some folks cry and love all creation besides. Lord James is one of that kind; when he's sober the only one he loves is himself."

Eureka got calmed down when we got to the yard.

"There!" says she. "That's enough of that. I'm going to be sensible and forget. But, Mr. Pratt, don't you ever, *ever* say romance or long lost to me again. I've had enough romance to last me through."

CHAPTER XIII

WE set up till 'most eleven, waiting for His Lordship to come back home, but he didn't come. And, to make a long story shorter, I might as well say right here that I ain't laid eyes on him since he flew out of Nate Scudder's parlor with the " 'ummer" after him. Somebody came to his room that night and took away his things. I presume 'twas him, but, if it was, he was mighty still about it. No, I ain't seen Lord James Hopper from that day to this. How he got off the Cape so quick and so quiet is a mystery. There's a freight train for Boston that leaves Wapatomac about three in the morning, and I shouldn't wonder if the brakemen of that train could tell a few things if they wanted to. But, as they ain't supposed to carry passengers, they won't tell.

Scudder made us a visit the first thing in the morning. He was wild-eyed and all het up. When he found that His Lordship had turned up missing he was hotter than ever. Going to sue somebody right off, as usual.

"How's Lady Christina this morning, Nate?" I

wanted to know. "How's it seem to have one of the nobility in the house?"

He fairly gurgled.

"I—I——" he stuttered, "I—— Somebody's going to pay for this. *Pay* for it; you understand?"

"Oh, that'll be all right," says I. "Think of the reward you're going to get. All you've got to do is to hang onto the lady till you get that reward. Judging from what little I've seen of her, I should think you might have to hire a couple of able-bodied men to help hang on, but that's nothing, considering."

I gathered from his remarks that him and Huldy Ann had been up all night and that the "hummer" was humming yet.

"She's a regular tiger," he growled; "a regular tiger. Yell! You never heard such yelling as she done. And when we tried to stop her I thought she'd scratch our eyes out. Half the town was hanging around the house till breakfast time. And all they done was laugh and carry on. Seemed to think 'twas funny. Funny! By cracky, somebody's going to pay for the fun. You hear *me*, somebody's going to pay for it. When I think of the time I wasted, all out of kindness for other folks, and the car fare I spent, and all, I—I——"

He 'most cried when he mentioned that car fare.

Nothing would do but he must see Doctor Wool right off. Seemed to have an idee that the Doctor would pay the reward, or the expenses, or something. He never made a bigger mistake in his life. Lysander said he was sorry, very sorry, but of course the domestic affairs of servants was not his business, and, without wishing to hurt anybody's feelings, he would suggest that Mr. Scudder did not holler so in his office or on the sanitarium grounds; it was disturbing to the patients. Nate went away, waving both arms and threatening to sue all creation, Lord James and Eureka especial.

Eureka and I talked about the affair most of that day, and I presume likely we'd have talked all the evening, too, if we'd had the chance. But we didn't have it. Something else happened that evening, and it put Hopper and the " 'ummer" out of our heads for good and all.

'Twas after supper and I went out to the barn to lock up. I was just taking the key out of the door when I felt a hand on my arm. I turned around. There, alongside of me, was Lot Deacon, as large as life—which was large enough, goodness knows.

He'd been away over a week, and I'd begun to think something must have happened to him; but it hadn't.

"Hello!" I sung out. "Well, for the land sakes, where did you come from?"

"Hush!" he whispers. "Don't make any noise. I came on the afternoon train, and I've been hanging around the woods ever since. I don't want anyone to know I'm here. Don't say anything, but come along. I want you."

I couldn't help saying something; however, I said it in a whisper.

"Did you find out——" I asked. He interrupted me, sharp.

"I found out what I went after," he says. "Now I mean to find out more. I want you to come with me to that room of Quill's."

"But—but he's there, ain't he?"

"No, I think he's gone out. There is no light in the window. And Wool's in his office, so the coast is clear. Come."

"But how are you going to get into that room? The door's always locked."

"I've got a key that will fit. I looked after that while I was away. Be quiet now."

I didn't say any more. We tiptoed into the house, up the stairs and along the hall to the door of the room where the Professor had been spending so much of his time. 'Twas locked, of course, but the Deacon man got a big bunch of keys out of his pocket and commenced to putter with the lock. The fifth key he tried fitted, and we tiptoed into the room, closing the door behind us. The smell of burnt rubber was so strong it pretty nigh choked us.

Deacon scratched a match, found a lamp and lit it. Then I pulled the window shades down tight, and we commenced to look around.

That room was a surprise party in its way. The carpet had been pulled off the floor, there was a pine table in the middle, and all around was the most curious mess of truck. Bottles by the dozen and little trays and tools and hammers and measuring things, even a little alcohol lamp and a sort of baby forge which was run by alcohol, too. And rubber—all kinds of rubber; big round chunks of the raw stuff, same as it comes from the place where they grow it; and strips of soft rubber like the bands they put around bundles; and pieces of hard, shiny stuff that didn't look like rubber at all.

I couldn't make head nor tail of the mess, but Deacon got more interested every second. He went snooping around, picking up this thing and that, looking at 'em, and handling 'em, and holding 'em to the lamp so's to see 'em plainer. All at once I heard him fetch his breath hard.

"Good Lord!" he says, almost forgetting to whisper. "Good Lord A'mighty——"

He had one of the hard, shiny pieces in his hand and was staring at it with all the eyes in his head.

"What is it?" says I.

He didn't answer for a second. When he did his voice sounded sort of scared and reverent.

"I—it can't be," he says. "It *can't* be. How could he do it here? Without the equipment or anything? He couldn't! and yet—and yet I believe he has. It's a new process; some new process, with chemicals. If it is—if it is, it is the biggest thing ——"

He stopped and went on twitching and pulling at the shiny, black thing in his hands.

"What *is* it?" I whispered. "What have you struck?"

He turned to me, and his eyes were shining and his mouth working.

"It's the answer," says he. "By the great and mighty, I believe it's the answer!"

Afore I could ask another question I heard something. So did he. We looked at each other.

"Some one's coming," he whispered, low and quick. "They may be coming here. We mustn't be seen. What will we do?"

We couldn't go out of the door we come in without walking right into that hall. I looked around. There was another room connecting with this one, the Professor's bedroom it was. I grabbed him by the arm and pulled him into it, closing the door easy astern of me; it was swelled and wouldn't latch, but I held it shut.

The person we'd heard in the hall had stopped and was knocking on the door to the room where the bottles and rubber and all the rest of it was.

We'd ought to have locked that door from the inside, but we hadn't. And we'd left the lamp burning, too. The knock—a mighty faint, careful knock it was—sounded again. Then some one said:

"Professor! Professor Quill, are you there?"

No answer, of course. Then I heard the door open and the person who had knocked came in. I knew who 'twas, for I recognized the voice, but I bent down to the keyhole of one door to make sure. 'Twas Miss Emeline, and she was alone. I felt Deacon's hand moving up and closing over my mouth. 'Twas plain he wanted me to keep that mouth shut.

"Professor," says Miss Emeline again. "Professor, where are you?"

She tried our door, but I hung onto it like grim death. She whispered the Professor's name again, and then she gave it up and went tiptoeing around that other room. Deacon and I kept still.

Next minute there was more footsteps in the hall,

heavy, solid footsteps, and I heard Miss Emeline give a little scream.

"Oh!" says she. "Oh, I——"

"Why, Miss Adams!" booms Doctor Wool's voice. "Miss Adams, what are you doing here?"

Again I thought 'twas time for us to be making ourselves scarce. I remembered there was a door from that bedroom to the hall, and the idee struck me that we might clear out that way. But, as I started to move, Deacon held me tight. For some reason or other he didn't seem to want to clear out.

I heard the Doc close the door of the other room. Then he says again:

"Why, Miss Adams, what are you doing here?"

I expected to hear some sort of excuse or apology. I sartin never expected to hear what I did. When she answered him 'twa'n't to make any excuses.

"Doctor Wool," she says, "why did you tell me that Professor Quill was working on a mathematical system in this room?"

He didn't answer on the jump. I wish I might have seen his face, but he was out of range of the keyhole.

"My dear Miss Adams," he purred. "Really I —I can't understand——"

"Why did you tell me that?"

"I told you because—because you asked me."

"I asked you for the truth and you told me **a** falsehood. Yes, a deliberate falsehood."

"A falsehood! Miss Adams, I am not accustomed to——"

It didn't make any difference to her what he was accustomed to. The "first family" blood was up; I never heard her speak so sharp and brisk. She flew back at him afore he could get his purr working good.

"You told me a falsehood. Anyone can see that the story of a mathematical system is ridiculous and untrue. He has been working at some experiment here, some chemical experiment, I am sure. It is perfectly plain. You knew that I was Professor Quill's friend; that we were old friends. Why have you deceived me in this way?"

He hesitated again. Then I cal'late he made up his mind to change his course. *That* tack was fetching him further from port every second, and I guess he see 'twas high time to 'bout ship. Anyhow, I heard him walk over to where she was.

"Miss Adams," he says, and the sugar was back in his voice now for sartin; every word leaked sweetness; "Miss Adams, will you—er—sit down. You and I must be frank with each other. This deception of mine—a harmless deception and meant only for the best—must cease. It has pained me ex-

tremely to deceive you at all. I shall deceive **you**
no longer. Sit down—please."

She didn't answer a word, but she set. I guess
likely he set, too, for I heard one of the Professor's
chairs creak as he came to anchor in it.

"Miss Adams," he purred, "I will explain."

Her tone wa'n't purry, by a consider'ble sight. If
she'd spoke to me that way I'd have shivered.

"If you will be so good," says she.

"Yes—yes, I will explain. It is true that I deceived you as to our good friend Quill's occupation
here. But it was a deception which he begged me
to practice upon you. Upon you and the rest—yes.
He has not been engaged in mathematical research;
it is research of another kind. I . . . You must be
prepared for a shock, my dear Miss Adams! it pains
me extremely to tell you, but I must. Professor
Quill came here because of the state of his health;
he told you that, did he not?"

"Yes; yes, he did. But what do you mean by
paining me? Is he worse?"

"He will never be better. He told you, I presume, as I did, that his ailment was a nervous one.
It is more than that."

"More? Oh, what *do* you mean?"

"I mean that our friend—my friend as well as
yours—is afflicted mentally."

310

I heard her give a little gasp. When she spoke her voice shook like a loose jib.

"Mentally?" she said. "Afflicted mentally? Oh, you don't mean——"

"I mean the worst. He is afflicted in his mind. He suffers from hallucinations. This—all this here —is one of them."

"Oh, *what* are you trying to tell me? Is he insane?"

"Not precisely that. Not that—now, or ever, let us hope. But he is mentally irresponsible. He suffers, as I said, from hallucinations, and they must be humored or the consequences will be alarming. He believes himself to be a great inventor. In other days—when you knew him in Brockton—he *had* invented, or discovered, several—er—well, chemical processes of some trifling value. Now, however, his hallucination is that he is on the trail of a great discovery; something in the"—he hesitated. I guess likely he was just going to tell the truth, and, not being used to it, it choked him—"something in the line of a new water-proof coating for—er—garments and the like. It is quite worthless, I fear, but his mental state requires that he be humored. He demanded this room for his—er—experiments. He particularly demanded that the experiments"—he kind of sneered when he said the word—"be kept a secret. They have been so kept, as you know. They must, for his sake, continue to be kept. I— er . . . Perhaps, Miss Adams, it would be safer for us to leave this room; he may return at any moment."

He got up from his chair, but she didn't. I didn't hear her move.

"Do his people know this? That his brain is affected, I mean?"

"Yes—ah, yes, certainly. Of course."

"Does the wealthy cousin who sent him here and is paying his expenses, know it?"

"Naturally."

"What is that cousin's name?"

"His name? The cousin's—er—name?"

"Yes. What is his name and where does he live?"

"He lives—he lives . . . I must entreat you to pardon me, Miss Adams, but I cannot tell you that. As you know—as both he and I told you when he first came—that cousin wishes to remain unknown. I have promised not to reveal his identity. Really, Miss Adams, I think we should go now. We can continue this conversation in my office."

Still she did not move.

"I wonder," she says, slow, "if you are telling me the truth—now."

"The truth! My *dear* Miss Adams! Really I——"

"Yes, the truth. Doctor Wool, I am troubled. I have been troubled, and perplexed, for some time. There are things I cannot understand."

"Indeed! I fear you are neglecting our chief guides here in this little haven of rest and true living. You are not thinking right, I fear. Remember, thought is all, and as we think, we are."

This was his sheet anchor, generally speaking. Give out from the pulpit that way, with his big voice rolling and purring, it usually done the business for the person that tried to argue with him. But now the anchor dragged.

"Oh, don't!" says Miss Emeline. "*Please* don't repeat that nonsense now."

"Nonsense! My *dear* Miss——"

"Yes, nonsense. I am beginning to believe it is nonsense. Doctor Wool, why have all the patients except myself and Professor Quill and—and Mr. Deacon, left this sanitarium of yours."

"Ours—*ours*, Miss Adams. Without you it might never have been."

"Yes, I suppose it *is* mine, in a sense. My money financed it. But why did all these people leave; and leave at once?"

"Some were cured; some were——"

313

"Nonsense! It was not because they were cured that they left. Why did they—Colonel Applegate in particular—hint to me that there was something wrong here. They did, and they hinted that I would learn some day what it was. And here is another thing: Why does it cost so much money to keep up this establishment?"

"The—er—question of servants; the—er—high cost of living; the——"

"There are fewer servants now than ever. And almost no patients. Yet you ask me for more and larger sums of money all the time. Only yesterday you asked me for five thousand dollars. I can't understand it. I can't afford it. My bankers tell me my income will be seriously impaired, if this keeps on. What do you do with all that money?"

I thought 'twas some question myself. I guess Deacon did, too, for I felt his hand tighten on my wrist. The Doctor cleared his throat afore he answered.

"Miss Adams," he purred, "I must confess that I am hurt. Your suspicions hurt me. Knowing my feeling toward you, as you do—my real feeling, my heart yearning——"

"Don't! Don't! I have forbidden you to speak of that."

"I *must* speak of it. There is not a moment of

my life that I do not think it. Miss Adams—Emeline——"

I heard her move now. He was follering her, I judged.

"Emeline," he said, "my dear Emeline, why do you continue to misjudge me? And repulse me? You know that my one ambition in life is to be worthy of you. Why do you repulse me always? Why not yield to my devotion and let me care for you through life? I worship you. I——"

"Don't! don't!" she cried. "I forbid you to touch me. I have told you that I could never marry you. Months ago, when I trusted you absolutely, I told you that. And now, when I—— Oh, who is it?"

It came mighty near being Lot Deacon. He was shoving his way past me. But some one else was in that other room ahead of him afore he could open our door.

"What is the matter?" says Professor Quill. "Miss Adams—Doctor Wool, what is it?"

He'd come along the hall without any of us hearing him, and had opened the door of the "experiment room" and walked in.

"What is it?" says he again, his meek little voice jumping. "Miss Adams, what is the matter?"

"Oh, oh, Jonathan! I'm *so* glad you came!"

315

panted Miss Emeline. "I'm so glad!" 'Twas the first time I'd ever heard her call him by his first name, and I guess she didn't know she did it.

"What is the matter? Doctor, what were you doing? Why don't you answer me?"

The Doctor answered. Answered pretty cool, too, considering how he'd been caught.

"Nothing is the matter, Professor," he said, soothing. "Calm yourself, my dear sir. Miss Adams and I—— Well, we are here, as you see. I felt obliged to disclose your secret to her. She had surmised it already."

"Then you know?" His voice showed how excited he was. "Then you know about it? Did he tell you, Emeline?"

"I told her," purred Wool. "Don't excite yourself, I beg."

His begging wa'n't much use, so fur's results went. The Professor kept right on.

"Then you know?" he asked again.

"Yes, I know. He told me."

"Of the process? The vulcanizing process? It is new! It is wonderful! It will revolutionize the vulcanizing of rubber, make it as hard and as tough as steel almost and at half the cost of the old, inferior way."

"She knows," says Wool, hasty. "She knows. Let us not speak of it now."

But Miss Emeline seemed to want to speak of it.

"Vulcanizing?" she said, as if she didn't understand. "Hard as steel? Why, how can you make water-proof garments as hard as steel?"

Wool laughed, or tried to. "You misunderstood me," he began. "I said——"

Quill cut him short. "Garments," he sang out. "It is not used for garments. It is a new vulcanizing process. I discovered it, myself. It is not for water-proofing at all. It is——"

"Hush!" Miss Emeline took her turn at interrupting. "So!" she says, slow, and speaking to Wool, I judged; "so! this is another falsehood—another one of your lies, is it. Don't answer me yet. I don't wish to hear you. I am going to have the truth if I can get it. Professor Quill, as an old friend of yours, a—a close friend, I think——"

"Emeline!" The Professor said it.

"Hush!" she says again. "Hush, please. I want you to answer me truthfully, Jonathan. I know you will if I ask it. Who is responsible for your being here and at work in this room? *Is* it your cousin—the mysterious cousin we have all heard about? Or is it that man there?"

There was only one other man in the room, so I,

for my part, hadn't any trouble guessing who she meant.

"Quill," says Wool, dropping his purr and speaking sharp and quick, "be careful."

The Professor was stammering something or other.

"Please, Jonathan!" begged Miss Emeline. "Please! Oh, don't *you* lie to me, or I shall never believe there is a truthful person in the world."

That done the business. The Professor's voice shook.

"I—I will not lie, Emeline," he said. "Doctor Wool brought me here. He is interested in my invention. I told him of it over a year ago and proved to him that I was on the right track. I owe so much to him. He is backing me with his money. He has kept me here and furnished me with the materials and money to continue experimenting. He —— Doctor, I beg your pardon. Forgive me for telling her. She asked me and I couldn't lie—to her."

The Doctor couldn't seem to find words to answer, and yet, if I'd been him, I should have cal'-lated I'd better answer then, or never. Afore he made a sound Miss Emeline spoke.

"*He* has backed you—with money?" she said. "*He*—with *his* money? Why, he has no money!

I have been supplying him with money to support this sanitarium. And so *much* money! I couldn't understand—— Oh!" as if all at once she had begun to understand; "O-oh! is it possible! Doctor Wool, have you been backing Professor Quill's experiment with *my* money? And pretending to me that it was needed to keep this sanitarium from becoming bankrupt. Is *this* where all the thousands I have advanced you have gone? Is it? But why —*why?*"

If she was knocked over by it, Quill was more so. "Thousands!" he sung out. "Of *your* money! Yours, Emeline! Oh, no! no! I would not have taken a penny of your money. I thought it was his. The experiments were too great a risk. I never— *never* would have permitted you to risk your money in them. You—of all people! The Doctor has done it on his own responsibility. I warned him, but he persisted in backing me. I thought it was his kindness of heart. I was so grateful to him. But not your money, Emeline! No! no! And not thousands! My experiments have not cost one thousand."

"But he has had thousands. Where have they gone?"

I was so interested in all this that I'd forgot I was on earth. What reminded me was being pushed

pretty nigh off of it. Lot Deacon gave me a shove
that sent me reeling, flung the bedroom door open,
and walked in.

"I guess I can answer that, Emeline," he said.
"Wool, you damned robber, I'll answer that; you
needn't bother."

There was an everlasting commotion in that other
room. While 'twas going on I walked in, too. I
didn't see why I should be the only animal outside
the show. My coming didn't make any difference;
nobody noticed *me*.

"You'll have to excuse me for listening, Emeline," says Deacon. "I didn't mean to first along,
but I couldn't get away. Afterward I thought I'd
better listen, for your sake. I'll answer that black-
guard there. You, Wool, you listen to me. I was
onto you the first day I came here. I've had some
experience with fakirs and scalawags in my time,
and I begun to suspect you as soon as I saw you.
Emeline, I'll tell you where your thousands have
gone to. That cuss there"—Miss Emeline shivered
when he said "cuss," but she looked where he
pointed—"is sharp and smart enough; I'll say that
for him. Somehow or other he got onto the Professor's vulcanizing process and saw what was in it.
It's a wonder, I do believe, and properly handled
it'll be worth millions to the company that exploits

320

it. Wool knew that. That's why he fetched Quill here and has kept him hid; so no one else would learn of the process. The 'mental affliction' was just another lie, like the 'mathematics' and the 'special exercises.' Mental affliction: Humph! Well, I'd like to be afflicted the same way. I'd be worth a heap more than I am now.

"And Wool——" he goes on. "Shut up, you! Don't you open your head, or I'll knock it off. This Wool has been forming a stock company with himself at the head of it and holding most of the stock. That's where your thousands have gone, Emeline. Well, what is it, Professor?"

Poor Quill was white as a sheet and wringing both hands.

"Oh, it can't be true!" he said. "It can't be! Your money, Emeline, yours! It is lost, and I am responsible! I! And I had hoped—I had hoped that some day I might be rich and could come to you and say——"

Miss Emeline said, "Hush, Jonathan," and stopped him from saying what he'd meant to say. What it was I could guess, and I saw Deacon look at 'em both pretty sharp. As for Doctor Wool, he laughed, laughed scornful and top-lofty.

"This is ridiculous, quite," he said. "My dear Miss Adams, I fear our new patient has been tarrying with the wine cup during his absence. I will explain to you later on, when we are free from interlopers and lunatics, and—er—eavesdroppers."

He started to march out of the room, but Lot stopped him.

"You wait a minute," says he. "I've got just a word or two more to say to you. I've been looking up your record. I know why you got out of the patent-medicine game. I know how near you came to going to state's prison when the Government analyzed your doped 'Willow Wine' and the rest of it. And, by the Almighty, you'll go there yet—for swindling—if you don't clear off these premises inside of twelve hours. I'll give you until noon to-morrow to skip for good. Now get!"

Lysander looked at him. "And suppose I don't choose to 'get'!" he sneers.

Deacon smiled, in a sort of joyful anticipation, as you might say.

"Then there'll be some damaged Wool in this neighborhood," says he. "Why, you fakir! you swindler of sick women! you——"

He b'iled right over, and the tongue-lashing he give that boss Right Liver beat anything ever I listened to. There was a heap of Scriptur' language in it, and more brimstone than you'd find in a match

322

factory. *I* didn't mind—I was having a good time —but poor Miss Emeline shrivelled and shivered.

"Oh, *Lot!*" says she, and started to go. Professor Quill jumped for'ard and offered her his arm. They left the room together, and Wool left, too, but he went the other way; Deacon saw to it that he didn't foller 'em.

"Whew!" says that South American ex-whaler, mopping his forehead. "Whew! Well, I feel *some* better, anyhow. Come on, Pratt; let's have a smoke."

"But—but don't you think you'd better go to Miss Emeline?" says I. "Maybe she needs you."

He looked down the hall. Miss Emeline and Quill were just at the top of the stairs, he helping her and she leaning heavy on his arm.

Deacon turned to me.

"Come on and have that smoke," says he.

CHAPTER XIV

HE told Eureka and me all about it later on, where he'd been and how he did what he called "getting onto Wool's little game," and the whole thing. 'Twas my suggestion that he go to Providence and hunt up Applegate that had helped him most. The Colonel had found out a little of Doc Lysander's record on his Brick Company annual meeting trip to Boston, and 'twas that that had made him decide to quit the sanitarium. He'd dropped a hint to the other patients, too, and they'd left on account of it. 'Twas through the Colonel that Deacon had got onto the forming of that stock company. That Wool was trying to form some kind of a company they learned, but just what 'twas for they couldn't be sure. So Deacon had come back to the Rest shop determined to get into the Professor's room by hook or by crook, and settle the question. Well, he had; there wa'n't no doubt about that.

I thought, of course, that Eureka would pretty nigh have a shock of paralysis when she found out that Lysander the Great, her idol and pet healer of all creation, was just a common swindler and black-guard. But she didn't; when she and I talked it over she took it surprising cool.

"I ain't so much surprised as you'd think," she says, sighing. "I ain't liked the way he's acted for ever so long. And one time, a couple of weeks ago, I heard him talking to Lord James, when they thought nobody was around, and what he said then didn't sound good to me. I never mentioned it, for what was the use? But I ain't so terrible astonished. You know what I believe? I believe that Hopper man knew more about it than any of the rest of us."

"Hopper!" I sung out. *"He* know about it! Rubbish!"

"No, 'tain't rubbish. After the way he treated his wife I'd believe anything bad of him."

I laughed out loud. "Ho! ho!" says I. "Eureka, your romances ain't working out according to *Home Comforter* rules, and you're put out on account of it. That's what's the matter with you."

She shook her head.

"I don't care," she says. "Anybody that would run away and leave his poor foreign wife to starve *is* no good."

I laughed again. "Starve!" says I. "She wouldn't starve. 'Twould take a regiment of mi-lishy to keep her from eating, if she was hungry.

The only wonder to me is that he could run fast enough to get away from her. Why do you cal'late he married her in the first place?"

"Maybe she married *him*," she says, and I agreed that that was most likely it.

"Speaking of marrying," says I, "I suppose Miss Emeline'll be Mrs. Deacon pretty soon."

She nodded.

"Yes," I went on, "I presume likely she will. Well, she's getting a mighty able man, if you asked me."

And again all she done was nod. Didn't seem to want to talk on that subject, and I thought she'd be crazy to talk about it.

"The poor old Professor won't be poor much longer," I said. "Deacon is wild over that vulcanizing process of his. He's going to back the old chap in putting it on the market, and they'll both of 'em be millionaires, if half of what Lot says is true. He ought to know; he's been in the rubber trade for a long spell."

That made her eyes flash. "Is Mr. Deacon going to do that?" she says. "Oh, ain't he a wonderful man!"

"Sartin is. Well, Eureka, there's one of your romances—his and Miss Emeline's—that *is* working out right. You ought to be tickled over that."

She said yes, she was; but she didn't look at me when she said it. I couldn't make her out on that line.

All that day Wool kept in his rooms, and nobody went nigh him. His twelve-hour limit was more than up, and I rather expected Deacon would put him off the premises by main strength, but he didn't. I hardly saw Lot nor Miss Emeline nor Professor Quill during that day; they kept to themselves, seemed so. And Doctor Wool kept to his.

But after supper I saw him, or he saw me. I was standing in the pines by the gate looking down the road in the dusk, and wondering who was coming along that road with a horse and team. I couldn't see the team, but I could hear the wheels and horse's hoofs. 'Twas awful still and a rattle and thump like that would carry half a mile.

I was leaning over the fence, looking and listening, when I heard a step astern of me. I turned, and there was Doctor Wool, a suit case in one hand and a bag in the other. He saw me at the same time.

"Evening, Doctor," says I.

"Ah—er—good evening, Pratt, good evening."

He said it as natural as life. Just as grand and condescending and purry as ever. You'd have thought I was some kind of a bug or hoptoad or

327

something, that he might have trod on if he'd wanted to, but didn't because of his kind heart. There wa'n't a flutter in his voice, nor a letdown in his majesty. Yet I knew now what he was and he knew I knew.

"A beautiful evening," says he, patting the weather on the head, so to speak.

"Yes, 'tis fine enough," I told him.

"You was—er—admiring the stars?"

"No-o, not exactly. Ain't many stars out yet. I was wondering whose horse and buggy this was coming down the road."

"A horse? And a buggy? Oh, yes, yes, I see." I could see, too, by this time.

"Wonder if whoever 'tis is coming here," says I.

He smiled. "I imagine so," he answered. "I imagine so—yes. If I am not mistaken, that is the vehicle which I ordered, by 'phone, from the livery stable."

"You ordered? Why——" And then I noticed the dunnage he was carrying, and the idee that he was clearing out came acrost my mind. "You ordered, hey?" says I. "Going to leave us, are you, Doc?"

He smiled again. "I am going away—for a time," he answered.

"Sho! I want to know!"

"You do know. Therefore your observation is a trifle superfluous. Avoid superfluities, Pratt; unless you can make them worth while. Ah, Simeon, is that you?"

Simeon—his last name was Smalley—was the chap that worked in the livery stable. He pulled up alongside the gate.

"Simeon," says Doctor Wool, "you are on time, are you not. That is well. Punctuality is a great aid in this life of ours. I admire you for it, Simeon."

Simeon's chest swelled out at that, as if he'd been praised by the President of the United States.

"I generally cal'late to be prompt," says he, vainglorious.

"I am sure you do. My valise—and my bag— may I trouble you?"

'Twa'n't a mite of trouble, you could see that. Simeon jumped for the dunnage and started to stow it in the buggy. I was grinning to myself. In his way, Lysander the Great was great even yet.

"Well, so long, Doctor," says I. "We sha'n't forget you. And you mustn't forget your motto. Think right, that's the thing, you know. If you think right, you'll probably be all right; anyhow, I'd risk you in the average crowd."

He stopped and looked at me, as if he was wondering whether to say what was in his mind or not.

And then he said it. For just one second I had a glimpse of the real Wool, underneath the purr and the padding. He put his mouth close to my ear.

"There is another motto I have found helpful in this world," he whispers. "It has helped me before and I rather guess I can depend on it yet. I'll pass it on to you, Pratt. This is it: 'There's an easy mark born every minute——' Ah, Simeon, you are ready, I see. Very good, so am I. Good-bye, Pratt. Good-bye. Drive on, Simeon."

Simeon drove on. And that's the last I'm ever likely to see of Doctor Lysander P. Wool. But I sha'n't forget him very soon.

When I'd got over the effects of that new "motto" of his, I headed for the kitchen to tell Eureka. She was alone there.

"Eureka," I sung out, busting with the news. "He's gone. He's skipped. He——"

I hadn't got any further than that when I was interrupted. The dining-room door opened and in came Miss Emeline. She was all shaky and white and she had an envelope and a little package in her hand. She didn't pay any attention to me, but went straight over to Eureka.

"Is Mr. Deacon here?" she asked.

She could see he wasn't there, of course, but she asked it just the same.

Eureka shook her head. I guess she noticed how queer Miss Emeline looked, same as I was noticing it.

"Has he been here? Do you know where he is?"

"No, ma'am," says Eureka.

"I ain't seen him since noon," says I.

"He will be here soon, I am sure. He may have gone over to the village. When he comes I—will you give him these, please?"

She put the envelope and the package on the table. Eureka and I looked at them and then at her.

"Why—why, yes'm," stammered Eureka, "I'll give 'em to him, if he comes. But maybe you'll see him afore I do. He——"

"No, no, I shall not. I—I am going to my room and I shall not see anyone. Give them to him, please. Oh, please do! Good night."

She was out of that kitchen like a shot. The door banged after her. Eureka and I stared at each other.

"Well!" says Eureka. *"Well*, I never in my life! What *do* you suppose made her act that way?"

I couldn't answer; 'twas long past supposing. And just then another door opened, the back one this time, and into the kitchen come the very person Miss Emeline had been asking about—Lot Deacon himself. And if you'll believe it, he looked full as pale and shook up as she had. And his first question was, names' excepted, just what hers had been.

"Is Emeline—Miss Adams—here?" he wanted to know.

Eureka shook her head. "No," says she. "But she has——"

He didn't wait for her to answer.

"That's good!" he says. "That's good. I was afraid she might be. I couldn't see her now; I couldn't."

He come to anchor in a chair, took off his tall hat—'twas the first time I'd seen him wear it since he first come and Miss Emeline asked him not to—and chucked it on the floor as if it had been the commonest old slouch that ever was.

"Oh!" squeals Eureka, horrified, and makes a dive for the hat, picks it up, and starts brushing it.

"What on earth is the matter, Mr. Deacon?" says I.

He didn't seem to hear me. In fact, all through what happened right after this he never seemed to sense that I was in the room at all.

"Eureka," he pants, mopping his forehead with

the silk handkerchief, "I've come to say good-bye. I'm going away."

And now 'twas Eureka's turn to get pale. She dropped the hat on the table and clasped her hands.

"Going *away!*" she says. "Going *away?* Not —not for good?"

"Yes, for good. My Lord! I've got to. I've *got* to. I can't stay here any longer. I've tried and tried. I've said to myself that I must stay. Over and over again I've said it. But I can't. I'm going."

Poor Eureka kept clasping her hands and unclasping 'em. "But—but Miss Emeline," she gasps. "How——"

"I know. *Don't* I know? I'm treating her like a low-down rascal, but I've got to do it. And sometimes I think she won't feel so bad, after all. It'll be a shock to her at first, but she'll get over it. It's all a mistake, this coming back of mine, anyhow. She ain't what she used to be and neither am I. We've both changed. I ain't fit for her. *I* ain't had any Boston training. *I* ain't got any high family connections. *I* don't use good grammar. When I get mad I swear, swear like the devil. I don't mean nothing by it; everybody cusses on a rubber plantation. But she don't understand. When I ripped that Wool crook up the back last night, she was scandalized. This morning she wouldn't hardly speak to me. Said she was grateful for all I'd done, and she was, too; but—but that ain't it. We ain't fitted for each other. She hadn't ought to marry me and—and, by the Almighty—I *can't* marry her. There! That's the truth and I'm darned glad to get it off my chest."

I couldn't say nothing; this was too many for me. I just stood and gaped, with my mouth open. However, if I'd stood on my head 'twouldn't have made any difference to that Lot man; 'twa'n't me he was talking to.

"Oh, Eureka," he went on, one word tumbling over the one in front of it, he was so worked up; "Oh, Eureka, you mustn't think I'm going to desert her. I ain't. I'm going to see that she gets her share of my money, just the same as if I had married her. And I'm going to look out for old Quill and his invention. I'll make him rich afore I get through, same as I said I would. But I sha'n't stay here. I can't. You don't know what I've been through since I landed in this place. I hate to go. In one way I can't hardly bear to go. I hate to leave *you*. You're a nice girl. You're my idea of a girl. Why, if 'twas you, I could plan for Paris and all that, same as I used to plan for— her. And how I used to plan it, poor fool that I

334

was! I'd see us walking together down them boulevards at night, with the lamps a-shining, same as I've really seen 'em time and time again. And the bands playing and the folks laughing and the shows going on. Whew!"

He stopped—for breath, I shouldn't wonder. Eureka's cheeks were red again and her eyes sparkled with the thought of all those wonderful things.

"Mustn't it be *lovely?*" says she.

"That's it. *You'd* appreciate it. If 'twas you, now, what a time we'd have, hey? You with that long sealskin and the diamonds and the jewelry I'd give you. You'd look fine in 'em, too; not like a clothespin. And me all dressed up to beat the cars and with money in my pocket. Nothing we couldn't have. Nothing too dear for us to buy. And we'd see it all, you and me, and—— Why! Why, for Heaven sakes! What are you doing? Crying?"

Eureka had been looking at him, her lips trembling. Now, all at once, she dropped into a chair by the table, put her head on her arms, and began to sob as if her heart was broke. I started towards her, but Lot Deacon got there first.

"What are you crying for, Eureka?" he sung out. "Good Lord! Good *Lord!* You—you ain't crying about *me?* You don't feel as bad as that because I'm going, do you?"

She only sobbed and sobbed.

"Great heavens above! *Do* you care, Eureka? Do you? Would you go to Paris with me? You shall have the sealskin and all the rest of it. I like you. I like you a heap. Why—why, one reason I couldn't bring myself to marry Emeline was because I'd come to like you so. Come on! I mean it. Say the word and you'll be Mrs. Lot Deacon afore to-morrow's half over. Yes, to-night, if you'll only say it. We'll go to the parson's in the village and—— *Do* you care, Eureka? Would you be willing to heave yourself away on an old rough, tough feller like me?"

She raised her head and looked at him.

"Oh, *wouldn't* I?" she breathed, sort of as if she'd got a glimpse of glory.

He bent over her and—— But there! I didn't see any more, nor hear any more, neither. I was out of that kitchen by this time. 'Cording to my notion, I'd seen and heard too much already.

They hunted me up by and by and found me hanging over the fence, holding my head on with both hands. When *that* bombshell bust I thought it had pretty nigh blowed it off.

"Come into the house," says Eureka. "Come in

336

quick, Mr. Pratt. Lot—Mr. Deacon, I mean—has got something to show you."

"Lot's the right name," crowed the Deacon man. "Don't you go putting any Misters on me. Come on, Pratt. I've got a surprise for you now that beats any you've struck yet."

I didn't believe it, but I followed him. On the kitchen table was the package and the envelope Miss Emeline had left. Both of 'em had been opened.

"See that, do you?" says Deacon. "See that, do you, Pratt, old horse? What is it?"

I knew what it was, all right. You couldn't mistake it if you had eyes in your head. 'Twas that diamond headlight ring he'd bought for Miss Emeline.

"What is it?" says he again.

"It's Miss Emeline's ring, ain't it?" says I.

He laughed out loud. "No, 'tain't," he crowed. "It was hers; now it's Eureka's. Here! you read that."

'Twas the note Miss Emeline had put into that envelope. I read it, and this was it:

> DEAR LOT:
>
> I don't know what you will think of me. I cannot say it myself and so I write it here, I cannot marry you. I simply cannot. You are a

good man, a good, kind-hearted man, and I am very, *very* grateful to you for all you have done for me and for Professor Quill. You must not think I do not appreciate that; I do; I do. But O Lot, I cannot marry you. We should not be happy together. I know it, and, down in your heart, I think you know it, too. Your coming back to me was wonderful. It was like you. But it was a mistake and, if you do not think so now, you will some day. We have changed, you and I, in all the years of separation, and my ways are not your ways any more. Please go. It is better we should not meet again, for my mind is made up and I shall not change it. I give you back your ring. Please forgive me, *please,* and do not think too harshly of one who will always be

Your friend,
EMELINE ADAMS.

P. S.—There is another reason for my writing this and I am going to give you that reason. Professor Quill wishes me to marry him and I am going to do it. He and I have known each other for a long time and he has become very dear to me.

"There!" whooped Lot Deacon. "There! Now everybody's conscience is clear and we're all happy. Hey, Pratt? Shake hands."

We shook hands, and we shook hard. Eureka's

pretty face was all streaked with tear-marks, but she smiled through 'em like a rainbow.

"But think," she says, "only think of her giving up a lover like *him* for one like old Mr. Quill!"

* * * * * *

Ah, well, that was last September, and now it's April once more. A pile of things have happened since that night in the kitchen.

Lot and Eureka and the Professor and Miss Emeline are married. The Deacons have been pretty much all over creation since, and, judging by Mrs. D.'s letters, he and she have enjoyed the real Paris and the rest of it full as much as they did day-dreaming about 'em. The Quills are up to Brookline, the vulcanizing invention has been incorporated and there's a whacking big factory being put up in East Cambridge. Neither Jonathan nor his wife will have to worry about finances, I cal'late, even if a dozen wolves in Wool's clothing turned up to rob 'em. Lot Deacon is president of the new company and Colonel Applegate is on the board of directors.

Young Clayton Saunders is head man in Applegate's broker place in Providence. The Colonel said any feller that could pull a trick like that one Clayton pulled by keeping him in that Doane shanty and buying Porcelain Brick Common at the lowest figger it's ever struck, was too good a financier for any other firm to get a hold of. Clayton and his wife—her that was Miss Hortense Todd—are mighty happy together, I understand. Mother-in-law, Mrs. Evangeline Cordova, is traveling in the Holy Land, and perhaps that accounts for some of the happiness. It's kind of rough on the Holy Land, though, the way I look at it.

Nate Scudder and Huldy Ann never collected that reward for fetching Lord James's missing bride back to him. They had trouble enough getting rid of the "'ummer" to last 'em one while. She wouldn't go for almost a fortni't; seemed to think Nate had her husband hid around the premises; and 'twa'n't until Nate got the constable and a passel of men to put her out that she quit. Even then they had to haul her out by main strength, and the hollering she done and the furniture she smashed has made talk enough to last Wapatomac all winter. Nate's still threatening to sue somebody for something or other, but he ain't collected a cent. I told him he could take the damages out of that "bill" of mine, but even that didn't seem to satisfy him. Christina boarded the cars for Boston and none of the Cape Codders has seen her since. I don't doubt she's got a job, though, working in somebody's family. If she once got it she wouldn't let go of it, I bet you. How Lord James ever managed to lose her beats me. I've had more respect for him ever since I saw her, on that account.

I've heard of him just once since he ran out of Scudder's parlor. That once was last week. Ed Baker's oldest boy, over to Wellmouth, has a job on one of the New York and Baltimore boats, second mate, he is—a pretty good job for such a young feller. He was home last week on a vacation, and he says to me:

"Say, Sol," he says, "I run afoul of an old acquaintance of yours in Baltimore two trips ago. I didn't exactly run afoul of him, but I saw him. I was on an electric car and he came out of one of the big hotels just as I was passing. 'Twas that English chap, the long-legged one with the half-mast side whiskers, that used to work for you and Hartley and Van Brunt over on Horsefoot Bar that summer, four or five years ago. I hadn't seen him since then, but I knew him in a minute. He's got a job, I guess, for he was carrying two fat valises for a big, fleshy, pompous feller that walked as if he owned all creation, and had a voice like an old-fashioned melodeon. He hailed a cab—the pompous feller did—and I heard the voice. 'Twa'n't one you'd forget in a hurry."

That made me wonder if the man with the voice could have been Doctor Lysander P. Wool. If it was, and His Lordship was with him, there might have been some sense in what Eureka said about their being thick and confidential at the sanatarium. Well, all I've got to say is that Baltimore better look out, that's all. That pair, working together, is enough to make a blind beggar put his pennies in his inside pocket.

So much for all hands connected with Sea Breeze Bluff Sanitarium for Right Living and Rest, except me. And I—well, I'm beginning to have a heap more faith in tea-leaf fortune-telling than I did one time. When Sophrony Gott saw that money coming to me in the teacup she sartin had her specs on, or else she's the best guesser in creation.

First thing that made me set up and take notice was a letter from Colonel Applegate. Inside it was a certificate for ten shares of Consolidated Porcelain Brick stock.

"From Saunders and me," he wrote. "If it hadn't been for you, Pratt, we should neither of us have made money on that deal. Keep it. If you dare to send it back we'll come down and shut you up in Doane's shanty and feed you on salt mackerel for a month."

So I kept it, though I didn't feel as if I'd ought

to, and every time the dividends come in I'm sort of ashamed to take 'em. Yet I don't know but I've earned 'em, in a way. If I hadn't swum out to that drifting skiff, the Consolidated Company might have been a president short, and if I hadn't run the *Dora Bassett* onto that Bayport flat, Clayton Saunders might not have had a wife.

But that ain't all. Lot Deacon writes me that I'm to be a shareholder in the vulcanizing business. "You've earned it," says he. " 'Twas you that gave me the tip to see Applegate about Wool. And 'twas you that was with me in that kitchen when I got the best wife on earth. No price is high enough for anybody connected with that piece of luck, and don't you forget it."

And, to cap the whole thing, Miss Emeline has put me in charge of the whole of her property at Wapatomac, house, land, and all the sanitarium furniture and fixings. She says she never cares to come there again. "There are pleasant memories connected with it, but so many that are unpleasant and that I wish to forget. I don't wish to sell it, but I know you will take care of it and keep it up, Solomon. So please take it, for my sake."

She won't take any rent, so you see, from being flat broke, I've come to be a landholder and a stockholder and mercy knows what all. There's only one trouble, and that is that hard cash is middling scurce, even yet. I can't sell my land nor my house nor my stocks, and it costs like fury to live up to 'em.

Eleazir Kendrick, my old partner in the fish-weir business, and me have thought serious of opening up the ex-sanitarium as a summer boarding house for city folks. We may do it; I shouldn't wonder if we did. *If* we do, I wonder what sort of freaks'll come to stop with us. They can't beat the Right Livers for freakiness, though; nobody could do that.

"And anyhow," I says to Eleazir, "I ain't real sure that it's safe to stay in this neighborhood. Philander Doane, the hermit chap, has sent me word that he bought a first-class violin with the money Saunders and Applegate give him, and he's got so he can play it fine. 'Tell Sol Pratt,' he sent word, 'that it come natural to me to play it, just the same as playing the concertina done. Tell him I'm coming over some day and play for him.'

"So you see," I says to Eleazir, "that maybe the safest thing for me to do is travel. If that violin makes any worse noise than Philander made on his concertina, *I* wouldn't risk hearing it. Maybe I better start for Chiny right now. 'Twould cost